SNAKES IN THE MEADOWS

Born on 5 January 1977, **Ayaz Kohli** is a 2007 batch IRS officer, presently serving as Joint Commissioner-GST, Mumbai.

He was born and brought up in Poonch district of Jammu and Kashmir. In 2007, he became the first person from his community and region to qualify the Civil Services.

Having seen the rise and repercussions of militancy from very close quarters, and moved by the plight of people of the border districts of Jammu and Kashmir, he decided to pen down his first novel, *Snakes In The Meadows*. His poem titled, 'Salvage Thy Pride,' has been a part of *Exodus* magazine released in the UK.

In this moving debut, Ayaz Kohli passionately traces stories of courage, love, loyalty and a fortitude that is inbred into the soul of the Pir Panjal region, the characters that populate this world and the politics that move them. *Snakes in the Meadows* is an encouraging start from a writer of promise.

—Dr. Shashi Tharoor,
author, Parliamentarian.

Snakes in the Meadows presents life as it existed in the traumatic days of terrorism in the border district of Poonch, in Jammu and Kashmir. The dilemma of the common man—either to live with compromised dignity and honour, or face possible death at the hands of Pakistan trained terrorists—has been brought out superbly. The author, while fictionalizing the events, has thrown light on life in the army, fighting militancy, disillusionment in the militant ranks over Pakistan brainwashing youth with wrong information about the condition of Muslims in India, and much more. Providing an insight into the social fabric of the region, the author has brought out the immense sense of nationalism in the villagers and their commitment to preserve their culture and traditions.

Despite introducing various characters from all walks of life to make the book interesting, the story does not move away from the basic theme of terrorism in the region, its adverse impact and the way local people deal with it. The weaving of facts with fiction makes this a brilliant novel, and the narrative style will keep the reader riveted from the first to the last page.

—Kuldeep Khoda,
Ex DGP, Jammu and Kashmir

SNAKES IN THE MEADOWS

Ayaz Kohli

Published by
Rupa Publications India Pvt. Ltd 2019
7/16, Ansari Road, Daryaganj
New Delhi 110002

Sales centres:
Allahabad Bengaluru Chennai
Hyderabad Jaipur Kathmandu
Kolkata Mumbai

Copyright © Ayaz Kohli 2019

All rights reserved.
No part of this publication may be reproduced, transmitted,
or stored in a retrieval system, in any form or by any means,
electronic, mechanical, photocopying, recording or otherwise,
without the prior permission of the publisher.

This is a work of fiction. Names, characters, places and incidents
are either the product of the author's imagination or are used
fictitiously and any resemblance to any actual person,
living or dead, events or locales is entirely coincidental.

ISBN: 978-93-5333-360-7

First impression 2019

10 9 8 7 6 5 4 3 2 1

The moral right of the author has been asserted.

Printed at HT Media Ltd, Gr. Noida

This book is sold subject to the condition that it shall not,
by way of trade or otherwise, be lent, resold, hired out, or otherwise circulated,
without the publisher's prior consent, in any form of binding or cover
other than that in which it is published.

Here's to the people of Murrah village of Poonch District in Jammu and Kashmir, India.
It was their courage and resilience that inspired me to write this book.
I salute the invincible spirit of the people of Pir Panjal.

Contents

Tales of Valour	1
Resilience or Relapse?	21
A World Apart	35
The Spring of 1994	75
Prevention and Pre-emption	97
The Vilest Millennium Bug	127
Trick or Treat: The Compromise	163
The Resistance to the Resistance	203
Sarp Vinaash: Destruction of the Snakes	233
Acknowledgements	277

How do you define misery?
How do you define sorrow?
What about horror?
Intimidation?
Subjugation?
How about unimaginable humiliation?
And systematic annihilation?

We are facing them all at once, and then some. Words almost fail me when I attempt to explain what we are going through.

I can't believe that you're unaware of our misery, oblivious to our suffering. And if you indeed don't know anything, well, you don't deserve to. But let me give you the benefit of the doubt.

I won't shock you with all the naked facts; I don't want you to relive your worst nightmares. For now, let me just tell you that Pathri Aali, our beloved village, is possessed. Our home, our Eden, isn't ours anymore—it belongs to monstrous snakes that lurk about in the meadows. These creatures have enslaved us; we are little more than their flock, petrified servants who have no choice but to do their masters' bidding. I don't have the courage to tell you what our masters make us do. They are bestial and ruthless, not thinking twice before trampling all our desires to satisfy their macabre whims. These new masters of the meadows are certainly not human or humane; they aren't even animals. They are vile ogres.

I am not asking for your help. My world has already been ruined, and you cannot salvage it. Chances are that by the time you read this, I would have been murdered. Sometimes I let myself dream that I will survive until the summer and eventually be buried in Pathri Pir. And then it strikes me—Pathri Pir isn't a shrine anymore; it is a graveyard.

You probably think that you are better off where you are, earning your bread in a distant land. But let me correct you: all that you are earning is ignominy. You may be saving your skin, but here at home, someone is paying for your cowardice.

I don't know if you'll be fortunate enough to survive this madness. But even if you do, what stories would you tell your children? Would you tell them tales of your spinelessness? Sing them ballads about how you abandoned your people because you were a selfish deserter?

I can't foresee any respite from our suffering. Not now, not in a decade. For us at Pathri Aali, there are only two choices: live like slaves, like instruments of their pleasure and abuse, or die with dignity. I have made my choice. And no, it's not the one you might assume I would make. Indeed it's the first one—a life of subjugation. It isn't a choice that can save my skin. Indeed, I want it devoured, if that can help some innocent.

Come back! Be the brave soul you were born to be. Death is inevitable; don't fear it. Bring to the children of our village something they have utterly forgotten: hope. If you can save Pathri Aali from annihilation, I assure you that you will find redemption. You will earn dignity to bequeath to your children, not tales of cowering behind walls. Don't just live to narrate the stories of your cowardice. Someone will tell a better story of how you died, rather than you telling your children how you lived.

Tales of Valour

One

Aslam was struggling to push the bull into the makeshift arena. The animal was particularly skittish that afternoon, scared of the ear-splitting beats of *dhols* reverberating in the hills and the enormous crowd.

'I will kill you if you lose today!' Aslam shouted at it.

But the bull was evidently unruffled by death threats for it promptly ran away, yet again. The cries from the audience became wilder.

Pathri Aali was witnessing the biggest event of the year—the bullfight. The mud-and-stone shanties of the village, built along stair-shaped rows, looked like seats in an amphitheatre. People squatted on roofs, excitedly waiting for the contesting bulls to fight each other. Pathri Aali was a small village built on a mountain slope, a few hundred feet above the shrine it was named after—the Pathri Pir. From the opposite hill, the village looked like mud-capped pebbles studded on a giant staircase.

On the roof of one of the crude houses, two cots stood side by side. Haji Mir Baksh and his friend, Avdal, sat on one, waiting for the bullfight to begin. Next to them sat two Army captains—Dr Himanshu Singh and Raman Negi. Haji Mir kept glancing at the Army officers, ensuring they were comfortable and entertained. He was, after all, the chivalrous host of the uniformed men who had accepted his invitation to witness the events.

Haji Mir had dyed his beard with henna the previous night, in preparation for the event. His kohl-rimmed eyes shone with pride whenever he smiled in appreciation of, nothing in particular. He kept talking till his voice was completely submerged by the beats of the dhols. Moreover, Haji Mir unhappily realized that his guests didn't seem to care for his narration. They stared steadfastly at the arena where the two beasts were about to lock horns.

The contest had a special significance for Haji Mir. In the last three years, his son Wazir hadn't won even once. On all three occasions, his bull had failed miserably at chasing away the opponent—a jet black bull from the neighbouring village. But this year, Haji Mir's younger son Aslam had vowed to avenge the family's consistent defeat.

Earlier that day, the villagers of Pathri Aali had offered alms and conducted a special prayer at the shrine of Pathri Pir. They had hoisted the *dhaal*—a white, triangular flag—on the sacred maple tree. It fluttered along with the other white and off-white flags raised on the tree over the years. The maple tree was believed to be centuries old; it was the only one of its kind among the thick evergreen Himalayan oaks along the mountain slope. It stood quietly beside the rivulet, absorbing the prayers of the villagers, safekeeping secrets from prying eyes.

Two megaliths also stood alongside the sacred maple, balanced rather mysteriously on the semi-eroded slope. They were built of rocks from the twin peaks of Tatta-Kutti, the highest peaks of the Pir Panjal Mountain range in whose lap nestled the village of Pathri Aali. If you were to ask the villagers, they would tell you that 'Jinns' or genies had transported these megaliths. They would also tell you that engraved on those stones were the footprints of the great saint, Pathri Pir.

Buried in the shrine were some passers-by who had visited and died during the summer. No one came here in the winter when those slopes were wrapped in gigantic sheets of snow that made passing impossible. The graves in Pathri Pir were considered sacred; the deceased became the companions of the Pir. Whenever Haji

Mir saw the shrine, he longed for its holy and absolute peace. If Allah so wished, he too would die during the summer.

❦

It was July 1987. The Gujjars in Pathri Aali had been able to feed their cattle well. The abundant rainfall that year had made the forest lush and luxuriant, the meadows full of tender grass. Butterflies fluttered over buttercups, Himalayan strawberries, and wild flowers. Tadpoles and pond skaters delighted in the water gushing forth from beneath every stone on the slope. No wonder then that the buffaloes had become especially healthy and strong. It was to express gratitude for these bounties of nature that the villagers had made offerings to the Pir.

The bullfight wasn't the only sport scheduled for the day. It was to be followed by several smaller events for which the youth of Pathri Aali had been rigorously training. But for the moment, it was the struggle of beast against beast. Haji Mir finally called out for silence. With the dhol shushed, the hills were resoundingly quiet but for the occasional barking of a few Bakarwali dogs[1] from the lowermost row of houses.

The two bulls stared at each other, snorting and thumping their feet for a few minutes. Suddenly, they banged their heads together. The sound resounded in the mountains, followed immediately by thunderous applause. The crowd cheered and jostled, pushing each other almost as vigorously as the competing bulls. Meanwhile, the bulls wrestled with all their might, oblivious to all else except the motive to emerge victorious.

Haji Mir wobbled and twirled in his cot as though he controlled the movements of his bull with a joystick. The wrinkles on his face deepened each time his bull winced. Eventually his face lit up. A

---

[1] A working breed of dog found in Jammu and Kashmir.

huge smile formed on his lips, exposing the only upper incisor left in his mouth. Aslam's bull had pushed its opponent into a bush and had won the contest. His village had won! The dhols resumed, no one daring to stop them as Aslam and his supporters stormed into the arena. Then the two Army officers, flanked by a dozen jawans, marched around the arena. They were met with a standing ovation from the audience.

Now that the bullfight was over, the audience would witness an exhibition of local sports. There would be *Gatka*—a stick fight that simulated a duel. There would also be *Bini Pakdai* (or *Bahan Pakdai*) where players had to free their wrists from the clutches of their opponents. The final event of the day was to be weightlifting. But as far as Haji Mir was concerned, the day's highlight was over. Everything else was merely 'satanic misdemeanour' or utterly vile and unnecessary. Avdal, however, disagreed. He believed that sporting events were a genuine show of strength and valour and not 'infantile husbandry games'.

Uninterested though he was, Haji Mir duly supervised the rest of the proceedings. Avdal awaited his favourite event: the lifting of a carved stone weighing a quintal. When everyone failed to lift the stone, claiming it was too slippery, Avdal smugly rose from his cot. But someone was quicker. A gaunt young boy emerged from the crowd and lifted the stone as if it was no heavier than a feather. He then walked towards the edge of the arena and threw the stone into the cow dung. The dhols rose to ear-splitting decibels.

'We need to respect the rules of the game,' Avdal whined, returning to his cot. 'I didn't like the way that boy tossed the stone out of the arena.'

Haji Mir gave Avdal a sympathetic smile. He knew exactly what Avdal didn't like. 'Come here, boy!' Haji Mir summoned the young victor, ignoring Avdal's displeasure.

The boy wore a grey salwar-kameez; a shawl was loosely wrapped around his shoulders. His cheekbones were prominent, rising above his rather sunken face almost like the Tatta-Kutti peaks.

Haji Mir smiled at the boy. 'Whose son are you?'

'Lal Din Khalifa's,' he replied.

The boy's response stunned Haji Mir. He glanced at Avdal with a silent question: 'Isn't he exactly like his deceased father?' It was, thought Haji Mir, as if Khalifa had been reborn!

Avdal shook his head in revulsion. The mere mention of Khalifa filled him with regret—a deep pang of resentment for not being in the village when Khalifa had been killed. Avdal had no love for Khalifa; in fact, he only had unwavering hatred. But the fact that it had taken twenty men to kill Khalifa made him the strongest man Pathri Aali had ever known. Khalifa, even in his death, had belittled Avdal's strength and reputation. Since his death, Avdal had routinely attempted to undo Khalifa's legend, but he hadn't met with any success. The villagers continued to eulogize the 'strongest man of the village who had single-handedly carried a heifer upslope'. Avdal found the whole story ridiculously overrated; after all, it hadn't been a heifer, only a calf.

'What is your name, boy?' asked Haji Mir.

'Mohammad Akram.'

Avdal grunted. As if erasing Khalifa's legend hadn't been hard enough, here was his younger version posing a fresh challenge. He stood staring at the receding figure of Akram, long after Haji Mir had dismissed him.

Avdal had settled in Pathri Aali a year after Khalifa's murder. He reared horses and loved them with all his heart. He couldn't bear as much as a thorn pricking any of his horses. But one summer, shortly after Khalifa's strength became a legend, Avdal was pleased to find one of his foals with a broken leg. Here was the perfect opportunity to shatter Khalifa's legend! Painstakingly, Avdal carried the injured foal on his shoulders from the meadow to the barn. 'I carried the poor colt on my shoulders,' narrated Avdal to anyone who cared to listen, conveniently forgetting that it had actually been a foal. 'It weighed more than a quintal, but I couldn't stop myself.' Pausing to breathe halfway through his emotional narrative, Avdal would slyly ask, 'The calf that Khalifa carried on his shoulders must have been about eighty kilos, no?'

But Avdal's not-so-subtle hints at attaining glory had all gone unrewarded. He had failed to dent the legend of Khalifa's strength. People's stubborn perceptions didn't allow the foal to pass off as a colt. Neither was a heifer relegated to being a calf.

Two

The furrows on Haji Mir's face were illuminated by the kerosene lamp that yielded light and smoke in equal measure. As he offered his evening prayers on a Saudi Arabian rug, his grandsons waited impatiently. The evening was story time; their grandfather would narrate fascinating folktales about *shers* (lions), the *Bann Budhi* (witch), and fairies.

Haji Mir adored his two grandsons—Riaz, five, and Kabir, four. Every evening, after his prayers, they would rush to his lap and demand a story. Their grandfather never disappointed them. On Thursdays though, they had to wait for a long time. Haji Mir's prayers would go on for hours. Finally, when the patience of the two children would run at its thinnest, he would curl his lips, blow on the milk saucer and the rice plate, and announce that he had imbued the food with Allah's blessings.

A few feet away, Parveen, Haji Mir's daughter-in-law, cooked chapattis for dinner. His wife, Hamida, and his elder son, Wazir, attended to the chores of the household, including feeding and milking the buffaloes. Aslam, his younger son, was a freewheeler. His daily routine comprised hanging out with his friends at desolate places, telling tall tales, and predicting the probabilities of weird, absurd events.

Among the many absurd probabilities that Aslam and his friends discussed, facing the *Bann Budhi* was the most hair-raising. She was the chimaera of the village—the witch that haunted the stories that Haji Mir told his grandsons every evening. The two boys were too young to examine the accounts critically, but

Aslam filled in for them. 'One needs courage and ingenious tricks to deal with the *Bann Budhi*,' he would tell his friends. 'If you snatch her golden comb, she will beg for life and promise not to trouble you again.'

'Why is that?' one of his pals would inquire.

'Her soul is ensconced in the golden comb!' Aslam would declare triumphantly.

Alternatively, one could also trick her to take her own life. This is what the Great-grandfather had done on his surreal adventures. Once, narrated Haji Mir, the Great-grandfather had gone hunting quails and partridges. At nightfall, he squatted by a bonfire, roasting his kill. It was then that the *Bann Budhi* stole up to him, silent as the grave. Had he uttered a single word, the *Bann Budhi* would have pulled his heart out with her golden comb. But she couldn't do any harm if her intended victim remained silent. The Great-grandfather was smart. He stayed mum, as though he had heard nothing but the crackle of burning twigs and he had seen nothing but the sparks rising from the fire. Frustrated, the *Bann Budhi* squatted in front of him, calling him names, ridiculing his actions. If he scratched his head, she mimicked him. If he rubbed his nose, she imitated him. Finally, he picked a burning log and scratched his back with the unlit side. The *Bann Budhi* picked one up too, but alas, she scraped her back with the burning side! Immediately her hairy body caught fire!

Sometimes, Haji Mir gave this story an alternate ending. In this version, the Great-grandfather sucked on his hookah, and the *Bann Budhi* sucked at his double-barrel gun, after which the Great-grandfather lost no time in pulling the trigger!

※

Haji Mir was an excellent storyteller. When he started telling his stories, Hamida and Wazir would join the kids, almost as enraptured. That evening, he was telling everyone's favourite story: the one where the Great-grandfather crossed the Pir Panjal Mountain near *Pir ki Galli,* on his way to Kashmir, and had the most thrilling rendezvous with jinns and fairies.

'They took him to the twin peaks of Tatta-Kutti, inside the palace of the fairies where torrents of milk flowed, and gardens were lined with gunny bags full of sweets!'

'Didn't Great-grandfather want to eat a sweet?' asked Riaz, very fond of sweets himself.

'Oh, very much, but before he could taste a treat, the jinns caught the human smell. It made their mouth water. But he couldn't be killed yet.'

'Why not?' enquired Kabir.

'Well, no human being could be killed without the sanction of the head of the clan. And the head had gone to Baghdad to pay homage to the holy shrine of Ghouse Pak. So the Great-grandfather was caged and booed by all the fairies and the jinns—all except one.'

'Who? Who?' Kabir was beside himself with curiosity.

'The head's daughter. She found the Great-grandfather extremely attractive and fell in love with him. If her suitor had known about her feelings, he would have gnawed the Great-grandfather alive!'

Hamida interrupted as always, saying, 'You don't remember it properly. The head's daughter didn't really fall in love; she had just always fancied marrying a human.'

Hamida's interruptions infuriated her grandsons and her husband alike.

Kabir complained, '*Daadi*, just keep quiet. *Daadaji*, what happened next?'

'The head's daughter hatched a plan to rescue the great-grandfather. She smeared henna on his hands, blackened his eyes with *surma*, and made him a toupee of her hair. When she was done with him, he looked exactly like a fairy. Then, the head's daughter opened his cage and showed him the palace gates. She thought that the jinn guarding the gates wouldn't recognize him and let him pass.'

'Did the jinn recognize him after all?' Riaz interjected.

'He did. "Your makeup is perfect", said the jinn, "but I have a strong sense of smell, especially for human flesh. I will let you pass only if the princess fairy does me a big favour." The head's daughter, deeply in love with the Great-grandfather, promised to marry the jinn if he spared his life. And that is how the Great-grandfather was flown home by the jinn, piggyback!'

Haji wanted to end the story there, but the kids were more interested in the fairies, the jinns, and their mysterious world than in the safe landing of the Great-grandfather.

'Did she marry the jinn then?'

'No, she didn't. She explained it to the Great-grandfather in his dreams. In exchange for saving his life, he had to marry her in the world of dreams. That was the pact. Most mornings, he woke up with henna smeared on his hands and his eyes blackened with *surma*.'

'Where is the world of dreams, *Daadaji*?'

Haji Mir grinned. 'The world of dreams is the one we create with our imagination. But for fairies and souls, it is as real as this world that we live in. Think of it as visiting a distant land, like my visit to Saudi Arabia.'

'What is a soul, *Daadaji*?'

'It is the part of us that we cannot see. When we die, the soul leaves our body and goes to heaven.'

Kabir and Riaz were thoroughly confused by now and felt that their grandfather was being rather complicated that evening. They could think of only one retort: 'What happened next?'

'Nothing. The story is over. Now go to bed.'

Most of Haji Mir's stories ended on this note. The kids could never get enough of him. As long as they remained awake, they would imagine events that succeeded the happenings in the stories, sometimes enlivening their imagination in their dreams. The next morning, one of them would declare, 'Look at my hands! The fairies have smeared henna on my palms!' The other kid, unwilling to be left behind, would also proclaim, 'Mine too!' It would be Parveen's simple explanations that steered them back to the real world, 'Both of you were playing with walnut skins last night.'

Apart from the folktales, the children of Pathri Aali also enjoyed the legends of the village. The most incredible of them featured Haji Mir as the grand hero. Hamida had exercised a blanket ban on that particular tale. Haji Mir had married Hamida two decades ago, after the death of his first wife. He had three daughters from his first wife, the eldest two years older than Hamida. Many of his grandchildren were older than Aslam, the only bachelor among his children. The grandiose tale pertained to the marriage of Haji Mir and his first wife, Mehar Bi, and it was one that Hamida vehemently detested.

But Hamida could not ensure that the ban on the story was honoured in other households. Haji Mir's eldest daughter often narrated the tale to her grandchildren with great pride and passion. There was no skipping or fast-forwarding, and no one to interrupt. Her story had a prelude too: 'My mother was beautiful. She was fair, with delicate hands, and her features were more exquisite than any woman in Pathri Aali.'

The incident had taken place decades back. Mehar Bi was fifteen years old when she received her first proposal of marriage. One of the men, Akbar, was a widower who offered her father five sheep and a heifer in exchange of his daughter's hand. Infuriated, Mehar Bi's father pushed Akbar out of his house; Akbar's turban fell off and hit the ground. Akbar was severely humiliated. He resolved to organize a *kahda* or abduction for marriage, with the help of his relatives.

One full moon night in May, Akbar marched towards Pathri Aali with twenty men, led by his brother-in-law. He wanted to avenge his humiliation, and fury ruled his head. Akbar and his gang attacked Mehar Bi's house, but it was guarded bravely by the men of Pathri Aali. For hours on end, they fought bravely together, not allowing Akbar or his men to enter through the doors and windows. But around midnight, two of the men of Pathri Aali were struck down. A rumour circulated that Mehar Bi, the girl they were fighting to protect, was not even present in the house. Thoroughly discouraged, the men of Pathri Aali abandoned their watch. Soon, the only person standing between the door and Akbar's men was Mehar Bi's father. He was beaten mercilessly until he fell to the ground, unconscious.

Akbar's party thoroughly searched the house but couldn't find Mehar Bi. Infuriated, they went on a rampage and invaded the remaining houses of the village, lashing out at the women and the children, ignoring their screams. Finally, they came to Haji Mir Baksh's house. At the door, a scrawny boy stood upright, brandishing an axe; the door was left ajar with two logs placed across it.

'I swear by the holy shrine of Pathri Pir that the first man who steps inside the door is a dead man,' Mir Baksh declared. The axe in his hand caught the moonlight and shone.

'Is that you, Mir Baksh?' Akbar laughed. 'You are so scrawny that if all of us urinate together, you will drown like an ant. Move aside and let me have the girl; hitting you would almost be an insult to my stick.'

'Do you dare to enter, Akbar?'

'Do you dare to stand here and threaten me? Get ready to meet your death tonight!' Akbar charged in with his stick. Mir Baksh stepped aside like lightning and the stick struck the logs placed on the door. The next thing Akbar knew was three fingers of his right hand were on the floor. Mir Baksh had inflicted a well-targeted, ferocious blow with his axe.

'Progeny of a pig! He cut my hand!' Akbar ran back, crying in pain. 'Kill him!' he commanded his men.

Akbar's men, although horrified by the incident, charged in groups of three and four to attack Mir Baksh. But each time their sticks hit nothing but the logs on the door. Akbar's brother-in-law decided to sidestep the logs by putting his leg inside the doorway and bending over to cross. But Mir Baksh's axe swung swiftly again. Torrents of blood gushed from the brother-in-law's thigh, the blood almost black in the moonlight.

With the two leading men badly injured, the rest of the party was dispirited. Nevertheless, they were unwilling to give up.

One of them complained: 'People will spit at us if they know that we were defeated by that mite of a boy!'

'Should we try to climb up the smoke hole?'

But unfortunately, that was the wrong thing to do! Mir Baksh's mother stood on guard near the vent, a hot griddle in her hand. She firmly struck the first man who tried to put his head inside the hole. He fell almost fifteen feet, breaking his neck and several bones.

Well and truly defeated, the men departed from Pathri Aali, carrying the injured on their shoulders and blaming their unpreparedness and misfortune for their humiliating loss.

Early the next morning, when Mehar Bi's father regained consciousness, he was shocked to see Mir Baksh still standing at the door, an axe in his hand, guarding the house like a Spartan. Later that day, the *kachehri* or the assembly of elders, pronounced their decision about Mehar Bi:

'The man who protected our honour and guarded the chastity of Pathri Aali without a care for his own life deserves whatever he desires and whatever we can afford. The kachehri is of the opinion that Mehar Bi be given in marriage to Mir Baksh.'

It was a grand wedding that was celebrated by the entire village as a symbol of good reigning victorious over evil.

And so another legend was born in Pathri Aali.

Three

'What was the story about that boy—what's his name? Wasim Akram? The one we saw earlier today, running down the slope?' Raman Negi, the Army captain who had watched the bullfight in Pathri Aali, asked Dr Himanshu. It was late in the evening in the Army camp at Jabari Hills, situated at a height of seven thousand feet. The peak overlooked the meadows and the hutments in the lap of Pir Panjal.

'Mohammad Akram, not Wasim Akram,' corrected Dr Himanshu.

Himanshu Singh lived in Buffliaz, a small town at the foothills of the mountains where the Army had a full-fledged establishment including a hospital. He visited Jabari Hills only on call. A dirt road with steep gradients and many broken stretches connected it with Buffliaz.

'He is Lal Din Khalifa's son,' continued Himanshu, 'the same boy who had visited the Army Medical Camp in Buffliaz last year, carrying his grandmother on his back all the way from his village for a glaucoma surgery.'

Himanshu remembered the incident clearly. After the surgery, when she was once again saddled on his back, Himanshu hadn't been able to contain his amazement. 'How old are you, boy?'

'I am fifteen,' Akram had replied.

'How did you manage to carry her all this way? Will you be able to carry her all the way back?'

'Oh yes. I will halt for a few moments midway, perhaps, if I can still see the sun.'

'You'll walk over fifteen kilometres up-slope with a woman on your back yet you are unsure whether you'll stop for a break?'

'Don't worry, Doctor,' the old woman had said. 'His father once carried an injured cow on his shoulders. The brutal villagers lynched him out of envy. My grandson has the same strength running in his veins. Anyway, I am nothing but a bundle of bones; my grandson is strong enough to carry many like me all at once!'

Himanshu had wanted to ask many more questions—about the injured cow, the lynching, and the purported envy. But he had decided not to delay their arduous journey. He could always ask Aslam about it later.

'The boy's father, Lal Din Khalifa, had quite a reputation in the village. People thought he was a giant,' Himanshu continued. 'I think they were rather scared of him.'

Major Dharam Pal Singh turned his attention from the Pakistan TV programme he was watching and interrupted, very uncharacteristically. 'I have heard that he once carried an injured heifer on his shoulders, all the way up the mountain.'

'It is possible, sir. His mother claimed the same. But for all his strength, Khalifa seems to have been a cruel man with a criminal bent of mind.'

Major Dharam Pal Singh was intrigued. 'Why do you say that?'

'Let me tell you some of the stories I have heard from the villagers. In early summer, when the meadows are parched, and fodder is difficult to get, the villagers have to travel to the cliffs opposite Pathri Aali for dried grass. It often takes them an entire day. Khalifa devised a plan to collect fodder without the hard work—he started looting the people. Many times, men returned home bruised or with broken bones. Women were harassed and molested. Once, when a group of six men confronted Khalifa near the Changa river, he injured them so badly that they were hospitalised with multiple fractures and haemorrhages.'

'Did no one ever complain against him?' Raman Negi enquired.

'Sure they did. Apparently the kachehri summoned Khalifa several times for his unacceptable behaviour, but he never showed up—a grave insult to the elders of the village. But finally, a day came when Khalifa committed the ultimate sin. A young woman returned to the village from the jungle, completely naked but for a bunch of leaves in her arms. Khalifa had not only raped her, but had hung her clothes atop a tall tree, almost like a flag of his accomplishment. He had demanded that the girl call her husband to climb up the tree to get them.'

'Why did he do that? Did he have some specific enmity with her?' Dharam Pal Singh had forgotten his favourite TV programme.

'It turns out her husband was among the men who had attacked him at Changa river. The men were furious. Nothing could appease them except slitting Khalifa's throat and drawing his blood. The elders of the village were against this extreme mission, but the young men had turned rebellious in rage.'

'Understandably so,' agreed both Raman Negi and the Major.

'So, the next morning, twenty men armed with sticks reached the Changa river once again. When Khalifa reached the riverbank, a group of men hiding above the cliff started rolling boulders at him. Some of them threw stones and wooden logs. A few of those did hit him, but his body seemed to be made of steel. He charged at the men with his stick, and they ran away helter-skelter. But the other group attacked Khalifa from behind and managed to throw him off-guard, toppling him over. Then they beat him ceaselessly until he lay perfectly still.'

'Until he died?' asked Dharam Pal Singh.

'No. The men believed that a person as vile as Khalifa deserved a worse death. So, they dunked him in the cold water of the river and then hit him some more. Some villagers claim that this is how they put a rabid dog to sleep. Do you know what the autopsy report stated?'

'What?' enquired Raman.

'It said that Khalifa had water in his lungs; he had died of drowning. That means, when he was dunked in the river, he was still alive! If the police hadn't recovered his dead body, he might have been scavenged by vultures. No one even mentioned giving him a burial; I think they'd have preferred it if the vultures had had a feast.'

Resilience or Relapse?

Four

When the election results had been declared, Adalat Shah had vowed to teach his enemies a lesson. 'Rigged elections! Sham elections! I will bring them to justice!' he had claimed. A year had gone by, and he was ambivalent about his vow. Domestic quarrels and failures in business had diluted his resolve. Adalat Shah believed that his wife was a nag. But he also knew that his business sense wasn't the best. Business had been the prerogative of his deceased father, the village moneylender who had amassed great wealth during Partition, and as the only son, he had been entrusted to carry it forward. It didn't matter how Adalat Shah had inherited his money or that his father was a swindler. A swarm of sycophants accompanied Adalat Shah all the time and smartly glossed over these unpleasant facts. More often than not, they blamed these 'rumours' on the 'undeserving competitor who won the assembly elections every year'.

The family business was in the town of Swarnpur. It was a small town by the banks of the Swarn river, from where most of the villages of Pir Panjal, including Pathri Aali, bought their daily supplies. Legend had it that the Swarn river used to carry grains of *swarn* or pure gold. Apparently, Alexander the Great had been mesmerized by the river. But Adalat Shah found nothing impressive about either the river or the town near it.

After the disappointing results of the latest assembly elections, Adalat Shah had lost all his political hopes. He was faced with the gigantic challenge of recovering the burgeoning debts of his business. He sat quietly at home, his mind in turmoil over a proposal that had come in earlier that day, via a trunk call. It could be the best opportunity to teach his political enemies a lesson. It could revive his business. But it was an opportunity put forward by his sworn enemy, Saghir Khan. It was a forbidden opportunity. What if it was a trap? Adalat Shah mulled over it for a long time and finally decided to lock his pessimism in the closet. Desperation can impair judgment, but Adalat Shah hoped he had made the right decision.

Saghir Khan was a notorious smuggler and double agent until the Inter-Services Intelligence (ISI) visualised a great motivator in him. They elevated him to the ranks of the most respected among the Mujahideen—a recruiter. He was awarded a new, respectable name—Ghazi Khan.

In the late sixties, Saghir Khan used to smuggle gold and drugs from Pakistan to India. Adalat Shah would find buyers for the smuggled goods. Their partnership yielded rich dividends until Saghir Khan ran out of luck. He spent a few years in an Indian jail but never named Adalat Shah or any of his accomplices. Upon release, he went straight to Shah's house to claim the gold that he had kept in his trust. But Adalat Shah refused to acknowledge any such agreement. Shocked, Saghir Khan stormed out of Adalat Shah's house warning of vengeance.

By the beginning of the 1980s, the ISI, under General Zia Ul Haq, watched every single bird that flew on the eastern horizon. With the agencies on both sides more alert than before, it was almost impossible for Saghir Khan to resume his illegal business. But Saghir Khan wasn't one to give up. He took his chances with a senior officer of the Indian Army, offering his secret services in exchange for protection. He brokered a similar deal with the agencies across the border, thereby becoming a double agent enlisted on the payrolls of both sides.

However, it soon became evident that he was two-timing the Indian Army. Although he narrowly escaped being caught by the Indian Army, the Pakistan Rangers managed to get the better of him. He landed in the District Jail, Rajanpur, and was then shifted to Central Jail, Sahiwal. Charged with drug smuggling and espionage, among many other charges, Saghir Khan was faced with lifelong imprisonment and possible execution. Highly improbable as it was, even if Saghir Khan managed to escape from jail, the authorities across the border also had the gallows ready for him.

Saghir Khan's confinement started taking a toll on his senses. He was haunted by visions and hallucinations that left him a shadow of his former self. Intimidated by his own thoughts, Saghir Khan started growing a beard and offering namaz five times a day. His body became frail and wobbly, but he kept recounting the many glories of Allah. And that continued for nearly six years.

One day, his prayers were finally heard. A senior ISI officer visited the Central Jail and enquired, 'Where is the fellow from Poonch?'

Immediately, Saghir Khan broke down before him. 'Sahib, I never worked for the Indian Army, but you won't believe me. I urge you to study the information I gave Pakistan about the strategic locations of the Indian forces. If any of it is proved false, you can hang me. I never cheated you, but here I am, imprisoned along with murderers and heinous criminals. Why?'

Over the years, Saghir Khan had garnered considerable experience in dealing with security agencies. He had sensed that the officer was keenly interested in him. He knew that there was something important that had brought him to Central Jail. 'Please, sir,' pleaded Saghir, 'give me a chance to prove my devotion to Pakistan and the path of Allah and Islam.'

The ISI officer decided to try him out. Saghir Khan was shifted to Muzaffarabad where many makeshift camps had been set up to train the youth to fight in Jammu and Kashmir. There, he diligently delved into the world of route planning, stealth, mines fields, landmarks, safe shelters, barbed wires, nocturnal movements, and other tactics for crossing the border.

For six months, Saghir Khan worked many shifts a day, indefatigably. One morning he was told: 'An officer from the ISI is coming to have a word with you. Wait in your tent.'

As he waited nervously inside his tent, Saghir Khan wondered whether it meant sending him back to Sahiwal Central Jail or offering him clemency. The wait was torturous.

It was late in the day when the ISI officer, wearing a golden salwar-kameez and Peshawari sandals, stormed into his tent accompanied by two gunmen. The officer wasted no time. 'The time has come for you to be elevated to a more responsible position. You know that the jihad in Kashmir is intended to liberate the people of Indian Occupied Kashmir. So, basically, the struggle belongs to the people of Indian Occupied Kashmir.'

'Yes, sir.'

'The men we are training here belong to countries like Afghanistan, Pakistan, Africa, and Turkey. We have some men from Kashmir too. But the jihad can be sustained only if the Mujahids get recruited from Indian Occupied Kashmir. Saghir Khan, I want you to become a recruiter for the Mujahideen.'

Saghir Khan was elated. His face lit up as if he had been waiting for this moment all the years he had been in captivity—dreaming, ideating. 'Sir, how can I do that? Are you going to release me?'

'No, you can't leave Pakistan. We will provide a house for you here in Azad Kashmir. You will have to set your network in motion to recruit deserving men from Indian Occupied Kashmir.'

'Sir, you know that Indian agencies are looking for me. All the communication between India and Pakistan is being monitored. Under such circumstances, there is only one solution to make such recruitment possible.'

'Tell me.'

'Sir, I can assure you that I will motivate the Kashmiri youth to join our cause. But to do that, I need to be allowed to move to Saudi Arabia.'

Saghir Khan suffered an entire month of silent treatment. As soon as he had proposed Saudi Arabia, the officer had left.

But after one month, Saghir Khan received good news. Under General Zia Ul Haq, Pakistan enjoyed great patronage from Saudi Arabia. The Saudi government agreed to receive Saghir Khan and put him under house arrest. He was issued a Pakistani passport in the name of Ghazi Khan and stationed at the outskirts of the holy city of Mecca. He was made to take an oath, swearing his allegiance to jihad and loyalty to Pakistan in front of the Holy Kaaba.

Soon after, the trunk call to Adalat Shah's residence had come—the call that had made him both anxious and excited.

'What do you want?' Adalat Shah had asked. 'Why are you calling me?'

'Adalat, we can forget our animosity in the name of Allah. But you'll have to join forces with me.'

'I don't understand.'

'Well, you probably know that our state will soon see an armed struggle. I am a recruiter for the jihad and am working from Saudi Arabia. You can help me in recruiting more mujahids for this noble cause.'

Adalat Shah was stunned. He had never expected Saghir Khan to be released from Pakistan jail, let alone hold a powerful position in Saudi Arabia.

'Please don't make such nonsensical offers to me. Don't you see that I have a political career?' Adalat Shah screamed into the phone before hanging up.

Five

When Aslam dropped out of school, no one questioned his decision. In Pathri Aali, this wasn't something that warranted parental admonition. But when he decided to resume his studies, quite a few eyebrows shot up. The villagers were beside themselves with curiosity when they saw him filling the form for the school final exam as a private candidate.

Although Aslam had never been particularly interested in studies, he hadn't quit school out of boredom. Indeed, it was a love bug that had got into him. Aslam was in love with Ashwar—a bright classmate and also a distant relative. One fine morning, Aslam had gone up to her when she was fetching water from the stream near Pathri Pir. In a rather vapid declaration of love, he had said to her, 'You are the reason I dropped out of school.'

'Me? How, exactly?'

'I didn't want you to know that I was a dumb student who cut a sorry figure when a teacher asked him a question.'

'But I still knew it,' she replied nonchalantly. 'Anyway, why do you care what I think of you?'

'I want to marry you. So, of course I care what you think of me.'

Ashwar lowered her eyes, suddenly shy and rather taken aback by the blunt proposal.

'So, what do you think? Will you marry me?' Aslam prodded.

'I can't marry a school dropout.' Ashwar replied, her shyness now gone. 'I will marry someone who is employed and can help me fulfil my dream.'

'What's your dream?'

'Why should I tell you?'

Aslam shrugged, 'Well, I must know the dream of the girl who is my dream.'

'Well, it's none of your business, but let me tell you nonetheless. I don't want you to think that I am a girl who just wants to marry a rich man.'

'I don't think that—'

'Aslam, I want to complete my schooling and study further. I want to become a teacher in the village high school.'

'Oh, so you think that a school dropout will not allow you to continue your studies?'

'Oh, come on; don't be so serious. I really can't think about marriage right now. And if you are desperate to find a wife, I'm sure you'll find another girl. You dropped out of school to get married, didn't you?' Ashwar didn't wait for a response and left.

Aslam watched her walking away, and pondered over all she had said.

'Ashwar, I swear by the holy shrine of Pathri Pir that I will wait until you attain your dream and are ready to marry me,' he shouted like a man possessed. She didn't reply but turned around, embarrassed, worried that someone might have heard him. 'By the way,' Aslam now lowered his voice and asked, 'you are sixteen years old already. How much more shall I have to wait?'

'Sixteen more years,' she giggled and turned away.

Stories of the budding romance spread in the village sooner than its consolidation. One morning, when Ashwar was leaving for school, her sister-in-law snatched away her bag. 'You don't have to go to school anymore. Your brother has decided that you'll be married off soon. Your studies are over, girl.'

'No! Please don't say that.' Ashwar was almost in tears. 'I beg you to please let me complete my schooling at the very least.'

But her sister-in-law had her own agenda. 'Don't be so cruel, Ashwar. Your brother has already done a lot for you. I can't see him struggle with your affairs anymore.'

Ashwar and her elder brother had lost their father when they were children. After their mother married another man, both of them were raised by their uncle. Her sister-in-law had joined the household about two years ago when her brother got married in an exchange arrangement that was not uncommon—in exchange for his wife, he had promised to marry Ashwar off to his brother-in-law, Hanif. It hardly mattered that Hanif was the widowed father of two children.

The stories about Aslam and Ashwar's love also reached the ears of Haji Mir. Being the head of the village, he tried to intervene and bring matters to an amicable solution. But that ended when Ashwar's brother, quite disrespectfully, told him not to 'poke his nose in their family matter'. Driven by self-respect and fuelled by ego, Haji Mir didn't attempt to heal his jilted son's heart. Aslam was commanded to stay away from 'other people's daughters and sisters'. On the day of Ashwar's marriage, Aslam remained a silent observer who could do little but watch his dreams and those of the girl he loved shatter.

Ashwar, too, had remained quiet throughout the whole ordeal, resigned to her fate. Within days of her marriage, her entire life changed. Hanif was now her reality as were her stepchildren—Manzoor, five, and Shamma, four years old. Both the children were amenable, affectionate, and evidently in dire need of maternal care. Spending time with them made her nostalgic for her own childhood. Hanif was also gentle and understanding—much more than she could have expected. They were a poor household, living with limited resources, but he had done his best to look after his family after the death of his first wife. In fact, his devotion to the household had earned him many critics: 'What kind of man does household chores like a woman? He cooks, washes utensils and clothes—there's nothing manly about him anymore!'

For almost a week, the new couple hardly spoke to each other. It was as though they were both struggling with unspeakable apologies. But Hanif broke the silence during dinner one night: 'Ashwar, I want to go to Saudi Arabia.'

She didn't respond, so he continued: 'I am finding it hard to run the house on the money I make here. There's an agent in Swarnpur who arranges visas for Saudi Arabia.'

Ashwar nodded silently. Working in Saudi Arabia—or *Soodia*, as it was popularly called—was a way of life for the villagers of Pathri Aali. Most of the men took up jobs as menial labourers. They looked after the camels or goats of Bedouins,[2] watered the gardens, and laid bricks or marble slabs in suburban buildings.

But there was another charm that beckoned many men—the promise of visiting their holy land. When they returned to the village, their pockets full, they anticipated a hero's welcome for conquering misery and poverty. They were given the title of Haji. It didn't seem important to these men to reveal the full details of their grand journey. Who wanted to know that they had, in reality, been deported by the Saudi government and hadn't even visited the Holy Kaaba, let alone perform the Hajj? It simply wasn't important.

Only a few knew the real story behind these spurious Hajis, one of them being Haji Mir. He knew what it took to perform the Hajj. He had, of course, performed it long back—in the early 1970s—travelling by ship that, in seven days, had taken him from Bombay to Jeddah. When he returned home, he was received like a hero, flanked by hundreds of men from the neighbouring villages.

---

[2] A group of nomadic Arab people.

He had got gifts for his visitors: the holy water of the *Zamzam* and date palms from the sacred land. The holy merchandise was on exibit for several days—a radio, finger-sized perfume bottles, a prayer mat, an overcoat and a bioscope. He had regaled them with fantastic stories about zooming cars, tall buildings, and the milky white lights on the streets of Mecca. Having memorized these stories, when Hamida started noticing discrepancies in his later retellings, she couldn't help but interrupt: 'It wasn't like that. Why can't you remember properly?'

Many months had passed since Ashwar's marriage, but Aslam couldn't forgive himself. He thought he alone was responsible for Ashwar's miseries. If stories about their affair hadn't circulated, perhaps her brother would have let her finish school. Aslam believed that he was Ashwar's second love; her first love was education. During their brief courtship, she had often tried to persuade him to join school again. It was time, he decided. He would appear for the matriculation exam even if she was unable to do so. He couldn't share her pain or misfortune, but he could at least step in to fulfil her aspiration.

He decided to meet Ashwar and tell her about his plans. One rainy afternoon, after Hanif had left for Saudi Arabia, he knocked on her door.

She yelled from inside, 'My husband is away. In his absence, I cannot let in any strange man. Go away!'

It was Aslam's turn to be embarrassed. He looked around to ensure that no one had heard her screaming, and hurried away.

Since that day, Aslam tried his best not to cross paths with Ashwar. He wouldn't meet her. He wasn't that weak. But, after they had migrated to their winter abodes, on a cold morning in January, when the village was covered in a sheet of white, Aslam found himself walking surreptitiously to Ashwar's house. It had snowed heavily the previous night and some of the rooftops were dangerously piled up with snow. When Ashwar and her stepchildren climbed up to the roof at sunrise armed with shovels, they found the job was already done.

'Look at that!' cried Manzoor. 'Who cleared the snow?' He was holding a small wooden shovel that his father had carved for him, and had been eager to get going with it. Manzoor and his sister Shamma had prayed for snowfall throughout the previous afternoon; they had dreamt of making a snowman, rolling snowballs, and drinking melted snow with milk and sugar. Manzoor had slept with the shovel by his pillow.

'You can help me shovel snow off my roof, son,' Lal Jaan called out from the neighbouring roof.

Ashwar smiled at her gratefully. 'Do you know who did it?'

'Yes. I saw him leaving a while ago. It was Aslam.'

Lal Jaan and Ashwar had developed a close bond over the months. Without children of her own, Lal Jaan thought of Ashwar as her own daughter. Before Ashwar's marriage, the older woman used to struggle with her household chores; her asthmatic and bedridden husband couldn't help her at all. Lately, Ashwar often checked in to help—cleaning the barn, feeding the cow, fetching water from the stream, making cow dung pats for fuel and chopping wood. All this was in addition to the arduous jobs she had at her own home, the most daunting being bathing and grooming her little stepchildren. In only eight months of marriage, Ashwar had turned into a scrawny, unsmiling, anaemic woman who didn't care about her appearance. The only joy remaining in her life was to read to the villagers who would come to her with letters from someone in Saudi Arabia.

Her husband rarely wrote to her from Saudi Arabia. The only letter she had received said that his work visa had been fake and that he was now living in hiding, working illegally as a labourer. He transferred whatever little he earned to the moneylender in Swarnpur from whom he had loaned the sum to purchase his air ticket.

A World Apart

Six

Buffliaz gave Himanshu the life that he had been yearning for years. Situated at the confluence of two rivers, Buffliaz reminded him of his childhood in Karnaprayag.

His transfer order to Buffliaz had come a year after he had joined the Army on Short Commission as a doctor. Many a morning, he would stand by the Swarn river and reflect on Nature. Nature, he believed, returns whatever you give her. Deep in his heart he felt that his transfer to this beautiful place had been somehow orchestrated by her.

Buffliaz offered Himanshu numerous opportunities to explore Nature. Sometimes he rode with Aslam on a Nissan 1 Ton—a mini truck that made for a bumpy journey. At other times, he walked down the hills, alone. In the summer, he scaled almost all the ridges surrounding Pathri Aali and sometimes went across the Pir Panjal mountains, all the way to the Kashmir Valley. Himanshu was a competent trekker, but he was extremely impressed by the prowess of Aslam. Whenever he spotted the boy on the hills, he tried to imitate the way he lifted his feet, turned his toes inwards, and used the sides of his feet to cross narrow paths.

Aslam enjoyed spending time with Himanshu, and assumed that the Sahib was struck with wanderlust. One morning, when they were trekking near Hill Kaka, Himanshu asked, 'Look, Aslam, what do you see?'

A giant deer was walking over the cliff, balancing itself as if suspended in air. It then jumped over to a cliffhanger with impeccable precision.

Himanshu noticed that Aslam's mouth had opened in awe of the deer's skills. 'Do you know what that is?'

Aslam shook his head.

'It's a Markhor. In Persian, Markhor means snake-eater.'

'Really? I can't believe that a deer can eat a snake.'

'No,' agreed Himanshu, 'but it can surely kill one with its hoofs.' Himanshu sat down under a giant Deodar tree. 'Aslam, these animals need protection from poachers and hunters. We, as human beings, are responsible for their protection. Imagine a day when these animals would live only in ancient tales, as though their existence was nothing but a story.'

'That would be awful, sir.'

'Only a few of these magnificent Markhors are left in Pir Panjal. You can help save them from extinction. One day, when you are married and tell your children about this amazing animal, wouldn't you regret not doing anything to save it? Only so your kids could see it too?'

Aslam smiled sheepishly. He couldn't get his head around the prospect of being a married man who told stories to his children as his father did.

While Himanshu focused his energy on the bounties of nature, especially the wild life that was being destroyed, Major Dharam Pal Singh was not at all impressed by Buffliaz.

'We are living a Spartan's life here,' he would rant before Himanshu. 'There is nothing interesting at all!'

Immediately after assuming his post at Jabari Hills, the Major had ordered the horse grazers to flee. He couldn't have 'untrustworthy people' so close to an Army establishment. He ordered the jawans to fiddle with the TV antenna till it received Doordarshan but it never did. The only crystal clear channel was Pakistan TV. Every evening, the Major sat drinking vodka, surfing channels and swearing. It was by accident that the Major discovered his second favourite indulgence after vodka—the serial *Dhoop Kinare* on Pakistan TV. One cold night, when he was more than a little inebriated, Dharam Pal Singh sat fiddling with the remote. He wanted to confront his enemies, but on the television was Marina Khan, the heroine of the serial. She looked straight into his eyes and smiled, and carved her way immediately into the Major's heart.

Although *Dhoop Kinare* made life a little more bearable for the Major, it was still pretty dull. He kept urging for a transfer to the battalion or corps headquarters. 'I have to look after my mother,' he would implore, 'She is arthritic and lives with my aged father in Haryana.' Dharam Pal's wife, Kavita Singh, did not stay with her in-laws; she lived with her parents and two sons in Dehradun.

Dharam Pal Singh had married young—at twenty-three. Two years after joining the Indian Army as a lieutenant, his marriage had been arranged to Kavita. She was a 'suitable girl'; her family had promised fifty thousand rupees in cash and a Bajaj Chetak scooter in dowry. But when after weeks of the wedding, the dowry didn't turn up, Kavita had to face humiliation and jeers from her mother-in-law. It got worse when her husband left for Jodhpur, leaving her behind.

Kavita embarked upon her plan to rid herself of a 'miserable life' and join her husband in Jodhpur. She wrote to her husband unconventional and cryptic letters, littered with blanks and empty spaces.

The half-empty letters filled with apparent longing riveted Dharam Pal like nothing ever had. Who needed words when the unsaid could be so powerful, so flexible, and so full of desire? He read these love letters over and over, filling in the blanks as he pleased, fantasizing about passionate intimacy with his wife, fondly making love to her in his imagination.

As the number of letters increased, so did the blanks and the lipstick marks. Dharam Pal could take it no more. He sent a telegram home: 'Dear Mummy, I am unwell. Please come immediately.'

Kavita and her mother-in-law came over to tend to the sick man. Within a fortnight, Dharam Pal's mother found it hard to justify her stay there. She was frequently rebuffed by her son, especially when he was sharing a private moment with his wife. Soon after, the offended woman boarded a train home, amidst an emotional farewell by her daughter-in-law who begged her to 'stay for some more days'.

Kavita hugged herself in joy after her mother-in-law left. She had finally attained what she wanted—a life with her husband, and the freedom to demand from him whatever her heart fancied. Initially, she seemed content with only his company; but as time passed, her demands gathered steam.

'Could you get me a camera?' 'I want imported Ray-Ban sunglasses and silk saris.' 'My brother needs a bicycle.'

Dharam Pal fulfilled all her whims by brokering deals with the fuelwood contractor, the vegetable supplier, and the grocery vendor, among others. These fellows were docile in obeying his wishes; after all, their contracts could be terminated anytime their 'goods didn't adhere to the prescribed standards'.

It all went very smoothly until a Junior Commissioned Officer, with a long arabic name that ended with Khan, got wind of Dharam Pal's scam—and ended up getting fired.

'You have once again proved that you people are traitors!' screamed Dharam Pal, the epitome of uprightness. 'You should have gone to Pakistan at the time of Partition. You can never be trusted. Get lost and never show me your bloody face again!'

Seven

The seventh floor of the Al Hijaz building on the outskirts of Mecca was aptly named The Seventh Heaven. Here lived Saghir Khan alias Ghazi Khan surrounded by state-of-the-art amenities. 'He deserves it too', thought anyone who saw him, for his tall frame, white robe, chequered scarf, and long, henna-dyed beard made him look like a saint. On his right hand he wore a silver ring studded with a lapis lazuli. The ring depicted the *Zulfiqar*—the bifurcated sword of Ali—and on its body was inscribed 'Allah Ho Akbar' in Arabic. He could often be found reclining on the couch in his living room, quietly fingering the beads of a rosary.

Ghazi Khan had many visitors, but no one could make eye contact with him for more than a moment. His face had the *noor*, the divine glow—the evidence that he was chosen by Allah for the noble cause of jihad. The only visitors who were indifferent to his 'divinity' were the Pakistani Intelligence officers. When they called at the Seventh Heaven, the servants had a day off. He wouldn't be a saint on those days.

Shortly after his relocation to Saudi Arabia, Saghir Khan requested that his wife and children join him there. The ISI conceded; a family under house arrest is better than a single, cunning man. His family crossed the Indo-Pak border much like him. New passports were issued to them by the Pakistani government. Saghir Khan was thrilled to see his family and confided in his wife about the fortune he had struck over the past few months.

'I have been running around like a petty thief all my life, risking everything and living without you. But for what? My life would have been miserable even if I had made a lot of money.'

'Why?' His wife raised her eyebrows.

'The Army and police would have constantly intimidated me. They would have made our life hell. But now, by divine guidance, I'm here with you and our children. What else do we need?'

He stood up, walked to the window, and lit a cigarette. 'I know what you are thinking,' he grinned at his wife, blowing smoke through the half-opened pane. 'But even Adam and Hawa were not given Eden without some prohibition.' He crushed the cigarette in a stone-studded marble ashtray and lay down beside his wife.

About fifty miles away lived Hanif, but his circumstances were hardly as rosy. True, he wasn't under house arrest and could roam around the entire countryside, but he wasn't safe anywhere. He had spent several months running between Mecca and Jeddah, avoiding the police, and unsure of whether he would eat the next day. Finally, he had managed to get work as an unauthorized daily wager in the outskirts of Taif. He worked at the construction site of a private house, doing menial labour and anything else that the site supervisor deemed necessary. Sometimes, Hanif felt that the supervisor had given him work only to accommodate a poor, desperate man in the Month of Fasting. The scorching heat of May had made both the fasting and the labour harder for Hanif. But he persevered because he had no choice. Like many other illegal workers from South Asia, his survival depended on changing locations constantly to avoid being nabbed and deported by the Saudi authorities.

It was at Taif that Hanif met Altaf Dastarkhan, a man from a village near Swarnpur. Altaf worked as a trucker with a company that supplied building materials. He greeted Hanif as no man had greeted him since he had come to Saudi Arabia. Desperate for help and overwhelmed by Altaf's kind greeting, Hanif broke down. 'I am in utter misery here. I was cheated by the visa agent in Swarnpur. I have to live in hiding, always afraid they'll catch and deport me.'

Altaf nodded sympathetically. 'You come to me on Monday, *inshallah*. I will help you.'

Hanif showed up early on Monday. Altaf took him along in a truck loaded with tiles. 'We are driving outside the city,' he announced. Hanif loved the use of the 'we'; he felt as if he was already employed as a loader with the construction material supplying company. His miseries would finally be over. He started drafting mental notes of gratitude for Altaf Dastarkhan, the son of his land, the man with the generous heart.

'Sometimes, we have to struggle, not for instant gratification but for something that will deliver dividends for our future generations,' Altaf broke into Hanif's thoughts. 'Do you understand what I mean?'

'Not really.'

'My father wanted me to follow his footsteps and be an ironsmith or a carpenter. He assumed that nothing would change, that nothing *could* change. Likewise, your forefathers never dared to undertake a struggle to rid them of their miseries. Don't you think we should struggle for a better future for our children?'

'Yes, of course. But then, our forefathers did struggle in the past, and so did their forefathers. Life is a struggle—'

'Hush! Have you forgotten what Islam teaches us? It tells us that we must persevere. Yes, our life is a constant struggle against the profanity of society and the cruelty of fortune. This struggle is called jihad. Let me explain—'

Hanif could not make much sense of Altaf's words. However, he kept shaking his head in apparent understanding, wondering, when Altaf would broach the subject of his salary, visa, and job.

'So, have you understood the idea?' Hanif concluded. 'If it's yes, you are welcome to join me. Once you understand the essence of our lives, problems like poverty will seem mere banalities.'

'Yes, yes. Of course!' Hanif agreed, jumping at anything that would drive away his poverty.

That evening Hanif was taken to the Seventh Heaven. Awed by the magnificence of the living room, Hanif prostrated himself on the carpet as a devotee does at a shrine. When he looked up, his eyes fell on a man whose face shone with divine light. He must be Ghazi Khan, the deity of the shrine. Hanif thought he was even more charismatic than Altaf had described en route. He was convinced that here was someone who could transform him into a pious, otherworldly ascetic who would attain ultimate happiness even without material comforts.

'I am aware of your miseries,' said Saghir Khan from his couch.

'I am poor and in debt, Sahib,' wailed Hanif, seating himself on the carpet in front of Saghir Khan. 'Even after working for nine months, I have been unable to repay the loan I took from a moneylender in Swarnpur. And my family, my children have nothing but…'

'Don't cry, my dear,' said Saghir Khan, calmly. 'Hopelessness is *kufr*, a sin. A devout Muslim should never be hopeless.'

'I must have committed many sins in my life. I must have hurt many. And I have missed prayers even in this holy land and in this holy month of fasting. But I have never lied to anyone or stolen from anyone. Neither have I ever betrayed the trust of anyone. Why is all this happening to me?' Hanif could not stop himself from breaking down. It was like confessing his sins to the dervish; his words flowed freely.

'It's not your fault that you are poor and indebted. It's not your fault that you were compelled to leave your home, the heaven on earth, our Kashmir. You had to earn your bread. My dear, all of us are indebted and poor, although in different contexts and proportions. Do you agree?'

'Ji, Sahib, without any doubt.'

'Good. Now tell me, who is to be blamed for our misery? What can we do?'

Hanif turned to Altaf in confusion, unsure of how to respond.

'I will tell you,' continued Saghir Khan, 'It's the *sarkar*, the puppet government that doesn't care about our fate. And it is those callous Indians who have occupied our Kashmir.'

Hanif was dumbstruck. He glanced at Altaf once more, but his companion only smiled, as if endorsing Saghir Khan's shocking revelation.

'Tell me, Hanif. What can you do for your family, your Kashmir, and Islam?' asked Saghir Khan.

'What can I do, Sahib? I am a poor man facing difficulties even in sustaining his family.'

'Not anymore,' Saghir Khan smiled, looking into Hanif's eyes.

'I don't understand.'

'The Mujahideen from different countries are undertaking training in Azad Kashmir. We are preparing for an armed struggle in our Kashmir, and for that, we need capable youths like you. I want you to undergo training for jihad.'

'What!' Hanif stared at Saghir Khan in sheer disbelief.

'Don't worry, you don't have to fight against the Indian Army. You will be taken to Azad Kashmir, and after the training is over, you can go directly to your family. As a mujahid, you are entitled to a monthly salary.' Saghir Khan leant back on the couch and stretched his legs. 'Nobody will ever know that you undertook training in Pakistan. And *inshallah*, within a few years, when Jammu and Kashmir gets independence, you will be celebrated like a war hero and hold a high office in an independent land. The rank of a mujahid is the highest in Allah's eyes. Always remember—*Jazak*

Allah, Subhan Allah! For a mujahid of Kashmir, there is heaven in this world and the next world too.'

Hanif sat silently, still in shock, as a bundle of Saudi Riyals wrapped in transparent paper was put on the table in front of him. 'Here's half of your monthly salary—7000 Riyals or 25,000 Indian rupees. The remaining amount will be given to you on the completion of your training. We understand that the family of a mujahid should not suffer financially for his obligations to Allah's cause.'

'Pick it up. Put it in your pocket,' encouraged Altaf.

'No.'

'Why not?' inquired Saghir Khan. 'This is jihad in the name of Allah, and you are entitled to a salary. Take it.'

'No.'

'But why not?'

'I think I am fine with carrying on the jihad of earning bread for my family through menial labour.'

'What?! Are you fooling yourself or us? You are working here without a work visa. Do you call that honest?'

'I have no other choice. I am a sinner, I know. But I am struggling to repay the loan that I took. I am doing whatever I can to feed my family.'

Altaf took a few steps closer to Hanif and put his hand on his shoulder. 'We are not asking you to do anything sinful. Even Khan Sahib has taken training in Pakistan. And there are many young men from our area undertaking training in Azad Kashmir. It's absolutely safe. *Wallah*, I swear.'

'Is this the help you promised me?' Hanif asked blankly.

Altaf and Saghir Khan looked at each other, confused and somewhat embarrassed.

'Take your time, give it a thought.' Saghir placed a comforting hand on Hanif's shoulder. 'As I see it, you have two options—you can live with dignity and peace in independent Kashmir. Or you can continue running from pillar to post, hiding like a rat, living in slimy holes. Even at this moment, the Saudi police could be right outside, waiting at the door to apprehend you.'

'NO! I will not pick up the gun.'

'Fine! Accept that you are a coward. It takes courage to pick up a gun for Allah's cause, and I can see that you lack it terribly. You have forgotten the horrors your parents faced at the time of the Indo-Pak Partition. Who is to guarantee that the nightmare won't recur? I can see you'll do nothing when the Indian Army pulls down the salwars of your women, just like they did in 1947!'

'Sahib, if I pick up the gun, will the Indian Army spare my women?'

Saghir continued, ignoring Hanif, 'Whether you like it or not, the time is coming when all of us will have to sacrifice our comforts and overcome our fears to protect the honour of our women, our mothers, our daughters, and our Kashmir. But people like you are good for nothing! You want to remain bystanders while people like Altaf Dastarkhan and Ghazi Khan fight for your cause. That won't happen, you coward! Sooner or later, you will have to pay for this jihad. You are one of those *Munafikin*, hypocrites who pretend to believe in Islam but never go to battle to fulfil their duties. Do you know the fate Allah has destined for you? On Judgement Day, your bones and flesh will be torn asunder, and you will be forever doomed!'

Hanif remained silent, infuriating Saghir Khan further.

'Tell me, you hypocrite, is it ethical to work here without a valid visa?'

'No, Sahib. But a valid visa is the right of respectable people like you. Poor people like me can't afford it.'

'Get out of here! May the wrath of Allah fall upon you!' Saghir Khan yelled as Altaf dragged Hanif to the elevator.

After Hanif's departure, the atmosphere inside the Seventh Heaven was closer to that of hell. Someone had dared to challenge the deity of the shrine! The servants, guards, and a few members of the neighbourhood who had gathered for Ramadhan prayer, looked on confused. Nobody said a word after the evening prayers and departed hurriedly to their homes. Saghir Khan summoned Altaf, his manner grave.

'Altaf, I want you to decide whether you seriously want to work for me or continue your trucker's job.'

'*Janab e Aala*, I am already working with you.'

'No. This is not the way I want you to work. I had trusted you with this holy job, and all you bring to me are idiots like—what was his name?'

'Hanif.'

'Hanif! Why did you bring him here? Don't you have better sense?'

'What do you want me to do?'

'Go to Swarnpur immediately. Convince Adalat Shah to work with me. If you manage that, you'll never again have to work as a trucker in this wilderness.'

'But *Janab e Aala*, I am a poor man. My visa is still valid for—'

Saghir Khan interrupted impatiently, 'I know. Just tell me how much money you want. And take this in advance.' Saghir Khan pointed to the packet of 7000 Riyals that Hanif had refused.

'No, *Janab e Aala*, you don't understand. I am willing to work for this noble cause without any money, I swear! My conscience is clear. But you know how Adalat Shah is. He doesn't even say his namaz unless he badly needs something done. To convince that kind of a man with such a paltry sum—'

'Oh my, behold the smart ironsmith! Strike the iron when it's red hot, huh? Look, I don't have more money to offer you. The Pakistanis already have their hands up my ass. But let me see.'

Saghir Khan lit a cigarette and walked to the balcony attached to the living room.

One week later, when the Eid moon sparkled in the sky, the Shah household had a generous visitor. Altaf Dastarkhan brought to Adalat Shah a special *Eidi*—a glittering gift from Saghir Khan.

Eight

Adalat Shah donned a karakul cap and a grey pinstripe salwar suit. He was specially dressed for the big occasion—addressing the Eid congregation in Swarnpur. The Mufti of the Jama Masjid left the pulpit to him, and he had specific plans for the address. Normally, Adalat Shah sat in the middle of the front row, behind the Mufti, taking little interest in the prayers. But today, something was different.

When Adalat Shah took the microphone, the crowd cheered. The valleys of Swarnpur reverberated with 'Allah Ho Akbar', 'Ya Rasul Allah' and 'Ya Ali'. People sat back, expecting a rousing speech about the appalling conditions of the roads, overflowing sewage, unregulated prices of essential commodities, and spineless leaders elected undeservedly during the assembly elections.

Adalat Shah began, after a quick and rather noisy mike testing, 'Phoo, Phoooo… Dear friends and elders, Aslam-o-Elikum and Eid Mubarak to all of you. Today, as usual, I am going to talk about the filth and the potholes. But, this year, the filth and the potholes I will talk about belong not in the gutters and roads of Swarnpur but in the attitude of our government. I am appalled at the way the government has been treating the people of Jammu and Kashmir.'

The audience was now fully attentive, hanging onto his every word. This was entirely unexpected and rather thrilling.

'Phoo, Phoooo… You witnessed how the assembly elections last year were rigged in favour of puppets and spineless buffoons,' went on Adalat Shah. 'They mocked people's aspirations and belief in the system. The prospects of our youth getting employment are as bleak as the restoration of the Babri Masjid!'

'Allah Ho Akbar', echoed the audience, now a sea of emotions.

'For a long time, our endurance has been misconstrued as our weakness. But we are in no mood for any reconciliation. Not anymore! Think of the Jews and how they had to bow in front of the people of Palestine. *Inshallah*, under the leadership of Yasser Arafat, they are finally going to taste liberty! We, too, have been pleading for a plebiscite in our state but now, time has come, and we must actively pursue our rights.'

At that point, sadly for him, Adalat Shah had to end his speech. It was time for the Eid prayer, and the Mufti was getting worried. Hurriedly, the Mufti cut short his speech to two 'phoos' and prayed 'May the cruel Prime Minister of Israel pay for his deeds! Glory to Islam and ignominy to non-believers!'

Adalat Shah and the Mufti were close associates. The Mufti was infamous for issuing fatwas at the slightest incitement. For instance, there was a fatwa against a particular haircut that his young nephew had dared to sport. There were fatwas against several beauty products, especially the ones his wife demanded money for. Women could not speak above certain decibels and were not to be heard ten feet away. Basically, everything that 'annoyed' Allah and his noble mullahs was banned. There was a fatwa against buying from the Hindu Khatri community. Sadly, Adalat Shah's business couldn't show appreciable increase and the write-off in favour of the Mufti, for endorsing the holy merchandise of Shah's products outweighed the profits thus earned. Sometimes, he rescinded fatwas too, and this was equally fascinating. The fatwa against riding scooters or 'satanic carriages' was withdrawn when Adalat Shah upgraded to a four-wheeler and his scooter was bought by the Mufti at a price that one good Muslim should offer to a fellow good Muslim. Riding then became *Sunnat* or the way of the Holy Prophet.

Adalat Shah usually maintained a distance from all such diktats. This is why it was surprising when he abandoned his secular outlook and gave an Eid address that was thoroughly inconsistent with his record. Perhaps the gathering had construed that the whole rhetoric was nothing but 'Phoo, Phoo'. No one—not even the Mufti—could understand the motive behind the rhetoric.

Well, except for one person. Somewhere in the middle rows sat a man called Altaf Dastarkhan who knew. Each time Adalat Shah began a new, provocative statement, he raised the slogan *'Nehra e Takbir'* in praise of Allah. The people responded with 'Allah Ho Akbar'. He had been quite pleased with Adalat Shah's speech. His discussion with Shah had borne fruit.

When Altaf had placed Shaghir Khan's proposal before Adalat Shah, the latter had taken long to deliberate upon it. Finally, Adalat Shah said, 'I have two conditions.'

'Tell me, *Janab e Aala*,' Altaf Dastarkhan was earnest and attentive.

'One: I will never deal directly with Saghir Khan in any manner. No telephones, no letters, no transactions, nothing.'

'Ji, *Janab e Aala*. All right.'

'And two—I need sixty-five thousand rupees per recruit. One hundred per cent advance.'

'*Janab e Aala*,' said Altaf, 'Please understand that I am not in the position to comment on this. All I can offer you now is twenty-five thousand rupees in advance for the deal.'

'I have a miserable track record of dealing with Saghir Khan. I cannot trust him.' Adalat Shah stared at the cash on the table.

'I know it, *Janab e Aala*, I know it. But now, you are dealing with me, not him.'

After Altaf Dastarkhan left, Adalat Shah did a few quick calculations. He then went to his bedroom, cheerfully humming a folk song.

'What is it? You seem happy,' his wife asked sleepily.

'Bring me my *bulbul*.' This was a special whisky he kept reserved for the choicest of occasions.

'It's Ramzan. You should not drink.'

'Ramzan is over, my dear, and so are our miseries. Get up! Bring me my bulbul, and yes, roast some beef. It's Eid, after all.'

A week later, at the beginning of June, after the frozen passes of Pir Panjal had thawed, four young men from Swarnpur prepared to cross the border. They were the 'first heroes' embarking on the grand mission of arms training in Muzaffarabad. One of them was Mumtaz Dastarkhan—Altaf Dastarkhan's teenage brother. Had his mother known what he was getting into, she would have done everything in her power to stop him.

One important task remained before they crossed the border—the oath-taking. Their hands on the Quran, all the young men said their pledge in the Jama Masjid of Swarnpur: 'I will devote myself to the cause of jihad and Allah. I will never name anyone involved directly or indirectly with the cause.'

Adalat Shah spoke to them, 'All of you are going to be our heroes. When you return home after the training, you will get a monthly salary of twenty thousand rupees. But that is peanuts compared to the status you'll achieve when Kashmir gains her independence.'

'*Janab e Aala*,' assured Altaf, 'It will be like a picnic to Azad Kashmir. No one will ever know.'

The Mufti joined in with his standard slogan: '*Islam ka bol bala, kufr ka muh kaala.*' (Glory to Islam and ignominy to non-believers)

Nine

Hanif was still enraged when he stepped out of the elevator at the Seventh Heaven. He must have walked about half a mile when, out of the blue, a police car came towards him. He stood in the middle of the road, frozen like a mummy, aghast that Saghir Khan's predicted 'doom for the hypocrites' was indeed coming true. Standing there in the path of the speeding car was not suicide. No, it was what Allah had willed for him as chastisement for his misdeeds and for being a useless, powerless individual. It was a desert storm that approached him, not a car, and the impact would tear his flesh and bones asunder.

Seconds later, the car had screeched to a halt. Hanif lay on the road, his legs and elbows bruised. But what was this, his flesh and bones seemed quite intact!

'*Haie yoo aami*? *Hal anta majnon*? (Are you blind? Are you crazy?)' the Saudi constable yelled.

Hanif was thrilled at how Allah had spared his life. After giving him medical care, the police transferred Hanif to the jail in Jeddah. Here lived many South Asians and East Africans in a queue for deportation. Hanif sat quietly in a corner, ignoring the animated conversation.

Ten days later, Hanif, along with many other illegal workers from India and Pakistan, was deported on board a Pakistan International Airlines flight to Mumbai through Karachi. Hanif had borrowed some money from one of his neighbours to buy the train ticket to Jammu. On his way home, he also purchased some clothes for his children from a flea market in Mumbai.

Back home after a miserable separation, Hanif gazed at his wife and children for hours on end. Shamma and Manzoor flaunted the mackintosh jackets and fleece trousers that their father 'had brought from Saudi Arabia'. Ashwar, however, didn't appear pleased with the unstitched piece of cloth that her husband had brought for her.

'There was absolutely no need for this,' she said flatly.

Hanif's return did little to lift the fortunes of the family; it couldn't even bring a smile on Ashwar's face. They sold the cow to repay Hanif's loan in entirety, once and for all. Salted black tea and corn chapattis became their staple diet for all three meals. Sometimes, Ashwar boiled some mustard leaves for a treat.

But for Shamma and Manzoor, their father's return meant a great deal. They were mesmerized when he told them about the cities of Saudi Arabia. They were amazed when he narrated that a glass of water in a moving airplane didn't spill. At night, they dreamt of the tall buildings in Mumbai and Jeddah, taller even than the deodar trees they played around every day.

Aslam sat for his matriculation exam with twenty other students. Everyone failed in most of the subjects. Aslam rejoiced the outcome.

'Are you crazy? Why are you happy when you've failed?'

'This is what it ought to be!'

No one pressed the matter; everyone believed that he had gone daft after Ashwar's marriage. But Aslam had a reason for his happiness—he believed that Ashwar was the deserving candidate, not him. If she had lost the opportunity to pass the exam, he had no right to the honour.

Ashwar, in her impoverished household, was indifferent to everything that happened in the village. Her world was confined to the four walls of her single-room house. She had convinced herself that education had been too grand a dream for a foolish daydreamer like her; her responsibility was towards Hanif and his children.

She had only one regret—that someone else knew about her secret dream. She hoped that Aslam would somehow forget her along with the dream she had told him about. How foolish it now sounded! How they must mock her in the village! Little did she know that Aslam had never breached her trust; he hadn't told anyone but his horse.

Not a day went without Aslam thinking about her. He recalled the beautiful time they had shared during their brief courtship. Sitting at the corner of the graveyard at the Pathri Pir shrine, amidst tall buttercups and Kashmir iris, the two had woven dreams about the future. Ashwar hesitated in talking about marriage, but Aslam would insist. He remembered their blissful moments to the minutest detail.

'Can't we talk about anything else?' Ashwar would complain.

'Okay, what do you want to talk about?' Aslam would try to hold her waist.

'That is a very inappropriate way to touch me.'

'Okay. Tell me how I should touch you then.'

'Well! You should not touch me at all!'

'Never?'

'Never!'

'Really, never?'

'Not until we get married.'

'Thank you, my dear. At least you mentioned the M word!'

'Are you happy now?'

'No.'

'Why not?'

'Because I can't touch you.'

'Oh God! Now I know why you called me here.'

'No, no. I mean, I can't touch you for another sixteen years. That makes me sad. Can't there be a concession?'

'All right,' Ashwar would smile. 'It will be either sixteen years or the day I become a schoolteacher. You can choose whichever happens first.'

'I know you will become a teacher within two or three years. You are really smart.'

'Thank you for the encouragement.'

'But Ashwar, you told me that you would marry someone who values your education and helps you achieve your dream. Isn't that so?'

'Of course, it is.'

'Ah, that means there's still scope for an early marriage.'

'No, my dear, that someone has to be a *mulazim,* a government employee, and not a dropout *majnu!*'

'Don't underestimate me, girl. I can still get a government job. Maybe I can become a police constable or an Army jawan.'

'That will be great. Aslam, the cop.'

'And his wife, the teacher.'

'It's late, Aslam. I should go now.' Ashwar had got up that day, her shirt speckled with grass and a flower stuck to her stole. Aslam didn't know it then, but the moment was to haunt him years later, reliving itself over and over in dreams. That day, however, Aslam had merely plucked the flower from her stole and put his hands around her waist.

'Why did you take it off? It was so pretty!'

'It was a Datura,' he explained, touching the spiny pod of the flower. 'Some flowers are to be seen, not touched. I hope you understand what and whom to keep close and when to maintain your distance.'

'That's very philosophical, Aslam, the cop,' she had teased.

'I am serious, Ashwar. The Datura is a poisonous, prickly flower that may intoxicate you. But I will never hurt you. Do remember that even if you forget everything else.'

Aslam's father, Haji Mir, had only grown in his heroic image after everyone heard the story of how he had married Mehar Bi. It so happened that another girl from a neighbouring village needed someone to protect her honour, and the villagers looked at Haji Mir. Surely, he wouldn't disappoint the community. Zaitoon, it seemed, was having a love affair with a married forest guard from another community. Her relationship had brought untold disgrace to both her home and village. When the kachehri summoned Zaitoon's father, the man pleaded in earnest, 'No *huzoor*, the forest guard is fifteen years older than my girl. He is exploiting my poor daughter. I promise she is utterly innocent!'

Haji Mir Baksh interrupted. 'You should have acted like a man. How can a forest guard exploit your daughter under your nose? And how can your daughter transgress?'

Everyone agreed with Haji Mir. The kachehri addressed the girl's father sharply, 'You must accept that your daughter is characterless. Both of you have shamed all of us.'

Sensing the sentiment of the gathering and accepting that he could never win the case, Zaitoon's father surrendered to his fate. But he wanted to have the last word. 'Haji Mir, you vow to protect the honour of our community. Maybe I failed to act. Maybe I was helpless and couldn't do anything. Maybe I was too weak to have the courage to kill the forest guard or punish my daughter. I am sure that the forest guard will abduct my daughter or maybe she will elope with him. I only have one request—punish me if you like, but please protect my daughter.'

'What do you want?' Haji Mir asked haughtily—a tone befitting a hero whose valour was being lauded yet again.

'Accept Zaitoon as your daughter-in-law.'

Alas, Haji Mir had never expected to face such a situation! He could now sense that celebrating his heroism was merely the ploy of a transgressor. Only a few moments ago, the kachehri had labelled the girl 'characterless', and now he was supposed to accept her as his daughter-in-law! Could he say that his son wouldn't agree to the marriage? No, that would undermine his credibility as a strong father and the head of the village.

No one from the kachehri spoke. All eyes were focused on Haji Mir in anticipation of his response.

Presently, Haji Mir cleared his throat and said, 'Around fifty years ago, when I stood in the way of Mehar Bi's abductors with an axe in my hands, I wasn't even a bit nervous. But today, when I have been asked to guard the honour of another daughter, I feel burdened by the load. My shoulders are now old. I leave the decision to the kachehri. Whatever you decide, I will accept.'

The crowd broke into a murmur. It was a difficult decision to take, especially as the verdict concerned someone who had always protected the village, had always been fair in his dealings. But that didn't mean justice worked differently for him than it did for others.

Avdal spoke after a few moments: 'The kachehri has decided that although the girl is guilty of bringing shame to our community, further shame awaits us unless we act now. If we stay quiet, the shame can be even more colossal—perhaps, unredeemable. To save our village from further ignominy, we have decided that Zaitoon will be married to Haji's son.'

Haji Mir appeared unmoved by the decision. He stared into the distance, avoiding eye contact with anyone. He could sniff a deep conspiracy in the way Avdal had handled the matter. Wasn't it terribly odd that Zaitoon's father had openly accepted that his daughter would elope with a married man? But nothing could be done now. Haji Mir always kept his word.

That evening, Aslam came home early. All his family members sat quietly, expressing solidarity with Aslam in their silence. It seemed there had been a disagreement between his parents. 'Why are you all so quiet?' Aslam's clear voice broke the hush.

Hamida responded, her voice strained and angry. 'Yes, tell him. Tell us all the decision of the kachehri.'

Haji Mir Baksh looked surprised. 'I have already told you.'

'Oh! So, you don't have the courage to repeat the same to your son? Neither did you have the gumption to refuse the kachehri.' Hamida looked at her son remorsefully. 'Son, your father has promised the kachehri that you will marry Zaitoon.'

'I cannot marry her,' Aslam stated flatly. It was impossible to read his face.

'You have to,' said Haji Mir. 'I have given them my *lafz*, my promise.'

'Why did you give them your word?' argued Hamida. 'Did you not stop for a moment to think about your son?'

'*You* keep quiet! Women should never speak against the decision of men. Don't you have any respect for my word? Moreover, there's nothing wrong with this girl!'

The kids were scared; they had never seen their grandfather so furious. Wazir gestured to his wife to take them to bed.

'Tell me,' repeated Haji Mir, 'what's wrong with this girl?'

'Nothing,' said Aslam.

'Then why can't you marry her?'

'I don't *want* to get married! Not now.'

'Oh! Do you have a pressing mission to accomplish? Are you going to become a dervish, a Sufi?'

Aslam remained silent. Haji Mir's voice resounded through the house.

'Accept your reality, son. Marrying Zaitoon is the only way to honour the *lafz* of your father. It's also the only solution to save the honour of Pathri Aali.'

Hamida sighed, realizing that nothing would make her husband change his mind. 'Do what your father wants, son. Sometimes you have to do things that you hate. The decisions taken by your elders may appear harsh, but, eventually, you'll find everything falls into place. Remember: The wish of your parents is what Allah wants you to follow. Allah will show you the right way.'

Wazir nodded. 'Yes, Aslam, our father has never let the village down. His command is like a divine decree for us. Denying it would be nothing short of sacrilege.'

Haji Mir saw the perfect chance to say the final word. 'All my life, I have lived as per my *asool*, my values. It is *asool* that distinguishes a good man from an evil man. Do you know the prime tenet of my *asool*? It says that I will always put my community before myself. So, son, whatever you do, remember that your old father has preached his *asool* his entire life. If my son doesn't honour my word, my entire life and everything I stand for will fall on its face.'

When Haji Mir began his evening prayers, Hamida sat beside Aslam. 'Son, did you know that I was very young when my mother told me I was going to marry your father? He was more than twice my age; his children were older than I was! I cried and resisted. I felt like I was presented as a trophy to your father for his heroism, just like his previous wife. But my mother told me that marriage is never an individual's choice. It is an arrangement to strengthen the communal bonds. In our society, the collective will prevails over individual aspirations. It is usually a girl who gets victimized in these conventions, but this time, you got unlucky. But, honestly, I don't think there is any fault with Zaitoon except that I find her rather silly.'

Aslam didn't comment on his mother's little revelation. He got up and walked out of the house.

There was very little time to prepare for Aslam's marriage. His family ran around arranging for things frenetically. Haji Mir trudged up to Jabari Hills to invite Major Dharam Pal Singh for his son's wedding.

Two days before his nikah, Aslam sneaked up to Ashwar's house. He half expected her to shoo him away like the last time, but surprisingly, she asked him in.

'Where's Hanif?' Aslam asked, looking around.

'He works at a road construction site near Buffliaz. He will come back in the evening.'

'And what about your children?'

'They have gone to school.'

'Oh yes, school is very important, isn't it?'

Ashwar gave him a watery smile, but Aslam didn't smile back.

'Anyway, I am here to invite you for my wedding.'

'Oh, yes! Congratulations! Your nephews invited me some time ago.' Ashwar paused for a moment before saying, 'I am glad you are getting married. Zaitoon is a nice girl.'

'Is she?'

'Of course, she is.'

'Ashwar, I want to offer you a gift. You cannot reject it as I am the groom. A groom must be granted whatever he wishes.' Aslam pulled out a piece of paper from his pocket.

'What is this?'

'It's the form for the matriculation exam. You have to fill it and give it to your husband. He will get a bank draft of a hundred and fifty rupees in your name and send it to the Board. Here's the money.'

'I cannot accept this, Aslam.'

'It's not a favour. Look at it as a loan that you can repay whenever you want.'

'No, Aslam, you don't understand. You are embarrassing me.

That isn't my dream anymore. Please, just let me live my life.'

'That's what I am trying to do.'

Ashwar raised her voice in frustration. 'Why can't you forget what I told you? That was childish, absolutely foolish! I am living my life, aren't I? Why can't you wake up and see the reality?'

'Why can't you tell me the truth?'

'What truth?'

'That you have succumbed to your misfortunes. That you are lying to yourself and me.'

'Aslam, please leave immediately. Why have you come here? Why don't you let go of the past? It's outrageous for you to visit me when my husband isn't here and attempt to tell me that my life is miserable!'

'Don't shout at me.'

Ashwar shoved the form and the money back into Aslam's hands. 'Please leave now. I will see you at your wedding feast.'

'No, you won't see me there if you don't accept my gift.'

'What? Is this a polite way of suggesting that we should not attend your wedding?'

'No, I am merely being honest with you.'

'Do whatever you want to; I don't care!' Ashwar tore the form, crushed the currency notes, and turned her back to him.

'*Alvida*, Ashwar. Goodbye!' Aslam said quietly as he walked away.

※

It was Thursday, the day before Aslam's wedding. Haji Mir had dyed his beard with henna and blackened his eyes with kohl; after all, it was the day when he would offer alms at Pathri Pir. That year, the bullfight had been cancelled on account of Aslam's wedding. But the celebration in the village was almost as grand.

'Do silence the dhols!' Haji said to Wazir, 'They shouldn't be beaten until we have offered the alms and mounted the dhaal. Also, call Aslam. He needs to accompany me to the shrine.'

The dhols were silenced within moments. But fresh chaos and confusion prevailed in Haji Mir's household. Aslam was nowhere to be found.

'Look everywhere, hurry!' Haji Mir ordered his friends and relatives.

The women started crying; they feared for the worst. Zaitoon's father was beside himself with rage. 'Have you sent your son somewhere? Just so he doesn't have to marry my daughter?'

'Have you lost your mind?' Haji asked scornfully. 'Do you think we will make all the arrangements for the wedding and then help our son escape?'

'I don't want to hear your empty arguments. Make them before the kachehri!'

Morning turned into afternoon and night but Aslam was nowhere to be found. Haji Mir sat on his prayer mat, chanting endless prayers for his son's return. Parveen vowed to walk barefoot to Pathri Pir if only Aslam was safe and sound. Hamida promised to fast on all Thursdays for the rest of her life if good news came of her son.

It was the most excruciating night in Haji Mir's life. For the past fifty years, he had savoured the night he had protected Mehar Bi and earned his heroic reputation. But he felt certain that this would be the night that would haunt him to his grave. Fingering the beads of his rosary, he prayed, 'Allah, please make the darkness of this night perpetual. I haven't the strength to face the morning. I can see only shame awaiting me at dawn—ignominy that would blind all the pride I have always held dear.'

The next morning, news of Aslam came. But it was heartbreaking news. Yes, Aslam had run away, confirmed a man who had seen him while returning from Swarnpur. He had spotted Aslam boarding a bus to Jammu.

Later that day, Haji Mir sat amid the kachehri like a deviant under trial. His beard was dishevelled, his eyes smudged.

'Now that Aslam has run away in the most disrespectful manner, what do you have to say?' Avdal asked out loud.

'What will he say?' Zaitoon's father interrupted furiously. 'It's easy to order others to control their children. It doesn't take much to label others weak and characterless. Now tell me, who is characterless? Who is a weak father?'

'Hush! Let him speak,' said Avdal. 'The kachehri demands a reply from Haji Mir, not you.'

'I am a man of my word,' Haji Mir said. 'Before this kachehri, I announce that because Aslam has run away from his duty, he has rendered himself dead for me. I denounce him as my son and reject his entitlement to my land. Since I had given my *lafz* to the kachehri that I will accept Zaitoon as my daughter-in-law, I am still willing to honour my promise. She can be the wife to Wazir, my only son.'

A murmur began in the crowd. Zaitoon's father scowled and said, 'Haji Mir, your *lafz* was to wed your younger son Aslam to my daughter. It wasn't just to accept her as your daughter-in-law.'

'Was it so, Avdal? Did the kachehri mention Aslam's name?' Haji Mir asked pointedly.

'No, but it was understood—'

'Don't give me assumptions and conjectures! Tell me if a name was pronounced in my *lafz*.'

'No,' replied Avdal.

Zaitoon's father was riled. 'But why would I plead to marry my daughter off to a married man?'

'How can I answer that?' Haji Mir argued. 'You are the master of tricks. Anyhow, you accepted that your daughter was preparing to elope with a married man. My son, Wazir, is gentle and faithful. He will treat your daughter with respect.'

The next day, Wazir took Zaitoon as his second wife, trying desperately to shake off the fact that she was supposed to have been the bride of his little brother.

Ten

Bumbai, as Aslam had expected, was a city of skyscrapers and giant ships. He looked, here and there, for masses of Hajj pilgrims and torrents of rainfall. Aslam shook a little whenever an avalanche of people jostled in and out of the numerous trains. The city was close to his father's description of it after his Hajj journey, but Aslam wondered why he had overlooked the tyrannical humidity. Come to think of it, there was plenty that his father had skipped in his tale.

A couple of days ago, Aslam had boarded a train to Mumbai. A fellow passenger had suggested that he travel to Bombay VT. But when he arrived, Aslam felt thoroughly out of place in his brown salwar-kameez. He decided to have a cup of tea. Perhaps it wouldn't be costly. As Aslam approached the tea trolley, a scrawny boy collided with him, almost pushing him on the railway track.

'I am sorry! Are you hurt?' said the boy.

'No.'

'Look, if you are hurt, you can grab me by the collar.'

The boy held Aslam's collars in demonstation. And just as he became a little suspicious, the boy, almost like lightning, picked Aslam's pocket and ran out of the station. Aslam ran after him the best he could. In retrospect, Aslam thought that the entire adventure had been a terrible idea. A man selling glasses of cold water put a hand on his shoulder. 'Would you like some water?'

'Yes! Thanks!'

Aslam finished the glassful in moments; water had never tasted so sweet.

'*Aath aane*,' demanded the water seller.
'*Aath aane*? For what?'
'For the water, what else?'
'You sell water? Is it *Zamzam*?'
'What is *Jamjam*?'
'*Zamzam* is the holy water from the *Zamzam* Well in Mecca. Don't you know that?'
'I don't *have* to know that. Just give me my money and leave.'
'All of you are thugs! Pickpockets!'
'Don't you dare insult me!' screamed the man, and lashed out at Aslam. A full-blown quarrel ensued between the two, and it took a police constable to control the situation. Aslam had to apologize for his remarks and for being unable to pay for the water.

Aslam's rosy picture of Mumbai evaporated within moments. That night, he slept hungry and without a roof for the first time in his life.

But Aslam's misfortunes were far from over. When he got up in the morning, his bag was missing. He looked around helplessly. What was he to do without his belongings?

Whatever sorrow had been piling up in Aslam, spilled though his eyes into the dust. As he stared at his tears falling endlessly, it started to rain. Aslam stood up, looked at the overcast sky, and yelled, 'You wouldn't even let me cry?! All right! Let me see how much worse it can get.'

With renewed resolve, Aslam decided to trace the route he had followed the day before. First, he walked to the railway station and ran his eyes up and down the platform. He stared at every beggar and hawker. No more was he a purposeless stroller. For several hours, Aslam sat outside the railway station, looking at everyone who walked out in his hope to ambush the pickpocket. Just when he was about to give up the seemingly pointless pursuit, he heard a man yelling, 'Pocket *mara*! He picked my pocket!'

Instantly, Aslam ran in the direction of the chaos, just in time to see the pickpocket escaping with a black handbag. A pot-bellied man ran after him, huffing and puffing.

'I will get him,' Aslam cried, running after the pickpocket once again.

The pickpocket was much faster than Aslam. Soon, he had outrun Aslam. He looked back and saw that the coast was clear. He walked with an air of arrogance till someone kicked him sharply in the shins.

'Motherfucker, jackal!' yelled Aslam, throwing in punches wherever he could. 'I have caught you now!'

The pickpocket, thoroughly taken aback, struggled for breath. Alas, noted Aslam, he wasn't the one who had picked his pocket the day before!

'Get up!' Aslam held the boy's collar, 'Where is your brother who snatched my money yesterday?'

By then, a crowd had gathered at the scene. The police arrived and handcuffed him, preparing to take him into custody.

'You can't take him like that!' Aslam protested. 'I need my money.'

'Come with us to the police station,' demanded the constable. 'We'll figure out what money you need.'

'There is no need for that,' announced someone from the crowd. Aslam saw that it was the pot-bellied man. 'You cannot arrest him; he has done no wrong.'

Aslam was surprised. 'Arrest me? Why? I am only asking for the money that this pickpocket's brother or friend, whoever it was, snatched from me yesterday.'

'I don't know anything about your money,' sobbed the pickpocket.

'You are lying!'

'Get into the jeep. Both of you!' The constable yelled, raising his baton.

'Why are you arresting me? Is it because I held this pickpocket and recovered someone's handbag? Or is it because you are shielding this pickpocket and his gang?'

'You can't arrest him,' the pot-bellied man insisted. 'You can't arrest someone who has helped the police nab a pickpocket.'

The constable scowled as he said to the pot-bellied man, 'You will have to come with me to the police station to lodge a complaint.'

'I'd prefer not to,' the man said flatly. 'There must be thousands of complaints against pickpockets at VT. Adding to the pile would hardly make a difference.'

The constable scowled again; it seemed about the only thing he could do. He pushed the pickpocket into his jeep and drove away.

The pot-bellied man gestured to Aslam to follow him. They walked to a juice vendor. 'How much money was snatched from you?'

'One hundred and twenty rupees.'

'One hundred and twenty rupees?' The man repeated while paying for two glasses of chilled sugarcane juice.

'Well, actually one hundred and ten rupees. But that was after I had to give ten rupees to eunuchs.'

The man took out two currency notes from his pocket and gave them to Aslam, 'Here's your money. I think I owe you this.'

'Oh! Thank you for the help!' Aslam put the money in his pocket. 'I can't say no because I can't afford to. But I'll consider this a loan. I will repay it as soon as I find a job.'

'What kind of job are you looking for?'

'Anything! A salesman, a potter, a labourer... Honestly, I would prefer to be a security guard. But then, beggars cannot be choosers, sir.'

'Well, in that case, you have already repaid your loan. Come with me.'

Aslam was overjoyed. The man hailed a taxi and gestured to him to step inside.

'Sir, could you please wait for only a moment? Also, could I borrow fifty paise from you?'

'Will a rupee do?'

'Much better,' said Aslam, as he pocketed the coin and ran to the water trolley near the railway gate.

'Here is your money,' he said to the man selling water. He still looked a little battered after their jostle. 'Thank you for the credit, and, once again, I am sorry for yesterday.'

The man stared at him, unsure how to respond, but Aslam had scampered off to the taxi.

'Sir, I didn't understand what you meant when you said I have already repaid my loan.'

'Well, it's because you are now a security guard.' The man smiled, lighting a cigarette.

Aslam muttered a 'thank you', still rather taken aback. Suddenly, *Bumbai* did not seem to be only a city of cheats and thugs. It was also the city of opportunities and hope.

'What's your name, young man?' Aslam's benefactor asked.

'Mohammad Aslam.'

'I am Badar Kaanchwala.'

Kaanchwala! What a strange name, thought Aslam. Or was it his business? Well, tons of strange things had happened to him already, and strange names were hardly that surprising. He sat back in the taxi, visualizing himself as a heroic security guard who would catch all the goons and pickpockets of Mumbai.

Aslam woke up in Badar Kaanchwala's house the next morning. Memories of the night before crept slowly into his mind. Had he been bragging about living in the border area where people aren't afraid even of cannon fire? Yes, he had certainly regaled his benefactor with tales of heroism—stories that embarrassed him in the harsh sunlight of the morning.

'Why did I pick a quarrel with the police? Why did I pocket Badar's money as if it belonged to me? What if Badar demands his money back at once?' Aslam thought, frantically replaying his actions of the day before. 'And look at my foolishness, I even made him wait for me and demanded fifty paise more! Why did I eat like a glutton at dinner, gobbling down the mutton korma and rotis as if I was finishing my very last meal?'

Aslam walked up to the window and surveyed the traffic. Thousands of cars and people seemed to be about even though the day had just begun.

'Did you sleep well?' Badar Kaanchwala came into his room and greeted him with a smile.

'Yes, sir. I slept very well.'

'Okay, now tell me. Do you have an identity card, like a driving licence or a ration card?'

'No, sir. My identity card was in the bag. I told you how it was stolen in the night.'

'You don't have to call me "Sir". I haven't been knighted! Just call me Badar Bhai.'

'Ji, Badar Bhai.'

'Since you don't have an ID card, we'll have to figure something out. There are a few formalities to be completed before I can employ you as a security guard. But don't worry, come and join me for breakfast first.'

※

Later that morning, when Aslam was riding in a taxi to his place of future employment, he ventured to ask, 'Badar Bhai, did you take offence to any of the things I did or said last night? I am not that kind of a person. It's just that I was—'

'Don't be absurd! Of course, I wasn't offended. I owe you

much more than you can imagine.'

'Was that bag very important?'

'Oh no! It only had some papers, packs of cigarettes, and perhaps about fifty rupees. But, to me, your efforts to recover it were worth lakhs of rupees.'

'Thank you, Badar Bhai.'

'By the way, last night you mentioned something about a jackal and lioness story. What is that about?'

Aslam was embarrassed. 'Nothing, Badar Bhai. It's only a folk tale.'

'Do tell me about it. I like folk tales.'

'Um, I can't tell you because it's…rather vulgar.'

'Haha, that is even better,' Badar said, lighting a cigarette, 'do I look like a saint to you?'

'Okay, if you insist,' Aslam began hesitantly. 'There was once a jackal that always pestered the cubs of the lioness. He would trouble them whenever she was away for hunting. He would ask them, "Where is your mother?", and they would reply, "Why do you want to know?"' Aslam paused.

'What did the jackal say then?'

'Err, he said he wanted to get dirty with the lioness.'

'He wanted to screw her?'

'Yes,' Aslam laughed sheepishly. 'So, one day the cubs told their mother about the jackal. She decided to hide behind a bush and wait for the jackal to come and annoy her cubs again. "Where's your mother?" the jackal asked, and the cubs replied, "Why?" Before the jackal could make his dirty comment, the lioness roared from the bushes. The jackal scampered off at top speed through a tunnel he had burrowed for himself. The lioness chased him, but unfortunately, her head got stuck inside the burrow. Her rear was exposed. So, the jackal came out from the other side and…'

Aslam laughed sheepishly once again as Badar Kaanchwala broke into guffaws. The taxi driver joined in the laughter, drowning out the music playing on the radio.

Aslam couldn't remember the last time he had laughed so heartily. The folk tale was banal and crass and almost unfunny, but there was something about the moment that was both hilarious and delightful. After his misery of the last few years, he felt free after a long, long time.

§

Muzdalifah. Muzdalifah. The strange name didn't quite settle on his lips. Aslam consistently mispronounced it for the first few days that he stood at the main gate of the building. It was a residential society, and he was the new security guard. Clad in a grey uniform and black boots, with a double barrel gun hanging on his shoulder, Aslam felt quite proud.

'Tell me again, what's the name? he asked his fellow guard on the second day of his duty.

'It's Muzdalifah, after the Muzdalifah ground in Mecca where the Prophet gave his last sermon.'

'Ah.'

When Aslam returned to his room after the day's duty, he often admired his reflection in the mirror. Ashwar would have praised his uniform.

'You are looking great, Aslam, the cop,' she would have smiled.

'I am not a cop, silly. I am a security guard.'

'Okay, Aslam the security guard.'

'Yes. But I draw a salary of nine hundred rupees a month. Is it enough for us?'

'Yes, it is.'

'Now that I am employed, will you marry me?'

But to this question, Aslam had no answer. The Ashwar in his imagination would always keep silent. His eyes would well up with tears, and he would lie down on the floor mat, sobbing, reliving memories of times he had spent with Ashwar. He had no regrets about running away from his wedding. He didn't care for his father's promises. But he did have one regret—if he had to run away, he wished he had run away earlier. He could have eloped with his love, his Ashwar.

It had been a few weeks since Aslam had assumed his new duty. He received a letter from his family, in response to a note he had sent them some time back. He had added a note for Ashwar in the letter, telling her how he felt about her and apologizing for not being able to help her achieve her dream. He pleaded with her yet again to take the matriculation exam.

The reply was harsh and to the point. His father had disowned him. Zaitoon was married to his elder brother, Wazir. Ashwar was 'not going to read any letters again', even if his family begged her. He would be better off not trying to contact them.

As much as Ashwar's words broke his heart, as did the news of his father's renunciation of him, Aslam was most deeply troubled by the news of his brother Wazir. It shattered him that Zaitoon, the girl he had wanted to get rid of, was now his brother's wife.

The Spring of 1994

Eleven

A few things united all the youngsters of Swarnpur—sports shoes, baggy pants, *fauji* haircut, cricket fever, and the songs of Kumar Sanu and Attah Ullah. The people of Swarnpur enjoyed their lives, oblivious to the mayhem on the other side of Pir Panjal. The only impediment to daily life was the interference of the Army jawans. They would frequently patrol villages, check identity cards, thrash a few young men for no specific reason, and ogle at the women.

In Altaf Dastarkhan's household, Attah Ullah was especially popular. His daughter loved playing his songs and humming along. The neighbourhood would often join in, for all of them staunchly believed that 'music becomes greater when shared'. Many an evening, Ajay Devgan would lip-sync to emotionally stirring lyrics: '*Humey toh apno ne loota, ghairon mein kahan dum tha. Meri kashti bhi wahin doobi, jahan paani kam tha*' (I was robbed by my friends; my foes couldn't defeat me. My boat capsized, unfortunately, where there was hardly any water).

Not everyone in the neighbourhood, however, enjoyed the musical extravaganza. To the ears of Mumtaz Dastarkhan, Altaf's brother, the music was no less than an auditory assault. He half-stood, half-staggered in a mud-covered trench, excavated five years ago by his brother. The only furniture he had was a cot, on which he sat all day, abusing people and making faces. He had an aluminium lunch box, a bucket of water, and a bin, but he often forgot to eat and drink. The contents would be littered all over, lost like Mumtaz's sense of time.

One of Mumtaz's friends, who had taken up arms training with him, had been shot dead by the Indian Army. Traumatized, Altaf had decided to send his brother underground—quite literally. His mother had protested and insisted Mumtaz to surrender instead. But the idea was booed by Altaf. 'You have no idea what they do to surrendered mujahids. The interrogation is so diabolic that even listening to it will kill you. The torture is inhuman. Once inside the jail, you rot there for the rest of your life! Do you want your son to suffer that fate?'

'The jail will be better than this grave you have excavated for your brother. How long will you keep him in this pit?'

'Don't worry,' Altaf reassured her. '*Inshallah*, Kashmir will soon be free. And then, you will be proud of your mujahid son, *Janab e Aala*.'

'I don't know what freedom you keep talking about. But if I had known what you were sending your brother into, I would never have let you do it. You brainwashed my son and drove him to this deathtrap!' The old woman wailed through the night, but Altaf stuck to his decision.

Sometimes, after midnight, Mumtaz would be brought out of his pit to meet his mother. Every time, he would walk around the courtyard until his mother forcefully made him sit.

'I want to walk, *Ma*,' he would implore.'I want to stand. I am sick to death of that stinking pit.'

His mother would scrutinize his skin, his hair, and lament about how much weight he had lost. 'Look at you! Is this what a mujahid looks like?' Look at these lice in your hair!' She would turn to Altaf and complain, 'You say maggots don't feast on mujahids in the grave. But look at your brother. They are eating him alive!'

Altaf didn't pay much attention to her wails. Such excursions were risky, and he didn't allow them for weeks if the village had recently witnessed a marriage or a funeral. In the winters and the monsoons, the snow and the rain made the pit even more miserable.

'Can't we cover the pit with a plastic sheet?' suggested his mother. 'No,' Altaf shook his head, 'The camouflage will be compromised.'

Altaf wasn't misplaced in his fears. Frequently, the Army would stand on Mumtaz's pit when they came along on their search operations. His mother would cry inconsolably and claim, 'He is among his forefathers, under the soil.' On some days, she was direct in her approach, even pointing the pit out to the Army jawans. But they never believed her. They ignored the barking of their Labradors too, for they assumed that their dogs were barking at the mongrel that Altaf had strategically tethered in front of the trench.

These encounters with Army jawans were spine-chilling for Altaf. Mumtaz, on the contrary, would sit patiently on his cot, pointing his rifle directly overhead, fancying pulling the trigger at the slightest provocation. When the last dog had ceased to bark, and the patrolling team had withdrawn, Altaf would whisper reassuringly, '*Chale gaye kaffir* (the infidels have left).' That would be Mumtaz's cue—he would commence uttering the vilest abuses possible, often targeted at the dogs that, he believed, always urinated around his pit.

It was supposed to have been a 'week-long hideout'. He had fancied himself emerging a war hero, to a welcome by young girls vying for the affections of a young mujahid. But the week transformed into months and years, and he increasingly grew disoriented. His only friend down there was a rat, who, on the third day of his captivity, suddenly came calling. He had possibly been drawn to the pit by the smell of food. It took the rat a couple of days to trust its host and eat directly from his hand. Ever since, his friend unfailingly showed up at breakfast and supper.

One morning, Mumtaz got some terrible news. He heard his brother instructing someone to throw a trapped rat away after drowning it in water. His friend didn't turn up in the pit that day—not even at supper. 'Why did you kill the rat?' he demanded, when Altaf lifted him from the pit for a brief respite.

His mother wailed. 'Look, my son has gone insane! Please don't send him back to that grave again!'

Altaf Dastarkhan sighed. He had had enough of the everyday chaos. He could find no peace. Moments later, he walked up to his brother with a gun and a small pouch of ammunition.

'Take your gun and ammunition and go wherever you want to. But yes, shoot all of us before you leave.'

Mumtaz smirked. 'Brother, if you think you can emotionally blackmail me into spending all my life in this pit, you are foolishly optimistic. I am going back to that stinking pit tonight not because I fear death, which will eventually come for me, but because I don't want my mother to wail over my disfigured body.'

'My son, I am already wailing about how you are buried alive. This is no life that you're leading!'

Altaf dropped a small gift down the pit as a consolation for the rat's death—a transistor. The mortal remains of the transistor were regurgitated from the pit the next morning. Mumtaz couldn't stand playing any music underground, even if the transistor had been willing.

❦

The furniture at 'The Guild' was in sharp contrast to that in Mumtaz Dastarkhan's pit. The Guild was Altaf Dastarkhan's retail outlet in Swarnpur, intended to provide gainful employment to skilled artisans. 'My conscience is clear. This noble venture will surely flourish!' Altaf had vowed on the first day. And indeed, it had.

On the other hand, Adalat Shah was ungrateful, though his retail business boomed and he drove a Maruti car while his son rode a Vespa scooter. He described his fortunes to his wife as 'just a mouthful of nectar from the bulbul'. His political ambitions hadn't completely waned, but then, he didn't do much to further them either. Adalat Shah no longer believed in the election process or the 'myth of a government run in accordance with the Indian Constitution'. Yes, one day, he would find himself in a prominent political position, but that would be for his invaluable contribution to the cause of Jammu and Kashmir. Adalat Shah was certain of it. He often said to his friends, 'Our sacrifices and the saplings we are planting will bloom into gardens. The fruits will be savoured by generations to come. And I will humbly acknowledge my anointment as the caretaker of this part of the garden.' The scope of 'this part' varied largely, ranging from Swarnpur to the entire Jammu region.

But, truth be told, Adalat Shah's saplings were late bloomers, most remaining dormant. Perhaps, he felt, the weather in the western region of Pir Panjal wasn't yet warm enough to make the saplings sprout.

Not all the mujahids lived underground lives like Mumtaz. Many of them from Pakistan and Afghanistan mingled with the locals, leading nocturnal lives. Among them was a fifteen-year-old boy called Humza. He laboured to join his fellow mujahids on their night strolls, but the youth was fatigued. His feet were swollen, and blood oozed from his wounds. One night, Humza stumbled and was left behind by his group. Alone and frightened, he somehow stumbled to the gate of the closest house he could find.

'Who are you, son?' inquired Lal Jaan as she opened her creaking door.

'I am a mujahid.'

Lal Jaan lost no time in pulling the boy inside and shutting the door. She boiled a wok of water to wash Humza's wounds and offered him corn chapattis with salted tea.

'What's your name?'

'Humza.'
'Are you Pakistani?'
'Yes. I am from Faisalabad.'
'Does it hurt?' Lal Jaan asked as she gently washed the wounds on his feet.
'Not as much as the wound here,' Humza patted his chest.
'Let me see it.'
'No *Mai*, you cannot see the wound. It is invisible.'
'Don't cry, son. What happened to you?' Lal Jaan's husband asked from his cot. His chronic asthma warranted long hours of bed rest.

'Four years ago, my father died of cancer. I was the eldest child. My mother sent me to a Madrasa, and looked after my siblings. She washed dishes and wiped floors in the neighbourhood. I couldn't see her suffer like that and offered to work at the welding shop where my father used to work. But my mother refused.'

'What else would a mother do, son,' surmised Lal Jaan. 'What did you do then?'

'In December 1993, a reputed maulana came to our Madrasa and told us about the horrific conditions of the Muslims in India. He told us how the Babri Masjid had been demolished. In fact, he also told us that the Muslims in India were not allowed to offer namaz; the mosques were permanently locked by security forces. Many of my friends were furious. They offered to take up the cause of jihad in Kashmir. Most of us came from poor families, but our miseries seemed insignificant compared to the plight of the Muslims in Kashmir.'

'Did you take up jihad then?'

'No, I was worried about my family. How could I abandon them to go for training in Azad Kashmir? I told the maulana that my mother was a widow and I had to earn bread for my family. It was a job I needed, not a cause. The maulana said to me,

"There can't be a better job than service to fulfil the will of Allah. We will look after your family. You will get a monthly salary of fifteen thousand rupees for two years. All you have to do is live in India Occupied Kashmir. After your tenure ends, you can join your family."'

Humza paused for breath and nibbled at the chapattis. 'The prospect of so much money allured me. I said so. But the maulana reminded me that money could never be compensation for Allah's cause. The real accrual is a paradise of the highest order—*Jannat Al Firdous*. He assured me that seven generations of a mujahid are entitled to enter that paradise. That winter, despite my mother's constant pleadings, I joined a training camp in Azad Kashmir. Two months ago, I crossed the border with several others. But what I saw wasn't what I was told. The mosques were not locked. I could distinctly hear the echo of the *Azaan*. I felt cheated. I asked my fellow mujahids, "What exactly is our plan? Why don't we confront the security forces? Why haven't we received our promised salaries yet?"'

'But weren't you told just to survive?' inquired Lal Jaan's husband.

'No, even that turned out to be a lie. Our commander beat me with a baton. He said that he would shoot me if I asked a question again. The shoes they gave me never fitted me; I must have developed a hundred sores walking on those treacherous hills.'

'You poor boy!' Lal Jaan's heart almost broke.

'Two days ago, I met a schoolteacher. He told me something that shook me from within. I realized how blind I had been. He said, "You must take care of your family. That is the most important jihad for you! Don't look for *Jannat al Firdaus* elsewhere, it's right under your mother's feet." I told my Commander that I wanted to return. He beat me again, this time with shoes, but made a radio call to Pakistan to apprise them of my decision.'

'And did they get any response?'

'The Commander told me, "You can go back but you will have to return all the expenditures we incurred on your training. Pakistan Police will hound you for spying and illegally crossing the Line Of Control. This is what they do with traitors." He snatched my gun and ammunition and even my shoes, saying, "These are for mujahids, not for turncoats like you," and led the group forward, leaving me behind. I tried to follow them for a while, but my feet hurt so much that I failed.'

'Don't cry, son,' Lal Jaan tried to console the boy. 'Allah will take care of you.'

'I am not worried about myself. But I am afraid they will harass my family.'

For the next few days, Lal Jaan's front door remained shut. Humza lay on a cot, scorching with fever. One night, when Humza felt well enough to sit up and sip some tea, he told them what he had decided, 'I am going to rejoin the group.'

'What!' cried Lal Jaan. 'Why do you want to go back to people who treated you like this?'

'I have to make amends.'

'But how will you find them?'

'I know how to reach them, *Mai.*'

Lal Jaan and her husband felt helpless, but they knew they couldn't detain him any longer. She gifted him a pair of her rubber shoes and hugged him before he left.

'Take care of yourself,' she called out, as he put on the shoes.

'*Mai,* I will never forget you. When my father died, my mother couldn't afford shoes for me. I never felt ashamed to wear her shoes while walking to the Madrasa. I don't know how, so many months ago, I stepped into shoes that fouled my judgement. But now, with your shoes and the love you have given me, I hope that I walk to my destiny.'

A week later, Pathri Aali was in mourning. It was perhaps the first time that the death of a mujahid was so openly grieved. The mujahid had been shot dead by the Army in an encounter in the adjacent village. Rumour had it that the boy didn't aim his gun at the Army jawans. Instead, he kept firing intermittently in the air, as if he was inviting his death.

The slain body of the mujahid, still in his uniform, was buried at Pathri Pir—to the sound of Islamic canons. Everything about that young mujahid was exotic: his looks, his salwar-kameez, his ammunition bag and scarf. And on his feet, surprisingly, were a pair of cheap ladies shoes.

Twelve

They say love can make miracles happen, that love is, in itself, a miracle. Only a few weeks after Humza's death, he was reborn. He came back to life in the form of Ashwar's newborn son. Lal Jaan was certain of it. There were astonishing similarities between Humza and Ashwar's baby, and Lal Jaan couldn't pass these off as a mere coincidence. She was Ashwar's chosen midwife and spoke to her excitedly about it.

'What are you going to call him?'

Ashwar shook her head blankly. 'I had expected a girl. I wanted to name her Ayesha.'

'Would you mind if I name him, then?'

'Not at all. What name do you have in mind?'

'Humza.'

Ashwar didn't really want her baby to be named after a mujahid, but she nodded. Lal Jaan proceeded to explain, 'If only you had seen that boy, you wouldn't have even considered any other name for the baby. They resemble each other like twins!'

'I can hardly notice any features on this baby, let alone spot any resemblance,' Ashwar said, perhaps to discourage Lal Jan.

'You will see, you will see.' Lal Jaan nodded.

Ashwar had only Lal Jaan's company in the days after her delivery. Hanif had availed his quota of a six-month leave and had to return to Saudi Arabia. He had been fortunate enough to secure a visa for Saudi Arabia once again, and there were no frauds this time. He worked as the caretaker of a deer farm owned by a wealthy Sheikh, and earned a handsome salary. During his vacation, he had expanded their house to three rooms with cemented walls. The cows now lived in a warm barn. Manzoor and Shamma had genuine gifts to show off to their friends: Casio digital wristwatches, miniature bioscopes, mini umbrellas with cartoon prints, and toy guns.

Among all the wealthy Sheikhs in Saudi Arabia, Hanif found his employer, Sheikh Saleh Bin Taha, the most generous. Deer rearing was his passion, and his flock consisted of quite a variety. There were gazelles, Oryx, and crossbreds of Arabian and African antelopes. Hanif looked after his flock with utter devotion. Such was his diligence that the family now trusted him completely. Sometimes, the Sheikh even trusted him with his harem and asked Hanif to take his many wives shopping. These visits usually rendered Hanif an object of great curiosity. The Sheikh's wives could never understand why Hanif had only one wife. They refused to believe that men in any part of the world could be monogamous.

Of course, the women hardly talked to him, but he could sense their surprise. It was usually only the Sheikh's eldest wife who posed questions to Hanif. The others remained veiled, never showing their face, and talking only in hushed voices. Nonetheless he was still successful in classifying them as 'Contour number two, three and four', the eldest being number one.

In the Sheikh's household, Eid was a grand affair. In the evening, one of the deer would be slaughtered and loaded on a truck for the feast. Hanif enjoyed Eid like never before; after all, he always received generous *Zakat* or alms during the festival.

There was only one thing about the Sheikh that sometimes worried Hanif—his paranoia. Now and then, he would get anxious about the honour and modesty of his wives. Hanif watched dumbstruck as he got cameras installed in various parts of the house. He was further stunned when the Sheikh handed him the responsibility of scrutinizing the tapes.

'I am indebted to you, *Ya* Sheikh Saleh. I can't say no to any work that you assign to me.'

'Well, Habibi, my dear, remember to keep this to yourself. I know you will.'

'I will! *Wallah*.'

Hanif despised the new assignment, but he tried to complete it faithfully. He sat for hours in his room, watching the tapes. Within a few days, the secrets behind the veils of the Sheikh's wives came to the forefront. Hanif winced when he saw all their faces for it came as quite a shock after the months of purdah. But when he occasionally spotted forbidden parts of their bodies, the details of which made him turn red, Hanif took his eyes off the tapes and recited, '*Astaghfir ullah*! God forbid such a sin!'

One day, the Sheikh's driver handed Hanif a stack of cassettes. One of them was highlighted with a permanent marker. Hanif had the shock of his life when he played it; he couldn't believe that such things existed. Too ashamed and embarrassed, Hanif didn't watch the rest and went off to meet the Sheikh.

'Please reassign this task to someone else. Please!' Hanif implored, unable to say anything else.

'Why? What happened? Did you find something wrong with any of my wives?'

'No, Sheikh Saleh. I haven't seen anything wrong about your wives, except that the clothes they wear at home are, well, unmentionable.'

'I see. I will ensure they dress up properly. Did you notice anything else?'

'No. Nothing at all.'

'Then? What's the matter?'

'Sheikh Saleh, I just saw one cassette, and it has thoroughly disturbed me. It's about white people in a filthy act.'

'Oh, dear Hanif, you scared me,' Sheikh Saleh sighed. 'That

tape is for me and not for you. I think that idiot driver of mine mixed the tapes up.'

Hanif did not give up his duties as a surveillance officer for Sheikh's wives. By February 1993, Hanif had been promoted from a cowboy who walked around the deer enclosure to a surveillance executive who sat in an air-conditioned chamber and monitored recorded footage. He had three assistants monitoring the deer farm, and he looked over them through live cameras. The cassettes were delivered to him by the driver. Despite Hanif's disapproval, the driver would also deliver malicious gossip.

'I don't want to listen to your tales,' Hanif would shush him.

'Ignorance is bliss,' the driver would retort, 'especially under these circumstances.'

Thirteen

Zaitoon wasn't having a good time in Haji Mir's house, and neither were the rest of the family members. Within days of her marriage, she started quarrelling with Parveen and her mother-in-law over petty issues. She quarrelled with Wazir too and even with Haji Mir Baksh, much to his disdain. Zaitoon saw her marriage as a terrible insult. She might have accepted Aslam as a compromise for accommodating the collective ego of her elders, but sharing a husband with another woman was more than she could endure. It offended her ego and lowered her self-esteem.

And just like that, by the end of yet another kachehri, Wazir divorced Zaitoon soon after the wedding. But if Haji Mir's family had expected peace after the divorce, they were bitterly disappointed. Avdal and his family started a spat with Haji Mir and his relatives. It started with a petty affair—a minor issue about the grazing rights for their horses and buffaloes. But it soon blew out of proportion. After the revenue clerk decided the matter in favour of Avdal, both sides fought each other with sticks. What followed was thoroughly ugly for Haji Mir—harassment from police, cumbersome litigation, and selling off property to pay for all those rigmaroles.

While that matter didn't seem to recede, Haji Mir was taken ill. For more than two years, he remained bedridden. The villagers, variously diagnosed the cause of his ailment—'It must be a curse for not keeping his *lafz* about Zaitoon,' said one. 'I think it is the melancholy due to Aslam's separation,' offered another. Haji Mir did not ask anyone to shut up; he had silently acknowledged the relegation of his authority ever since Aslam had let him down.

It had been six years since Aslam had run away. But his family was still in mourning. Their troubles never seemed to end. Hamida often tried to convince her husband to reconsider his decision of disowning Aslam.

'Why do you still hold a grudge against your son? Why do you care for people who have been our enemies in the guise of friends and relatives? They would never like to see our son return to his house, but you are still succumbing to their tricks.

'You have always been too worried about what others think of you. But let me tell you, however much you try to rebuild your image now, your enemies will not be impressed. They will berate you even if you sacrifice all of us for this village. The price of your so-called principles is the happiness of your family. And now that they have claimed our grazing land, do you still want to disown your son so your enemies can enjoy our meadows?'

'I don't want any further discussion. If your son had any goodness left in him, he would have returned to the village and pleaded for mercy before the members of the kachehri. But he hasn't come back; he never will!'

Aslam had been manning the gate of Muzdalifah for over four years when he was appointed the supervisor in one of Badar Kaanchwala's glass factories. On the first day of his new job, Badar Kaanchwala told him, 'You are a supervisor now. Keep your eyes and ears open but mouth shut.'

The new job didn't please Aslam. It wasn't a reward for doing his previous job efficiently; in fact, it was the result of failing at his duties.

A few months after the demolition of the Babri Masjid, the Muslim residential society was attacked by a Hindu mob. Aslam couldn't handle the situation. He fired a few shots in the air and many were injured in the stampede that followed. Aslam had to spend two nights in a local jail before Badar Kaanchwala bailed him out.

'Why did you fire?' Badar shouted at Aslam—something he had never done before.

'I thought I was given a gun to protect Muzdalifah.'

'Not like that! You had to guard the society against burglars and thieves. You are not a cop who can fire at rioters!'

Aslam kept quiet for a moment and then smiled before replying, 'They looked like burglars to me.'

'It's not funny at all. They could have lynched you. You may still be their target. I'll have to see what can be done.'

Badar Kaanchwala's partner was rather displeased at Aslam's new role. 'Could you trust someone who unthinkingly fires his gun at a crowd?' But Badar managed to persuade him. 'I know this man well. His character is as clean as the glasses we manufacture. He only needs to toughen up.'

'Why don't you familiarize yourself with the accounts? It will help me out as well,' suggested the accountant.

But Aslam hated accounts. He found it very difficult to take stock of raw material and finished goods. As for checking the inventory of sale and damage, it made him cringe. Requesting the accountant to manage the account registers, Aslam busied himself with unloading the delicate glass slabs. He also supervised the labourers who handled the glass slabs. Even though Aslam had spent the week doing a task different from what Badar had commanded, he had done it diligently. His employer would be pleased. But the man who met Aslam after a week was the epitome of rage.

'What do you think you are doing?' Badar demanded. Aslam had never seen him so furious before.

'Badar Bhai, have I done something wrong?'

'You don't have to pick glass slabs! This is not what I sent you here for. You cannot be trusted with any job, not even that of a security guard or a labourer!'

Aslam sat quietly in his seat.

'You have disappointed me, Aslam. You don't understand the job that I have assigned to you, do you?'

'No.'

'Do you know that the damage of raw material is not even 1 per cent of the loss that I suffer? I don't care much about it! The major problem I face here is labour trouble.'

'Labour trouble?'

'Yes. The labour unions are nothing but mouthpieces of goons. Two months ago, I had a big order from a housing society to supply toughened glass. Do you know what the labourers did? They went on strike for over ten days! I couldn't supply the material in time, and my bank guarantee had to be liquidated.'

'Ohh!'

'You see it now, do you? And worst, who do you think got the contract in my place? The person who sponsored the strike!'

'Why didn't you fire the workers?'

'I can't. The labour union is strong. They will ensure no one ever works for me again.'

'So, what do you want me to do?'

'I sent you here to be a supervisor. I was hoping you could motivate the labourers and, if possible, spot the black sheep.'

'That's a very difficult task, Badar Bhai.'

'Is it? I don't think it is more difficult than cracking that inane jackal and lioness joke! Think of it as hunting for the jackals in the garb of lions.'

'But Badar Bhai, what's the use of finding the black sheep if you can't fire them?'

'See, firing them is not the only solution. I have other ways of dealing with them.'

Aslam didn't understand much, but he wanted to do anything he could for his generous employer. Badar Kanchwala had done a lot for him, and it was all he could do to help him. 'I'll try my best.'

Being suspicious wasn't in Aslam's nature. But from that day, he roamed the factory every morning and looked into the eyes of each worker. He attracted many puzzled looks, but the labourers mostly let him be. At the end of the month, when Aslam got his salary, he looked at the accountant with a confused look. 'Have you made a mistake in counting? Is this really my salary?'

'I have made no mistake,' said the accountant. 'It is my job to know everyone's salary.'

Aslam could never understand why his salary had become more than thrice as much! He had to do something to justify his keep.

He kept his eyes skinned for the next few days. It was extremely difficult to identify the troublemakers from among fifty workers. Sometimes, he felt there weren't any; it was all an unfounded apprehension. But by the next month, Aslam had recommended two names to Badar Kaanchwala. He wondered how his boss would deal with them. In the very next week, one of them was arrested by the police in a case of theft. The other quit his job; people gossiped that he had received a threat from the underworld. Aslam marvelled at the ingenious solutions his boss had come up with to tackle the errant workers. Indeed, firing them would have been tame in comparison.

Within six months, Aslam had become a shrewd manager with a thick beard and a receding hairline. He felt quite powerful and enjoyed the favours that many workers sent his way. When a few workers complained to Badar about Aslam's arrogance, he brushed them away. To his partners, he said, 'The glass has been toughened. Isn't that what we specialize in?'

Aslam rarely thought about his family now. He had no desire to return to his village. He did feel sorry for his sister-in-law,

Parveen, and his nephews, but that couldn't be helped.

His feelings for Ashwar, however, assumed a hyper-real dimension. He was unable to relate to her in the real world anymore but imagined that they were together in a dreamworld. She was the fairy from his father's stories. She taught in a high school, lived at the edge of a stream, and waited for him impatiently every evening. She still looked as tender as ever, elegantly wearing her black salwar-kameez. Sometimes, he had a nightmare that she was being pricked by hundreds of Datura pods, and he couldn't pull them off. It turned out to be Ashwar's little joke; her entire stole was made of Datura! But even in his dreamworld, he could never touch her. Sometimes, he howled in the middle of the night, only to be silenced by the collective swearing of his two roommates: '*Saale*, crazy, *majnu*!'

Both his roommates knew about his incomplete love story. They sympathized with him and did their best to console him the following morning.

Once, one of his friends suggested, 'Why don't you abduct Ashwar?'

Aslam laughed hysterically at the suggestion. '*Kahda* is what we call abduction. If I dare to do that, my father wouldn't think twice before breaking my skull with a stick. Anyway, I don't want to disturb her anymore. She is happily married.'

'Then, why don't you forget her?'

'I can't. She doesn't let me.'

'What do you mean?'

'I can't explain it. I have a feeling that I must remain committed to her.'

'You have gone crazy. Absolutely crazy! *Devdas*! How can you be committed to a happily married woman?'

'I don't know.'

In April 1994, after about a year of his appointment as a supervisor, Aslam sent a money order of five thousand rupees to his father. Haji Mir was baffled when the postman started to count the cash. The postman usually delivered only court summons, or, at times, letters of the men working in Saudi Arabia.

'Whose money is it?' Haji asked the postman.

The postman jeered, 'The name and address are yours. The thumb impression is yours. And now you ask me whose money it is?'

'You mean it is my money? Five thousand rupees? Who would send me so much money from Saudi Arabia?'

'Who said it's from Saudi Arabia? It's from Bombay, from someone named Shabir Ahmed.'

'But I don't know anyone named Shabir Ahmed!'

'So? You have already given your thumb impression on the receipt, and I have counted the money for you. My duty is done. You can decide what you want to do with the money.'

'Can I send it back to the Bombay address?' he asked.

'Yes, you can,' the postman appeared disgruntled as he took out a form and a pen.

'You don't have to do that,' interrupted Hamida, snatching the money from Haji's hands.

'This is not our money.'

'It is ours. He is our son. He isn't asking for anything; instead, he is giving you something.'

'Hamida, this is someone called Shabir. It isn't your son Aslam.'

The postman appeared bored. 'Should I stay or go?'

'Please leave,' Hamida replied, 'Thank you for bringing us the money.'

Hamida turned to her husband and said, 'You well know who has sent us the money. A minor change in the name couldn't have misled you.'

'All of you have become uncontrollable! Now that I am weak,

you don't care to understand why I was refusing the money. My decisions mean nothing to you.'

'Your illness has nothing to do with it. I will always respect you, and so will everyone in this house. But we are starving. We don't even have money to buy your medicines. Riaz and Kabir are insulted by their teacher every day for not wearing the school uniform. If Aslam wants to help us, why don't you let him? You know that Zaitoon wasn't the right match for him.'

'Get them their uniforms,' said Haji Mir, looking away. He could never bear it if anyone saw him weep.

Prevention and Pre-emption

Fourteen

Dharam Pal Singh was now a lieutenant colonel. Despite his transfer after the promotion, his family continued to live in Dehradun. He wasn't complaining. Budhpora wasn't the kind of place he would have liked his family to stay in. It was a small town in the Kashmir Valley, famous for silk carpets and infamous for harbouring dreaded militants. The streets and by-lanes of Budhpora trembled under the boots of Army jawans who patrolled night and day. Although guns were sparingly used, the batons swung dangerously in the hands of the soldiers as they disciplined one civilian after another.

Dharam Pal Singh's name had become synonymous with spine-chilling terror. When he prowled, whispers would pass from one corner to another; it was as if the deer in the jungle had sensed the tiger approaching. He never made a spectacle of his prey. Indeed, he mauled, battered, and crushed his prey as if it was the most natural route to 'discipline'. He had a rather ugly nickname in the town—*Bresh* or terrifying monster.

'Don't mind the nickname; it is a town tradition to cook up disparaging nicknames,' said Ramzan Butt, one of Dharam Pal's confidants and drinking partners.

'And what do they call you?'

'Nothing, sir.'

'How dare you hide things from me?' Dharam Pal Singh raised both his voice and his pistol. 'Tell me what they call you!'

Ramzan trembled. '*Pyolu*,' he whispered.

'*Pyolu*? What does that mean?'

'It means testicles. Balls.'

Dharam Pal Singh broke into hysterical laughter. '*Pyolu*! Whose *Pyolu* are you? Mine?'

Ramzan nodded. Taking in the derisive laughter was infinitely preferable to being shot.

Ramzan was never addressed by his name again. He twitched his nose each time Dharam Pal Singh addressed him as *Pyolu*. Many of these occasions were unnecessary. 'Right *Pyolu?*' he would ask, 'How is your family, *Pyolu?* Come, sit here, *Pyolu*.' It infuriated Ramzan more than anything else in the world. Well, at least until something worse turned up.

One evening, after Dharam Pal Singh returned from Dehradun, he said to Ramzan, 'I know you don't like being called *Pyolu*. So, let's raise a toast to your new name. It is basically your old name with a minor modification.'

'What is it?'

'From now on, instead of calling you Ramjan, I will call you Ramjaane. Cheers!'

Ramzan winced. He used to hate it when Dharam Pal occasionally mispronounced his name as 'Ramjan', but this latest frill was obnoxious.

'Why Ramjaane, sir?'

'Oh! I must explain,' Dharam Pal Singh stopped laughing and sipped his vodka. 'You are the hero of the movie, Ramjaane. It's a Shahrukh Khan's film where his name is Ramjaane. Interesting, isn't it?'

Dharam Pal Singh was content with his present posting. He had been utterly hopeless at Jabari Hills, but his enthusiasm and zeal in Budhpora were immense. In fact, the zeal often transgressed limits and translated into merciless beating, threats, intimidation, unwarranted detention, and collateral damage to life and property.

'I was rusting in Jabari Hills,' he told a gathering during a party hosted in his honour by the General Officer Commanding(GOC). Four militants had been killed by the Army under his command.

Dharam Pal Singh's exploits in Budhpora were remembered for years to come. He was idolized for how he dealt with enemies and hated for how he oppressed innocent people. Finally, when he was promoted and transferred from Budhpora, opinions were divided on whether it was a reward or a punishment.

One random night, more vodka running in his veins than blood, he commanded his men to search every house in town.

Milind Kumar, a captain under him, tried to make him see reason, 'Sir, I think, we should not go for a house-to-house search at such an hour. The women and children will be scared. It's against protocol too—'

Dharam Pal Singh flared up at once. '*Saala, behenchod*! Did I ask for your opinion? Have you forgotten my most important rule? *I* am the one who does the thinking! Rule number two: I don't have any soft corner for traitors and those who support them. And rule number three: only cowards follow precedence and protocol. The Army has no place for cowards. Anyone who deviates from my rules would be an enemy of the nation, and you well know how I handle enemies!'

No one dared to argue. Dharam Pal Singh was armed with the most dangerous of weapons—hatred and rage.

One of the Majors gathered enough courage to ask, 'Is there any information, sir?'

'If there's no information, won't you ever go for a search, Major? Don't you know that those motherfuckers are always out there, sheltered by the *kattuas*, the circumcised?'

That night was a truly horrible one for Bodhpura. The residents of Masjid Mohalla, in particular, faced unsolicited rough treatment.

'All the men! Come out at once!' The jawans knocked peremptorily at the doors, rousing many children from sleep. 'Take out your ID-cards. Stand still, you motherfuckers!'

Men were hit with batons as if silk carpets were being dusted. Children cried and women wailed; their sobs could be heard from miles away. An unfortunate family that had come to Masjid Mohalla from a nearby village, seeking a marriage alliance for their son, didn't know what they had walked into.

The son shouted, 'You ask us whatever you want. But don't misbehave with the women.' His father tried to gag his mouth, but it was too late. The *Bresh*, zeroed down on his tender prey.

His father pleaded for mercy. 'Sir, forgive him; he is just a kid.'

'Is he a kid? He is eighteen years old. Most militants are of that age group,' Dharam Pal Singh announced furiously, holding the identity card of that boy. 'Ah yes! There you are! He is not even from Masjid Mohalla.'

'Sir, they are our guests,' interrupted the host. 'They have come from a nearby village to ask for our daughter's hand in marriage.'

'Shut up, you motherfucker *kattua!* I know you offer your daughters to the militants. They come at night, sleep with your daughters and sisters, and disappear by the day.' He started beating the boy with fists and kicks until he fainted.

'You have fainted,' he said, poking the boy's belly with the barrel of his rifle. 'Has your heroism evaporated?'

Dharam Pal Singh constantly needed someone to feed the Bresh in him. That particular night, the boy was that someone. He dragged the boy along with four other men to the Army base for further interrogation. Before leaving, he shouted out an inebriated warning to the resident's—'Don't give shelter, food and women to militants. Not unless you want to die! And if you do, I'll be willing to help you.'

Captain Milind got the boy admitted to the Military Hospital. He had to spend a couple of weeks there before he recovered, albeit partially, from intestinal haemorrhage, broken ligaments, and a dislocated left shoulder. But his many injuries appeared trivial when compared to his shattered mental strength. Captain Milind frequently went to visit him and tried to cheer the boy up. But he had been broken beyond repair. On the day of his discharge, Dharam Pal Singh addressed a few sharp words to his father, 'Thank your stars that he is alive. But if he makes any further attempts to be a hero, I assure you it would be fatal.'

'*Meharbaani, karam aap ka janab*,' the father replied, shedding tears. 'You have been very generous.'

The Masjid Mohalla incident didn't go down well with the other officers, especially with Captain Milind. But Dharam Pal Singh struck gold with it. It was what brought him Ramzan, the trusted confidant he could fall back upon.

The morning after the Army picked up men for questioning, a civilian requested a meeting with him.

'Who is he?' demanded Dharam Pal. 'Some bloody politician?'

'I don't know, sir. Should I tell him to go away?'

'No. Bring him to the lounge. I will kick his ass if he dares to politicize the incident.'

'Who are you?' Dharam Pal Singh asked his visitor, wasting no time.

'Good morning, sir. I am Ramzan Butt from Masjid Mohalla,' the visitor introduced himself.

'Ramjan?'

'Yes, sir.'

'What brings you here?'

'Sahib, I have a request to make. It is about the men you picked up from Masjid Mohalla in the night—'

'Who told you we picked up any men from Masjid Mohalla? Are you a politician—an activist or something?'

'No sir, I am not a politician or an activist. I am a petty

contractor. I used to supply vegetables to the Army before the contract was awarded to another contractor.'

'So? What can I do for you?' Dharam Pal appeared bored. The miseries of others didn't interest him.

'Sir, among the men you picked up from Masjid Mohalla is a young boy. His father is a shopkeeper. If you release him today, he is ready to give you a hefty compensation. I assure you the boy is clean. He studies in the tenth grade.'

'Elaborate the compensation,' Dharam Pal Singh asked, his voice steady.

'Ten thousand rupees.'

'How dare you? Bloody civilian! You think I am like those police *walas*?'

'No sir. But they must realize that their freedom is not for free. Only then will they value it. Don't you agree?'

This was a new notion of freedom for Dharam Pal. He felt as if he suddenly had a counter narrative to the freedom struggle of the 'ungrateful' Kashmiri separatists. 'I will agree to twenty-five thousand. And let me tell you, I don't believe in negotiation.'

'Okay sir, no negotiation,' Ramzan said. 'Twenty-five thousand it will be.'

Dharam Pal Singh breathed in deeply; what a wonderful thing it was that he had raided the Masjid Mohallah that night. His eyes fell on a rather odd cap on his visitor's head. 'What is that cap you are wearing?'

'It's a Karakul cap, sir.'

'Karakul?'

'Yes, sir. The skin of a baby lamb. You can keep it if you want it, sir.'

'Really?'

'Yes. Only for ten thousand rupees.'

'Ten thousand? That's too expensive.'

'Yes, sir. These caps are expensive. In our culture, our cap is a symbol of our respect.'

'And you are selling your respect to me?' Dharam Pal Singh chuckled.

'Sir, this cap is not as important to me right now as the proposition I have for you.'

'What proposition?'

'People must value their freedom, and they must know its price.'

'So?'

'So, to begin with, you can pick up more young boys from well-off families and then release them after they are appreciative of their freedom. Just like this boy!'

Dharam Pal Singh laughed haughtily.

'Drinks?' he inquired of his potential partner.

'Sure, sir.'

'And the appropriate prices of their freedom will be charged?'

'Oh yes, sir. The whole town has enough means to buy their children's freedom. This is a carpet weavers' town. Silk carpets sell excellently!'

※

Soon after the Masjid Mohalla incident, Ramzan became a sought-after man in Budhpora. Just like people, even the torture cells had nicknames befitting their reputations. Ramzan would ask parents before they could make their pleas. 'Did I tell you about the "Papa and Kaangri"? You don't want to hear what they do in those torture cells.' He never failed to weep with the aggrieved parents. 'Oh *Khudaya*!' he would sob, 'When will the cruelty of the Army end? Until how long will we be intimidated like this?' Sometimes, he would feign a plea, 'Please find someone else for the job. The Army is so harsh that they will shoot me one day. Or worse, they will throw me into a cell.'

Helpless parents would throw themselves at his feet, pleading, begging.

'You don't understand. They are hungry wolves that India has unleashed upon us. We have to satiate their hunger.' The hunger would usually amount to a hefty sum of money, a chunk of which he appropriated for his services.

Dharam Pal Singh's clandestine arrangement wasn't as hush-hush as he had hoped. Many officers knew about it. One day, Captain Milind stopped Ramzan at the main gate and threatened him to never return. He also reprimanded two jawans associated with the 'Catch and Release' scam. Milind's behaviour, naturally, didn't go down well with Dharam Pal.

'How dare you stop him!' yelled Dharam Pal. 'Ramzan is *my* informant. And the two jawans are daring and dedicated. You were trying to demoralize them! I will recommend an inquiry against you for insubordination.'

And so the scam continued unabated. It flourished so much that even the Brigade Headquarters got wind of it. A brigadier enquired Dharam Pal about the allegation of 'Catch and Release'. 'Oh, it is false, sir. Totally blown out of proportion!' Dharam Pal responded calmly. He didn't stop to think that perhaps he needed to be on his guard.

Dharam Pal's arrogance extended not only to his peers and juniors but also to the local police. During a joint operation of the police and the Army, many mercenaries were killed in an ambush. Dharam Pal was furious. He walked up to the subinspector who was placing the dead bodies in the police van. 'I am not surprised. You guys are always eager to take credit for *our* achievements.'

'What?'

'Don't *what* me! Put the dead bodies in the Army truck!'

'But the legal process is—'

'Don't fuck with me, officer,' Dharam Pal Singh warned the

subinspector. 'And don't preach at me with legal formalities. Keep your rotten rules for thieves and pickpockets!'

Dharam Pal had a long list of people who needed to be 'disciplined', Captain Milind's name being at the top. He was asked to do tasks that normally befitted jawans. He was sent for search operations in areas that Ramzan had sworn were 'militant havens'. But each time Milind returned empty-handed, Dharam Pal Singh would be deeply annoyed. His leave application for attending his brother's wedding was rejected. To add insult to the injury, Dharam Pal Singh ordered him to go to Srinagar and book air tickets for his family on the very day of the wedding.

'My wife and children are coming to visit me,' Dharam Pal nonchalantly announced. 'By the way, I just remembered—isn't your brother's wedding today? What does he do?'

'He is a teacher, sir.'

'That's good. Very good indeed. No challenge whatsoever. You should also consider an alternate profession.'

Captain Milind was enraged, but he kept mum. He stormed out of the office and returned with a handgun. For a moment, Dharam Pal felt as if he was going to shoot at him, but Milind redirected the gun just in time and put it on the table. 'Here's my handgun, sir. I would rather teach in a private school than carry out domestic chores for inconsiderate bosses.'

Dharam Pal Singh's insults were so loud that the entire battalion heard them. 'It's almost like a coup situation here!' he informed authorities at the Brigade office. 'Captain Milind just threatened to shoot me with a handgun!'

Captain Milind faced an inquiry, the outcome of which seemed to take forever to arrive. But whatever it would be, Milind knew that his career was almost over.

Dharam Pal's wife Kavita hadn't changed her greedy ways; her demands were still as grand as ever. Sometimes, Dharam Pal would lash out, 'Do you think I have a money tree in my backyard? Can't you appreciate that I am risking my life every day to earn each penny? But all you want to do is show off!'

'I know you don't love me anymore,' Kavita would complain. 'Don't you remember that you had promised me you would fulfil all my wishes? But, of course, that was different. We were newly married. Now, after all these years, and after I have given you two lovely sons, you don't care for me anymore. Why should you, anyway? I have become fat and ugly!'

'Oh God. You are ridiculous. I don't deny you anything; I am only saying that I'd rather invest in property than in things we don't really need!'

'Oh, so a car is unnecessary. Of course, it is! How can you understand my situation when you have all sorts of vehicles at your disposal here? Do you know the school bus driver is so arrogant that he doesn't stop even for one extra minute? The neighbours taunt me if I ask them for a lift to the market. You have no idea of the humiliation I face every day.'

Dharam Pal gave up. He had never been good at negotiations. He got his wife a brand-new Maruti car. Much to his surprise, Kavita drove it from the showroom to their house in Dehradun. 'I knew that my loving hubby would buy me a car. So, I learnt to drive beforehand,' she explained.

'You always take me for granted, don't you?' Dharam Pal sighed, finally understanding that he had been tricked. He forgot about it eventually, especially after his wife had thoroughly thanked him in bed.

In the first week of November 1995, Budhpora became a

battleground between the security forces and the civilians. Skilful men pelted police parties with stones. News channels ran stories of boys disappearing from police custody. People gossiped about fake encounters and ransom being charged by notorious officers. Meanwhile, without a care for anything that was transpiring, Dharam Pal Singh sent in an appeal for out-of-turn promotion.

The fiery sentiment in the town didn't ruffle Dharam Pal. He went along one afternoon with a convoy, surveying the street in front of the girls' high school. Hundreds of young girls in white uniforms walked past; it was break time. Dharam Pal was especially struck with one of them—a real beauty, he observed.

'Drive over to that girl,' he instructed his driver and ogled at her when she stood still, trembling with fear. 'What's your name?' he asked the girl. She must have been about sixteen.

She didn't speak. Her legs shook in fright.

'Show me your ID card.'

She shook her head, indicating that she didn't have one.

Dharam Pal Singh noted her name and address and let her go. The driver gave her a sympathetic look, but that was all he could do.

'You know, women too have raised an extremist group in Kashmir,' he asserted later, to anyone who cared to listen. 'We have to keep an eye on them.' His juniors nodded even while they themselves were occupied with the shameless ogling.

That evening, Dharam Pal Singh drank to the girl. 'Humera! What a pretty name! You are beautiful, Humera. You must become my princess. I promise that I will burn Budhpora down if I don't find you in my arms in the next few days. Only your beauty can melt the heart of this *Bresh*.'

The next morning, when Ramzan came to meet him, he told Ramzan about Humera.

Ramzan was displeased. 'Sir, I would suggest you avoid drinking too much. I also think you need the company of your wife for a few days.'

Dharam Pal Singh grabbed Ramzan's collar. 'How dare you try to counsel me! You bloody *Pyolu*! Look, here is her name and address. Find out every detail about her. We will pick up any male member of her family, and then you know what the ransom is going to be. And don't worry, you will get your share in cash. But if that girl doesn't come to me in the next few days, I have plans that you won't enjoy in the least.'

Ramzan couldn't afford to annoy the *Bresh*. He returned in the evening with some news. 'She lives at the fringe of the town, sir,' said Ramzan, 'her home is near the paddy fields. Her father is the only other member of her family; he survived a mine blast some years ago. The poor fellow is blind, but a skilful carpet weaver. People say he can tell you the number of knots on a carpet only by touching it. Oh, and he has a special nickname: *Zaluru*.'

'*Jaluru*? What does that mean?'

'It means the spider. In his house is a wooden pillar from which silk strings emerge in every direction; they go up to the kitchen, the bathroom, the veranda, and even outdoors. They say he only has to touch those strings to figure out that a stranger is inside his house. I am rather doubtful about that last bit.'

'Doubtful? It is nothing but a bundle of crap! I am not interested in his nicknames; tell me about that girl!'

'Sir, I heard that a militant proposed to her some time ago. She refused. When he tried to force himself upon her, she ran away to her relatives in Srinagar. They say that the militant is still after her.'

'Son of a bitch! Anyway, before that motherfucker militant gets her, I want her with me.'

'But how, sir?'

'We will pick up her father.'

'That will draw much ire, sir. He is blind, and the whole

town will march on the streets in his support. And you know how agitated people are these days.'

'But I can't wait, Ramjan!'

'Please wait for some time, sir. I promise I will get her to you.'

'All right, but make this your top priority. You have no idea what I am going through.'

'Well, I can imagine, sir,' Ramzan grinned.

Earlier that day, Ramzan had chatted for hours with Humera's uncle. He owned a tea stall in Masjid Mohalla. Her uncle knew Ramzan's reputation and had chosen his words carefully.

'She still plays with her dolls,' her uncle had said with a smile. 'Once, when she was ten years old, I asked her what she wanted to be when she grew up. Can you guess what she told me?'

Ramzan shook his head.

'She said she would become a corn doll.'

'Corn doll?'

'Yes. I was surprised too. I asked her, "Why so?"'

'What did she say?'

'She said she wanted to have a large family. She wanted brothers and sisters and cousins, a family as big as a cornfield. She would often play with dolls made out of corns; she would braid the husk into twin plaits. In fact, she has one corn doll for everyone who died in the blast that killed her family members.'

Armed with some information about Humera, although abstract, Ramzan went to visit her father the next morning. The blind man seemed to stare straight into his eyes. For a moment, Ramzan wondered if his blindness was a ruse.

'Why are you here?' asked her father. 'What do you want?'

'I am Ramzan Butt.'

'Oh! Ramzan! Have you come as the messiah or the informer?'

Ramzan avoided the question. Instead, he said, 'Sir, I have learnt that your daughter is brilliant. But her studies are suffering because she is being pestered by militants.'

'All untrue! Neither is she good in studies nor does anyone trouble her. What business is it of yours anyway?'

'It doesn't concern me, but I know someone very influential and resourceful who wants her to excel in her studies. He wants her to have a career. To make this happen, he has proposed a monthly scholarship for your daughter. Or, if she is willing, he can get her a job in Delhi.'

'Why do so much for a regular girl from Budhpora?'

'Think of it as a reward for her courage. She has bravely saved her honour from notorious militants and shown the will to continue her studies.'

'Well, who is that messiah?'

'He is a colonel in the Army.'

The blind man's brows stiffened. 'What's his name?'

'Dharam Pal Singh.'

The next thing Ramzan knew was a silk rope around his neck. It almost stranguled him and yet, the blind man didn't loosen his grip. Ramzan felt certain his neck would break within moments. Seeing no opportunity to free himself of the death grip, he resorted to drama. 'How will a blind man know if I am dead?' he thought to himself and pretended dead.

The noose was loosened. 'I am letting you go. No, it's not because I have even an iota of mercy for you. It's just that I don't want to go to jail and leave my daughter at the mercy of rabid dogs like Dharam Pal Singh.'

'*Zaluru*! You have made a mistake by sparing my life,' Ramzan said in warning as he hurried out of the house. 'Be ready for the consequences!'

A few evenings later, Dharam Pal Singh, Ramzan, and two Jawans sneaked out of the battalion to execute the most heinous crime ever committed in Budhpora. The day he had been almost killed by Humera's father, Ramzan had rushed straight to Dharam Pal, showing his bruises and cooking up stories about the torture that he had been put through. 'He said such disgusting things about you that I am ashamed to repeat them, sir. I tell you, the only way to get Humera is to abduct her.'

And so, on a cold evening of November, Ramzan guided the Gypsy van to Humera's doorstep. It was a full moon night, and the sky was clear. The car's headlights were turned off.

'Do you think I am too drunk?' asked Dharam Pal Singh.

'No sir, you are always in control,' Ramzan responded loyally.

Dharam Pal knocked at the door a few times, but no one came to open it. Impatient, he ordered the jawans to break it open. The neighbourhood fell into a hush as the blind man howled like an injured wolf. A gunshot broke the silence of the night, and the old man could be heard no more. The team then proceeded to search for Humera. They looked for her everywhere—below the beds, inside the cupboards, in the kitchen, under the folded carpets, and even inside canisters too small even for a cat. Finally, Ramzan discovered her hiding inside the granary. Triumphant, he dragged her to Dharam Pal Singh.

'Keep quiet,' he said to the sobbing girl, 'or I will shoot you!'

No one came to her rescue as he pushed her inside the car, her mouth gagged. It was only the street dogs who protested at all, barking and growling furiously. Dharam Pal shot at them like a wild man. But their sacrifice didn't go in vain; it gave Humera an opportunity to escape. She ran barefoot towards the fields, and the party followed her relentlessly. The fields were flooded with cold water. Humera slipped and fell several times, but managed to rise and regain her balance.

'Stop, or I will shoot you!' Dharam Pal Singh roared, ready with his gun yet again. He fired a few bullets in the air to scare her. But she kept running. Humera had almost reached the village on the other side of the field when a bullet pierced her shoulder bone. Somehow, she managed to keep running and knocked frantically on the doors of all the houses she could see. No door opened. No one came out to help her. Crazed, she ran towards the mud silos outside the village and climbed a wooden ladder leading to the terrace. She dived into a heap of corn kept for drying, gathered some of the grains over her body and closed her eyes, terrified.

Early the next morning, the villagers discovered her dead body buried under a heap of reddened corn. Several doors in the village were bloodied too, bearing the haunting imprint of a girl's bloodstained fingers. The villagers lowered their heads in shame. Would she have been alive today had even one door opened for her?

Humera was buried in the village graveyard. When spring came next year, her grave became a shrine, surrounded by sprouts of golden corn. Someone built a marble stone near her grave and engraved it with a couplet by Mirza Ghalib:

> 'Sab kahan kuchh lala-o-gul mein numaya ho gayien
> Khaak mein kya surtein hongi ke pinha ho gayein.'

> Of all the good souls in earth's bosom,
> Some as poppies and roses germinated,
> The buried figures, are they there?
> Into myriad secrets surely they mutated.

Fifteen

Himanshu applied for another Short Commission with the Army in Jammu, pending the approval of which, he decided to consult at a small medical shop in the market. The nameplate proudly stated: 'Dr. Himanshu Singh, MBBS, MD/MS prep. Ex-Army doctor.'

'What on earth is MD/MS prep.?' Himanshu asked the shop owner.

'It means you are preparing for MD and MS. Anything wrong with that?'

Himanshu laughed. 'In that case, why don't you write: "Asp. President of India"?'

'Asp.?'

'Aspiring, of course!'

The shop owner looked thoughtful, evidently considering the proposal. Himanshu shook his head, wondering the reception his clinic would get. And indeed, it turned out to be, well, fascinating. Patients came to visit citing diseases he had never heard of. They also proposed unthinkable causes; their self-diagnosis left Himanshu in a daze. Sometimes, they suggested cures too; it usually involved a glucose drip or injection.

On the morning of his birthday, someone called Himanshu at the shop. The shop owner, waving the telephone receiver in his hand, said, 'It's your uncle. He sounds upset.'

Himanshu reluctantly held the receiver to his ear. 'What has happened, uncle?'

'Come home immediately,' his uncle blabbered. He didn't say any more but hung up.

On his way home, Himanshu was a worried man. He wondered if his uncle and aunt had quarrelled yet again. Or was it a medical emergency? Could it be a birthday surprise? Surely not, Himanshu brushed off that last bit. He was too old to expect those.

Himanshu had been adopted by his maternal uncle when he was ten years old, after his parents had died in an accident at Karnprayag.

It turned out to be a birthday shock. At home, his aunt stood threateningly with a bottle of kerosene in her hand. 'Choose right now!' she shouted at his uncle. 'It's either me or Himanshu.'

'What are you doing?!' Himanshu tried to snatch the kerosene from her, but she was quicker. She poured some kerosene on her torso and screamed again, 'I will set myself ablaze, I swear!'

Himanshu left the room. He sat by the cradle of his baby cousin, born only a few weeks ago. The infant had started crying loudly due to the commotion his mother had raised.

His aunt stormed out of the room and shoved Himanshu away. 'Don't touch my child's cradle!'

'I had told you not to force me to remarry,' his uncle shook his head, his voice breaking. 'Your *mami* doesn't want you to live with us anymore. She has asked me to choose between the two of you.'

'I understand, uncle. Give me an hour to pack my luggage.'

'No! You are not going anywhere. You are my son. No one can force me to disown you.'

Himanshu ignored him and walked to his room. He started stuffing his belongings into suitcases.

'So you have decided to leave me. What a great surprise for your uncle on your thirty-third birthday! Did you think I had forgotten your birthday? I never have! But how could I wish you, my son, when the house was in utter chaos?'

'Don't worry, uncle. Things will calm down after I leave.'

'Himanshu,' his uncle said clearly, his voice not shaking any more. 'If you have decided to leave, I won't stop you. But here are my two conditions. You can make your choice.'

'What conditions?'

'Before my second marriage, I had made half of my property in your name. I never told you, but she knows.'

'What? What do you want me to do?' Himanshu was thunderstruck, unable to think.

His uncle brought out a sheaf of papers from the cabinet. 'Here's the first option: take these papers, sell your property, and buy yourself a house away from this madness.'

'And the other option?'

'Sell it to me. I have already written a cheque befitting its price. Here it is.'

'What if I say no to both these options?'

'Don't, son. You will break my heart.'

Sixteen

It was the year of the Assembly Elections in Jammu and Kashmir. For the first time in his life since he had contested about two decades ago, Adalat Shah was not a candidate. He *couldn't* be a candidate; he was in jail.

Six months ago, in December 1995, Adalat Shah had been charged with treason, sedition, and waging a covert war against India. The warden of the jail had little love for Adalat Shah and did everything in his power to make his life miserable. The prosecution had taken a long time to prepare the charge sheet against him. One hundred and fifty-nine people had been named as prosecution witnesses from different parts of the state. When the trial had finally begun, Adalat Shah could sense that it would go on forever. With each passing day, his acquittal seemed unlikelier.

Disgruntled with his prospects, Adalat Shah spent his time in jail sticking to his own rhetoric—sham election, puppet government. Unfortunately, there were no takers for his opinion. Sometimes, when his arguments turned into insinuations about Pakistan, Kashmir, jihad, and communal riots, he was beaten up by the other prisoners.

When the day of his second hearing finally arrived, he slipped on the floor and broke his left arm. The judge refused to hear the case, much to the dismay of the prosecution, and ordered that Adalat Shah be transferred to another jail. He also ordered an inquiry into his allegation that the other inmates constantly tortured him.

When Adalat Shah was shifted to another prison, he got temporary relief from the perpetual torture. At the new jail, his family could visit him more often, and that was something. His former friends, including the Mufti of Jama Mosque, never came to meet him.

Adalat Shah's imprisonment had come as a big shock to everyone in the know. 'You are making a big mistake,' he had threatened the police officers, 'you will escort me back to my house in half an hour!'

He had made several phone calls to important people, including a senior party leader. But the politician had been unavailable. 'Sir will call you back as soon as possible,' assured his assistant. At the police station, Adalat Shah had to wait for over an hour before the Station House Officer (SHO) came to see him.

'Who among you is Jahalat Shah?'

Adalat Shah stood up slowly, dusted his buttocks, and replied, 'It's not Jahalat! It's Adalat, you ignorant man!' It is possible that Adalat Shah might have been gentler in his tone had he not assumed that he would be released within moments. Surely, by then, someone would have arranged for his release. As it turned out, the arrogance led to a severe beating.

'This is a police station, not your father's house!' asserted the SHO. 'Don't tell me who you are. I have so much evidence against you that you will rot in jail for the rest of your life.'

His time in jail broke him sooner than he had expected. He lost faith in his friends, and even in his family. He grew more confident that his wife was disloyal to him—something he had already accused her of a few weeks ago. 'You are not my blood!' he had said to his son, fuming because of a rather trivial disagreement. His son had pointed a shotgun at him, which his wife had managed to snatch away just in time.

Although Adalat Shah was losing faith in his family and friends, there was someone who surprised him with warmth. Altaf Dastarkhan visited him every week. He had even attempted to bail him out, although unsuccessfully. It was ironical that of all the people, it was Altaf whose intentions had always seemed murky to Adalat Shah. He would always make fun of Altaf when he would proclaim, 'My conscience is clear, *Janab e Aala*.' But, it seemed, Altaf was his only real friend, at least in these times of need.

He confided in Altaf one day, 'My brother, forgive me for doubting your intentions. I never valued you until all my loved ones deserted me. Who your true friends are becomes evident only when you are in trouble. I understand that now.'

'You don't have to apologize, brother,' Altaf reassured him. 'I am sorry that you are behind bars. But I shall not rest until I get you your freedom. I swear by my children's lives!' He hesitated before continuing, 'Brother, there is something I have to tell you. But I don't know if I should.'

'What is it? Tell me.'

Altaf drew closer to Adalat Shah and whispered, 'I may be wrong, but I think something is going on between your wife and Wani Sahib. People have also started to gossip.'

Adalat Shah closed his eyes, apparently in agony. He recalled how the acquaintance between his wife and Wani, a senior politician, had created a chasm of doubt between them.

'But we cannot be sure, brother. I don't want you to jump to any conclusions.'

'No, Altaf, I think you are right. Only a true friend can share something like this. Can I request you to do me a favour?'

'Of course, brother.'

'I have a cousin in financial difficulties. Could you please withdraw fifteen thousand rupees from my account in Swarn Valley Bank and give her the money? I will sign the withdrawal slip.'

Altaf Dastarkhan did many favours for Adalat Shah. The 'cousin' was the beneficiary of many of these. On occasion, he even brought her to meet Adalat Shah in jail. Impressed by Altaf's unflinching loyalty, he trusted him with his secret.

'Altaf, I think you know that she is not just my cousin. She is my girlfriend.'

'I sensed it, brother.'

'Look, I can't trust my wife anymore. I am afraid that she will spend all my savings, and my children will have nothing to live on. It saddens me that after all my hard work, I have only about one lakh rupees in my saving account. But whatever it is, I don't want that woman to squander it. Could you withdraw all the money and deposit it into my girlfriend's account?'

Altaf agreed. He came to Adalat Shah with receipts and passbooks, showing them to him despite protests. 'I don't need to see all this; I trust you completely.'

The requests came in full steam, and Altaf fulfilled them all, never refusing Adalat Shah. But one day, Adalat Shah made a rather unusual request. 'Well,' he said hesitantly, 'it isn't a matter of great importance, but I would love it if you could help me.'

'Tell me *Janab e Aala*. Please don't hesitate.'

'I have kept a makeup box in my cement store. I had purchased it for my girlfriend a few days before I got arrested.'

'Do you want me to get it from the cement store and give it to her?'

'That would be excellent.'

'Of course, I will do it, brother.'

Saghir Khan now lived between Jeddah and Muree, Pakistan. Interestingly, he had won his freedom exactly ten days before Adalat Shah lost his. After Adalat Shah had grown the recruitment business by leaps and bounds, Saghir Khan was entrusted with an even more challenging task: fund raising. He happily accepted the new task, but not without negotiating new clauses. 'I want full citizenship of Pakistan, a royalty of fifty thousand Pakistani rupees per month, and a bungalow in Muree. I also want all the charges against me to be dropped.'

Saghir Khan more than lived up to the expectations from him. His charisma never failed to convince wealthy Sheikhs to part with their money. What could be a better way of laundering some sinful indulgences than giving alms for a 'noble cause'? Soon, Saghir Khan opened a Madrasa each in Lahore, Rawalpindi and Muzaffarabad. He lived comfortably, and the elusive peace almost seemed attainable.

His family, however, had completely dissociated from him. His children had never enjoyed living in Jeddah because they found it too restrictive. Muree, a hill station, appealed to them for an occasional holiday, but it wasn't where they wanted to spend their lives.

'Why did you choose to stay in a bungalow in Muree?' his youngest daughter demanded. 'You could have asked for a penthouse in Islamabad or Karachi.'

'I was born and brought up in the hills. You won't understand it, but this place seems like home.'

Indeed, she did understand. She vividly remembered the last glimpse of her ancestral place when her mother had smuggled her children to Pakistan. But she didn't care. All his children chose to pursue careers. Saghir Khan's eldest daughter got a job with a national bank in Pakistan. His sons ran a slaughterhouse in Lahore. On weekends, when the family would get together, they would collectively lament about the miserable life in Saudi Arabia.

'It was suffocating!' said the eldest daughter. 'You can't step out of your house without permission, you can't socialize with people, you can't have any friends! All you have to do is stay indoors and offer prayers.'

'And then you wait for the next day to offer prayers again!'

chuckled one of the sons.

Lament although they did about the lack of liberties in Saudi Arabia, they could not overlook the lavish lifestyle they enjoyed. 'People here are so backward, ignorant, and ill-mannered,' they would claim. 'Even the beggars in Saudi Arabia are not as miserable.'

Apart from Saudi Arabia, the only country they were all praises for was the USA. 'You know, that is why Saudi Arabia had its charms,' the eldest daughter observed, 'we had access to American culture. You know, shopping malls, Chevrolet and GM cars, football, pop music, even driving on the right side. I loved that!'

The father and the children lived a dual social life; he between mendicancy in Jeddah and magnanimity in Pakistan, and they between the realities they despised and the fallacies they feigned to have savoured.

Seventeen

Motivated to be a liberator of Kashmir, Mumtaz Dastarkhan spent the best years of his life in a trench, begging for his own freedom. After his mother died, he rarely saw sunlight. He got rather violent, even threatening to murder Altaf's daughter, if she dared to play music.

One night, he decided that any form of escape would be better than spending a single more moment in the death-hole. He wanted to run away with his gun and ammunition at the very first opportunity. Life wasn't important for him anymore; a proper death, a death with dignity and a proper burial was all that he desired. Of late he was being haunted by a recurrent nightmare—he would turn into a rat and would be killed by drowning. He started clawing his way out of the pit, knowing that the roof wasn't too thick.

Little did he know that Altaf had covered the pit with a tin sheet and piled heaps of fodder. It suddenly dawned on Mumtaz why his brother had retracted his bucket and aluminium lunch box—he was afraid that Mumtaz might try to use the metallic objects and carve an escape tunnel, or commit suicide. But that wasn't what Mumtaz wanted in the least. Suicide was no way for a man to die! He wanted the death of a soldier, a death that people would remember him for. At least in death, he had to redeem the humiliation that had been his life.

Mumtaz stopped trying to escape. He refused to eat the meals that Altaf sent down in plastic bags. He would wail all day, 'Mercy, my brother! Mercy! I am losing my senses. Please let me out. I don't want anything from you but that!'

His brother would try his best to reassure him, 'Just a few more days, my brother, and you will live like a prince. It won't be more than a month, I promise. Please don't give up hope.'

'Hope is a useless thing,' Mumtaz would declare without emotion.

Sometimes, during nights, Mumtaz would wail so loudly that Altaf was forced to circulate a strange explanation. The villagers started murmuring about an apparition that haunted the cemetery and cried every night.

On the day of Adalat Shah's arrest, Mumtaz finally got his freedom. Altaf Dastarkhan, fearing his own arrest, rushed to the Army camp. An inebriated officer called Major Joshi met him there. A deal was brokered, albeit a hard negotiation, amid several pleadings and blunt refusals.

Late that night, Altaf brought Mumtaz out of the pit. He hadn't left the pit for weeks on end, and he staggered as he stood up, unsure of his own limbs.

'You are free now, brother,' Altaf said. 'Didn't I promise you that?'

Altaf held his brother's arms and helped him walk inside the house. He switched on the light, but Mumtaz screamed in protest. Disoriented as he was, Mumtaz staggered to the kitchen, only to come back with a chopper that he held against the neck of his neice.

'Brother!' shouted Altaf, 'You are free now! Please don't hurt her.'

'Oh! So, I am free now! Why was I imprisoned?'

'No one imprisoned you. You are a mujahid—'

'Shut your mouth! Shut your mouth at once, or I will kill her!'

Indeed, Altaf had overestimated his brother's disorientation. 'Give me my gun, ammunition, warm clothes and food. I will not hurt her unless you dare to disobey me.'

Altaf's wife was petrified. She brought out everything that

Mumtaz wanted, including the gun and the ammunition.

Mumtaz inspected the gun; it appeared heavier than he remembered. 'Will it fire?' he asked his brother, pointing it at his niece even as she screamed her heart out.

Altaf tried to placate his brother. 'Please don't hurt her, dear brother. She is innocent. You think I have wronged you, don't you? Then shoot me!'

Mumtaz was unmoved. He sneered in disgust at his hosts and at the food laid out.

8

Major Joshi had cancelled drinks for that evening. His focus was on the capture of a mujahid who had been in hiding for several years. His jawans crouched on the bank of the Swarn, ready for an ambush. It was a cold night, and the chilly wind almost froze their fingers and toes. But even after five hours of waiting, there was no sign of the mouse they had laid the trap for.

The Major was irritated; he had rarely spent an evening sober. 'It's going to be two o'clock in the morning! *Saala, madarchod* will never come.'

'Sahib,' a jawan alerted suddenly, 'there's someone on the bridge!'

And Swarnpur woke up to a light and sound show as never before. Flares illuminated the Swarn river and it shone, living up to its legend of a river of gold.

Major Joshi wanted to be sure of his prized trophy. He imagined the headlines he would be making: 'Most dreaded militant of Swarnpur gunned down by Major Joshi'; 'Seven years on and seven hours of gun battle'; 'Major Joshi finally gets the better of Mumtaz Dastarkhan'; 'Most notorious militant of Pir Panjal killed by the Army in a protracted gun battle'. He was determined to not let anything go amiss.

Mumtaz lay quietly on the bridge, unruffled. He knew his

enemies would want to capture him without any casualties. But he couldn't let that happen. Making mental notes of headlines proclaiming his own glorification, Mumtaz decided to shoot his first bullet on Indian soil. He could spot the green helmet of a soldier directly below, and took aim. But unfortunately for him, the gun misfired. Stunned for a moment, Mumtaz realized the shocking truth—the gun was defective! It wouldn't fire and Altaf had known it all along.

Mumtaz tossed his gun into the Swarn, brandished the dagger he had and yelled out whatever had accumulated during the long years of suppression. The dying beast raised a final cry that shook the villagers huddled indoors. Some villagers interpreted it as, 'Altaf you are lower than a pig,' and others as 'Allah! My life has been lower than a pig's.'

The apparition had presented itself on the bridge for a fraction of a moment and disappeared. 'Where is he?' Major Joshi finally broke his silence, 'Fire!'

The bridge was riddled with bullets fired by the puzzled Jawans. There was no visible target, but it had to be there. They fired till a soldier confirmed there was nobody on the bridge. Eventually, it was the Major who discovered Mumtaz. To his shock and relief he saw Mumtaz Dastarkhan's corpse staring at him from under the river, his fingers still wrapped around a knife.

Mumtaz was buried beside his forefathers. At his funeral, the village Maulvi prayed, 'Today, we also extend our hands for the peace of the spirit that haunted the cemetery for the last few months.'

Some of the villagers winked at each other. 'Aameen!'

The Vilest Millennium Bug

Eighteen

Haji Mir wept for his son. He didn't let anyone see him weeping, but he did. It had been eleven years since Aslam had left home. He sent in the occasional money order but no letters.

Every evening at 7.40 p.m., Haji Mir tuned in to the news bulletin on Radio Kashmir. The monsoon had made the radio rather noisy; it would whoop, hiss, and whistle before Haji Mir could make out a single word. But for his respect for the holy land from which he had brought it, many a times Haji felt like banging his radio on a wall. But Hamida had no such attachment to the chaotic device.

'Just like you, your radio is old now. It coughs more than it talks.'

'Hush!'

'What do you listen for, anyway? Your son will not make it to the headlines.'

In the last few years, most of the men of Pathri Aali had migrated to Saudi Arabia. It wasn't unemployment that drove them away, but the threat to their lives if they chose to stay on at home. Pathri Aali was witness to a deathly tug of war. On one side were the militants who constantly persuaded them to join the jihad. On the other hand was the Army that regularly picked them up for 'questioning'.

By April 1997, militants commanded the diktats of daily life in Pathri Aali. The villagers were divided in their opinions. While one section, led by Avdal, endorsed the wishes of the militants, another section, led by Haji Mir, resisted them. But Haji Mir found himself too weak to lead much of a protest. It especially broke his heart when the militants banned the bullfight he loved, along with the local sports. Such activities were, apparently, 'un-Islamic'. As it transpired, many things about that village and about its dwellers turned out to be 'un-Islamic'—traditions, occupations, even some names and, basically, everything that the Mujahideen could use against them. Haji remained quiet when the militants beat up the trumpeters and destroyed their dhols. The community of trumpeters, having lost their livelihood, relocated to a small town in the neighbouring district. But they had a terrible time there. This mass migration was looked down upon by the townsfolk, and soon they found themselves being apprehended for all sorts of petty crimes like theft, pickpocketing, shoplifting, and even prostitution.

But Haji Mir found it impossible to contain his fury when the militants banned the mounting of dhaals at the shrine of Pathri Pir. That, too, was declared un-Islamic.

One of Haji Mir's supporters was Lal Jaan who, although frail, had an unflinching voice when it came to confronting the militants. One evening, when a few militants dropped in uninvited at her house and demanded dinner, she exploded.

'How can you expect a helpless old couple to feed uninvited guests? Did we invite you to break bread with us?'

'This is not how you talk with the Mujahideen, you rotten old woman,' one of them lashed back. 'Don't you have any respect for us? We are here to fight for your freedom.'

'Freedom? From whom?'

'From the Indian occupation, of course!'

'We will be happy if we get freedom from you militants.'

'Don't call us militants! We are the Mujahideen.'

'You are right. You aren't militants but murderers!' Lal Jaan yelled. She might have been killed that night but for her husband who apologized profusely.

With Avdal, on the other hand, the militants were pleased. He happily supplied them with horses to carry munition. He didn't do anything to displease them. Not until one evening when a militant caught his granddaughter listening to music on the radio. Avdal slapped his daughter for effect. 'Music is *haraam;* it is profane! Don't you know that?'

Haji Mir was not ignorant of Avdal's relationship with the militants. He believed that Avdal was also using the militants against him and his family. There were rumours that the militants had promised to restore the meadows of Jabari Hills to Avdal and his ilk after forcing the Army to retreat. Haji Mir was afraid of how Avdal was handling the situation.

'He doesn't understand,' Haji Mir complained to Hamida. 'These are troubled times. One step in the wrong direction can push Pathri Aali to peril; all of us can be destroyed! Internal hostilities should be the last thing Avdal should encourage in such times.'

The next monsoon, the road to Jabari Hills was almost destroyed and flooded; the flash floods made it harder for the Army to march on foot from Buffliaz to Jabari Hills. There were stretches where the Army had to pass through the river valley, and it was here that they were most vulnerable to being ambushed by militants. The Changa riverbed was especially notorious. It had only a makeshift bridge built with a tree trunk, and that too had been washed away. The Army was particularly cautious while crossing this riverbed, trudging lightly on the slippery gravel and keeping their guns close.

It was an afternoon in July 1998 when tragedy struck the Army. The aftermath of the disaster changed the course of life in Pathri Aali. A few jawans had already crossed the river bed when gunfire reverberated in the hills. Before the Army could react, the militants had surrounded them. Eight Army officers were killed that afternoon, including a young lieutenant who was to go on leave to get married. The dead bodies were carried by the river and washed up on the shore, miles away. The militants escaped unhurt.

After the incident, the search parties at odd times of the day and night became even more insistent and violent in Pathri Aali. The Army lashed out at the men with rifle butts and batons. The women were slapped and children were made targets of vulgar, disparaging abuse.

No one dared to question the Army officers—no one but Lal Jaan. She often raised her voice fearlessly, 'Did we invite the militants here? Where were you when they crossed the border? First, you help them cross the border and then torture us for their whereabouts!'

Haji Mir knew that it wouldn't do to sit still anymore, even if he couldn't do much. He, grabbed his cane and, with great difficulty, dragged his withered body uphill to the Army camp at Jabari Hills. Even if he could do nothing else, he would at least get some of the innocent men free.

'Janab,' Haji Mir said breathlessly to the new Major. He hadn't seen him before. 'My boys are innocent. We are poor people, but we have never engaged in any anti-national or illegal activity.'

'Okay, let's assume you aren't lying. But tell me, how come you have never given any information about the militants? It is impossible that you haven't ever seen them.' The Major scratched his nose, closely watching Haji Mir.

'Yes, you are right, sir. They are everywhere. They come demanding food even if we haven't eaten in days. But we have to feed them. What can we do when someone demands food at gunpoint?'

'Do you know where they hide? Somewhere near your village?'

'I don't know, sir.'

'There you are.' The Major sounded annoyed. 'Do they jump down straight from heaven, get food, and disappear into thin air?'

'I don't know where they hide, sir. I am speaking the truth.'

'So, you are saying you aren't shielding these militants?'

'Why should we shield them, sir? We are helpless in front of them.'

'Oho! I distinctly remember that when a young militant died some years ago, your entire village mourned his death. But I didn't see any grief when a young Army officer died only recently.'

'He was not a militant, sir. He was a poor, helpless boy who was given a gun and forced to become a mujahid. For you, yes, he might be a militant. But he had no choice; he wanted to help his family. Sir, you know that the Pakistanis give monetary compensation to the family of a deceased mujahid.'

'Don't tell me what I know!'

'Don't be angry, sir,' continued Haji Mir, 'but when the young Army officer died, your men beat us as if we were animals. They tortured our women and children. We mourned yet again, but this time for our own miseries.'

'I am sorry about that,' said the Major, 'but what do you expect from my men when their mates get killed in front of their eyes? How can they carry the coffin of a young boy whose parents and fiancé were eagerly waiting for his return, their eyes on the road?'

Haji Mir sighed and closed his eyes. He thought of his son, Aslam, whom he hadn't seen in years. He had longed to see his son dressed as a groom, but the day would probably never arrive. 'I know how it feels, sir,' said Haji Mir. 'If anyone knows how it feels when your son goes away, never to return, it is me.'

A week later, the Indian Army was pulled out from Jabari Hills. A colonel—no one knew who it was—had prepared a secret report stating that Jabari Hills was rife with militants and the Army was nothing but a 'couple of sitting ducks'. Moreover, Jabari Hills had such poor connectivity with the Army base that it would be more prudent to pull the Army out until the *pakka* road was restored.

The militants rejoiced. To commemorate their mini victory,

they slaughtered Haji Mir's bull. When Haji Mir tried to protest, they only had one response, 'Thank Allah that it's your bull we are killing, not you.'

Ten days later, a fresh team of twenty-two militants arrived in Pathri Aali. Most of them were from Pakistan. The team was led by Zuber Ali, a stout man in his late forties. Before becoming an area commander for the Mujahideen, he had mostly lived in the villages of southern Kashmir. When the Pakistani Army was preparing for the Kargil War, many militants were recalled from Kashmir and pushed into Kargil through Skardu, a city in the Gilgit-Baltistan region of Pakistan. Zuber had also been one of them, but he had managed to avert his recall. 'I have an excellent plan for controlling the Pir Panjal Mountains,' he had revealed. 'I can execute it only if you let me stay.'

Zuber had lied. The real reason he had refused to leave was different. A year ago, he had been spared from the gallows in Pakistan. He had been under trial for triple murders, but the Pakistani authorities had decided to spare his life. After all, his commitment to jihad in Kashmir was unparalleled. Even though Zuber had escaped death that day, it still followed him about. On most nights, he had horrifying nightmares. He feared that he would be called back and imprisoned any day. And this time he would certainly be hanged. The very thought of returning to Pakistan made him tremble.

A few months ago, when he had been in the Pulwama district of Kashmir, Zuber had met his namesake—a young boy who went to college. Zuber gave him a nickname—Junior. In the evening, both Zubers would chat about guns, the battles of the Prophet's time, topography of Kashmir, Cricket World Cups, and other random subjects. Junior was talkative and often bragged about the trivia he had collected over the years. It was during one such discussion that the boy came up with a proposal that would later become

Zuber's excuse for avoiding his return to Pakistan.

'Did you know that the Islamic forces almost won the Battle of Uhud?' the boy had asked.

'Yes, they would have won had the archers not left the hillock. You have told me that about a thousand times.'

'That's the point. That's the whole point!' he jumped off the chair and stood in front of Zuber and his colleague, Khalil.

'What?' Zuber smirked, 'Have you gone crazy?'

'No, I am not crazy. But don't you see? We can win this battle too, but only if we can place archers on a certain hill that I have identified in Pir Panjal.'

'Hold your horses,' interrupted Zuber. 'Let me tell you something once and for all.'

'What?'

'We are not here to fight the way you think we should. I am no war expert, but I have undergone arms training in Muzaffarabad. A retired Army Officer taught us all about strategic and tactical warfare. I knew it then, and I know it now—I don't want *anything* to do with it! I joined this jihad after spending many years in jail in Pakistan. I had only two choices—death by hanging or jihad in Kashmir. What would you have chosen had you been in my shoes?'

'So, you are saying you *don't* want to kill the enemy?'

'I want to relax, my dear Junior. Killing time is infinitely more important.' He winked at Khalil, who smiled back. 'So, stop preaching at me about Islamic battles and the rest of your gibberish.'

Junior looked appalled, opened his mouth to protest, but decided against it. Zuber and Khalil were dreaded criminals in Multan, Pakistan. But in southern Kashmir, they were revered dervishes. People invited them for dinners, named their babies after them, and sought their blessings for new ventures. And, like all the other dervishes of Pir Panjal, their blessings came at a cost—the promise that they wouldn't be annoyed.

Junior's parents disliked his conversations with Zuber. They sent him to Srinagar, afraid that he might invite trouble from the Mujahideen. Surely, the physical distance would make both parties forget the whole affair. His parents were, therefore, unpleasantly surprised when Zuber and Khalil came to visit their son during one of his home visits.

Junior's mother fell on Zuber's feet. 'Mercy, my brother! He is just a kid. He is like your son. Why are you after him?'

'We are not after him. But he has to answer some questions.'

'What do you want?' Junior enquired, hiding behind a cabinet in the hall.

'Tell me, Junior, to how many people did you reveal my secrets?'

'What secrets?'

'Don't pretend! Okay, let me remind you. Do you remember I told you that I had been in jail in Pakistan? That I didn't intend to kill my enemies but merely pass my time?'

'Yes, I remember. But I never told anyone.'

'He never lies, brother,' Junior's mother rushed to her son and embraced him.

'Let me decide that,' said Zuber, and hit her with a baton. She didn't protest as he gagged her with a scarf and locked her inside the bathroom.

'Now,' Zuber sat back in the chair, 'tell me the truth. Don't even attempt to lie again.'

Junior started crying. His father looked on helplessly.

'Crying will not save you. Answering my questions honestly can.'

'All right,' wailed Junior. 'I told a couple of guys in the college hostel. They were bragging about their interactions with Mujahideen, so, I narrated mine.'

'Ah! Finally! So, what exactly did you tell them?'

'I told them that you were seeking my help to wage war

against India. You wanted to capture a strategic location, and I had presented to you the Uhud Model.'

'What?' Zuber slapped Junior. 'What *bakwas!* What bullshit! What the hell is the Uhud Model?'

'I told you about it earlier. Remember, the Battle of Uhud? Just like the hillock in that battle, there is a strategic hill in Pir Panjal. If archers are mounted there, it can decide the war against the enemy.'

'Archers?'

'Yes, modern archers. You know, canons, artillery.'

'And they believed this crap?'

'Not until I showed them the photographs and maps of the hill.'

'You have those too?' Khalil shook his head in disbelief. 'Do you have them here?'

'Yes. In my bag.'

Zuber whistled as he inspected the papers that Junior brought out from his bag. To Junior's father, he said, 'Your kid invites trouble. It is because of him that the Pakistanis have got wind of my plans. It is his fault that I am being recalled.'

'You won't have to go,' Junior protested. 'Just share with them my Uhud Model.'

Zuber frowned. 'Where is this strategic hill?'

'It's the hill overlooking the village of Hill Kaka,' replied Junior. They were his last words before Zuber shot him dead. And his father.

A few days later, Zuber sent an elaborate plan through his messenger. He included the photographs and maps of the Pir Panjal mountains and explained things exactly as Junior had.

'Remember the details carefully,' he told his messenger. 'The key to Kashmir is Pir Panjal. It doesn't connect Kashmir with India; in fact, it separates Kashmir. If we blow up the sole bridge connecting Kashmir and India, we can effectively separate Kashmir.'

'But how can we do that?' The messenger made a few quick notes.

'We have to reach a particular location that I have identified. It is a spot that the Indian Army has left unattended, and it is located at a very high altitude. But this point overlooks all the strategic points of Pir Panjal.'

'So, if we can take that hill, the war can be won.'

'No, we don't even have to fight for that hill; it's unoccupied. We just need to occupy a nearby hill. It is called Jabari Hills.'

Initially, Zuber had little faith in Junior's grand plan. He had intended to use it only to prevent his recall. But, when the Army decided to retreat from Jabari Hills, and he was elevated to the rank of an Area Commander, he realized that the plan had merit.

Nineteen

By the end of 1999, when the rest of the world was awaiting the new millennium, Swarnpur found itself bitten by the vilest millennium bug. It had become the cradle of militancy, and within that cradle, Pathri Aali suffered like an insignificant speck left to its destiny. Every evening, as the sun set and left behind rapidly falling darkness, women and children abandoned their homes. They would seek shelter in safe houses that they believed would protect them from their predators. Many turned up at Haji Mir's house, and Lal Jaan also found herself with more visitors than ever before. Ashwar, along with Shamma and Humza, carried blankets and bedspreads to Lal Jaan's house every night. Whenever a dog barked at night, everyone would tremble. The unknown fears that lurked outside made their throats turn dry, and their hearts almost stop. In this year of the new millennium, it seemed as if every night was a night of *Qayamat,* of annihilation. To them every night seemed like a millennium.

One night, screams tore the silence intermittently, most of them coming from the neighbouring village. Haji Mir wanted to enquire about the commotion, but Hamida and Wazir stopped him from stepping outside.

Haji Mir didn't protest. He knew that he was all they had, and being with them was critical. But the very next morning, he set off to make enquiries. For about the first time in his life, Haji Mir missed his morning prayer. Walking with more confidence than he felt, he stormed into Avdal's house. Avdal hadn't spoken to him in a long time, but that didn't matter.

'Is everything okay? What happened last night?' Haji Mir came straight to the point.

'Quiet!' Avdal warned, 'The Mujahideen are sleeping inside.'

'What were those screams we heard last night?'

'I have no idea.'

'Yes, you do. What are you hiding from me?'

'Go home, Haji,' Avdal said, 'don't get your old body in more trouble than you're already in.'

'I won't go until you tell me what you're hiding.'

'For Allah's sake! Please go home,' Avdal shoved him outside. He lowered his voice and added, 'I will come over to your house and tell you. We cannot talk here.'

§

'We have been shamed! We have been shamed so atrociously that you'll almost refuse to believe it,' Zaitoon's father cried in front of Haji Mir. He looked battered, having aged rapidly over the years.

'What do you mean?'

'My daughter, Zaitoon!' cried her father. 'They have been ravishing her for several days. They pounce on her like animals, all at once, and she is left shattered. It breaks my very soul to watch her like that. Last night, we tried to confront them. But in response, they beat us all. They threatened to behead us if we resisted their advances on Zaitoon.'

'Who are "they"? Those militants?'

'Yes,' answered Avdal.

'And yet you are sheltering them in your house?'

'You don't poke a sleeping bear, Haji,' said Avdal. 'It would be suicide.'

'Yes, we don't poke a bear; we kill it when it turns grisly! This is what we did to Khalifa.'

'You talk about killing! Look at yourself. You can't even walk erect without your cane! There are many Khalifas out there, Haji, but this time they are equipped with guns and daggers. You cannot fight them with your cane.'

'How many of them are sleeping in your house?'

'Two.'

'We have to confront them! Surely we can do something—'

'We cannot. They are mindless and diabolic, but they are armed. They are so cruel they will shoot us all at one go.'

'So, what do you suggest? That we wait for them to dishonour our daughters and wives? It could be your daughter next, Avdal.'

'I suggest that we wait for their area commander, Zuber, to return. He has been away for a while, and that's what has given these boys the advantage. I am sure Zuber will take them to task once he learns what they did. After all, they call themselves mujahids. They are true Muslims.'

Haji Mir was restless. He didn't want to wait for Zuber to return and bring the wrongdoers to justice. But he was powerless. After the Army had retreated from Jabari Hills, it had become clear to the people of Pathri Aali that they couldn't expect any mercy from the militants. All the matters concerning the village were decided by Zuber Ali; the kachehri was un-Islamic. It was Zuber Ali who had pronounced a 'just' chastisement for Lal Jaan to punish her for her attitude towards the Mujahideen. 'Give her fifty lashes,' he had ordered. The old woman had been lashed with a nylon rope—the one she used to tether her cow with—for they didn't have a leather whip. Her husband kept pleading for mercy as two militants pinned her to the straw mat and flogged her until she fainted.

After the militants had gone, her husband smeared some turmeric paste on her bruises. 'You should not have talked like that,' he said, weeping. 'We are powerless in front of them.'

'They killed my son.'

For a while, her husband feared the worst. Had the torture made her lose her mind? 'We don't have children, Lal Jaan. What son are you talking of?'

'My son, Humza. They killed him.'

'Humza? Ashwar's son?'

'No! My Humza. Have you forgotten him, you old man?'

Hamida was in a state. She kept requesting Haji Mir to maintain his calm when he went to meet the area commander at Avdal's house that evening.

'Don't forget that he has no sympathy for us. Be humble and submissive.'

'It is going to be a pointless meeting. What can I expect from a man who whipped an old woman mercilessly?'

'Don't say such things,' Hamida complained. 'You'll only put us in further trouble.'

'What do you want me to do? Tell them that they are right and we are wrong? That we are their slaves?'

'Why do you want to pick up arms for a lousy girl like Zaitoon? She must have flirted with the men and swayed them—'

'Don't talk nonsense!' Haji Mir was incensed. 'You want revenge because you got an unsuitable daughter-in-law. But I seek to salvage the honour of Pathri Aali. I may be weak, but I am still strong enough to confront them.'

'And what if they turn against you? Don't forget that Zaitoon's father had also confronted them and they threatened to behead him!'

'I have never lived with "what ifs". What if they decide to destroy every household in Pathri Aali? Trust me, if we don't act now, they will. They have no respect for us—not for our shrines, our women, our culture, our kachehri, not even our elders. But we cannot sit numb and tolerate their atrocities like we have no dignity.'

'I know you will do as you please,' Hamida said, resignedly. 'But do remember that we are no match for them. You can't beat their guns with your arguments.'

Haji Mir, though frail with age and prolonged illness, was rejuvenated by the challenge at hand. He felt as if Pathri Aali's fate would be decided in the meeting with the area commander. Things were about to change. He detested Zuber and the hold he had over the villagers.

Zuber Ali, Khalil, and two other militants entered Avdal's house. Everyone except Haji Mir stood up to greet them. Zuber stared at Haji Mir. 'Don't you know how to greet a guest and a mujahid?'

Avdal intervened, '*Janab*, he is feeble and old. Forgive him.'

The meeting had begun on a bad note. Zuber came straight to the point; his tone was demeaning. 'So what's the matter, Avdal?'

'*Janab*, we request you to look into the matter of, err… maltreatment of our women.'

'What maltreatment? And who is the complainant?'

'*Janab*, this man here,' Avdal tapped Zaitoon's father on the shoulder, 'He complains of something shameful that happened with his daughter. Why don't you speak up?'

'*Janab*,' Zaitoon's father submitted, 'your boys, Abu Sufyan and Musa, have sinned. They abused my daughter. Please show mercy on us, master!'

'Don't cry. I will address Abu Sufyan and Musa. Does anyone have any other complaint?'

It could have well been a redundant question. Zuber seemed impatient to leave, not listen to complaints. In any case, the sight of the AK-47 rifles dangling from his shoulders made any further complaining difficult. The villagers had come prepared to discuss a million grievances but no one uttered a word. Haji Mir looked around disdainfully. Subjugation to anarchy was not Haji Mir's principle. He glared at Zuber as he stood up, and enquired, his voice unwavering, 'Is the justice you vowed to deliver according to Islamic tenets?'

Zuber couldn't believe someone would dare to stop him on his way out. 'Have you gone crazy?' he asked. 'Do you want to die today?'

'Today is better than tomorrow. Especially if "addressing" those rapists is the justice you have decided to deliver.'

Zuber was furious. He brandished his rifle warningly, glowering at Haji Mir. 'What makes you question my judgement? How dare you insinuate that I disobey Islamic tenets?'

'I question it because I am not afraid like all the other men here. Before I came to this meeting, they pleaded with me to keep quiet. All of them wanted to talk about the atrocities your men commit every day, but the fear of your gun silenced them. Look at this father here,' he pointed to Zaitoon's father who sat shrivelled in a corner. 'He was pleading with you as if it was a sacrilege to complain about rape! He pleaded not to bring your boys to justice but to show mercy on him for complaining!'

'So, how would you like them to complain? What would you want me to do?' Zuber sneered, his eyes gleaming.

'I only have one question. Before you declared our kachehri un-Islamic, we at least had a mechanism to resolve our problems. Now, if you vow to deliver justice as per Islamic laws, tell me, where are the culprits? Why aren't they being stoned to death?'

'I have to inquire into the matter first,' Zuber managed to say. 'Then, I assure you, justice will be delivered.'

'All right,' said Haji Mir. 'I will wait. We will all wait.'

The next morning, Zuber and Khalil came to Haji Mir's house. The two accused militants were with them. Haji was dragged out of his house and taken to a barn at the end of the settlement.

While his family members endlessly cried for mercy, Haji Mir was pushed, beaten, and threatened. Old as he was, he couldn't do much to protect himself.

The villagers were faced with a horrific prospect. The hero of Pathri Aali had been dragged out and beaten like a stray animal. For many, Haji Mir had been the only beacon of hope. But their beacon was rapidly burning out.

Zuber was not done with Haji Mir. He had him tied like an animal and screamed at him, 'Get ready to answer my questions. If you evade them, be ready to get slaughtered as per Islamic tenets!'

Haji Mir nodded slightly. His entire body hurt.

'Now,' said Zuber, 'the court begins its proceedings. Haji Mir, I have learnt that you are a *mukhbir* of India. Tell me, what information have you been giving to the Army about our movements?'

'What kind of a question is that? What happened to the proceeding you started yesterday?'

'Do you want another beating? Answer what you are being asked! What is your connection with the Indian Army?'

'When they were here, we hardly knew about your movements. That's what I told them.'

'Really? I have heard that you often invited them to your home. They used to sleep in your house and have your women as bedfellows. Is that true?'

Haji Mir fumed. He stared at Zuber, shook his head in disgust, and spat on the floor. The crowd around them had thickened, but no one protested. Wazir was locked up in the house. He didn't try to escape. He knew that if he confronted them, they would kill him along with his father? His father had made him promise something the night before.

'If something happens to me, promise me you will stand guard. You will protect your family. You will never abandon them like Aslam.'

'I promise. That's my *lafz*.'

Among the crowd were many of Haji's relatives and well-wishers. They longed to help him, for no one could bear to see him beaten so mercilessly. But going against the Mujahideen wasn't an option. They stood rooted to the ground and prayed. The young men from whom courage could be expected, had left for Saudi Arabia. Haji's grandsons, Riaz and Kabir, had also left the village. The only surviving hero, perhaps, was Haji Mir himself, but he was old and powerless now.

And how could Pathri Aali forget Avdal? Hamida, Parveen and Wazir were not so sure. They thought it was possible that Avdal was behind the ordeal. The long enmity between the two families had completely broken their trust in Avdal. But crisis can erase differences.

'I had warned him. I had warned him!' said Avdal angrily when Hamida approached him for help.

'Don't go, father,' Avdal's daughter pleaded. 'They will be after you just like they're after him.'

'I have to. Don't stop me. Haji Mir is egoistic and rather stupid, but these militants are barbaric.'

'But, what if they start beating you too?'

'I cannot silence my conscience anymore.'

Avdal walked up to Zuber, much to the joy of the gathered crowd. 'Mercy, my master!' he pleaded with folded hands. 'Haji Mir is old. He doesn't have control over his senses. The separation from his son has demented him.' 'And are *you* in your senses?' asked Zuber. 'I had ordered everyone to stay away, but you still interfered.'

'Do you have anything to say?' asked Zuber, turning to Haji Mir. 'Don't you disagree with Avdal? Don't you find anything wrong with the way he is begging me for mercy?'

'Please let him go, master. He is only a weak, mentally unstable old man.'

'You keep quiet!' Zuber tried to shove Avdal. 'You cannot compel me to do anything.'

But Zuber was unaware of Avdal's strength. He couldn't move him even an inch towards the door.

Embarrassed, and desperate to prove his strength, Zuber shouted to his men, 'Tie his hands! Beat him until he shuts up!'

'Why are you torturing us?' Haji managed to ask between beatings. 'Are you so insecure about yourself and the justice you claim to deliver?'

'You are an informer for India!' Zuber lashed out. 'You are a traitor of Islam.'

'You don't really need an allegation since you have already made up your mind to kill me. No one will ask you to justify yet another killing. What happened to the justice you promised yesterday?'

Haji's questions both prolonged their torture and made their deaths certain. His pointed barbs enraged Zuber, more so because he hadn't an answer. Haji Mir was attempting to reason with the unreasonable, trying to invoke a conscience in someone whose heart had been blackened by savagery, damaged beyond repair. Perhaps, things would have been different had Avdal and Haji correctly estimated Zuber's barbarism. Perhaps, if Avdal's hands hadn't been tied, he could have put up a fight. But in Pathri Aali that year, the odds weren't in their favour. The two men were tortured until sunset and, finally, slaughtered. Both their necks bled; their heads were turned towards Mecca.

Moments after Haji and Avdal breathed their last, Zuber felt the pang of deep regret. So intense was his disappointment that he almost wished he could resuscitate Haji Mir and answer his darned question. Khalil had answered it for him when both of them had grinned at the anguish of the mourning villagers.

'Khalil, I don't like how this man kept pestering me about

justice. Tell me, what would you have done with these boys?'

'Nothing!' replied Khalil, nonchalantly. 'They are mujahids.'

'So?'

'We, the Mujahideen, go to the highest heaven. Right?'

'Yes…'

'What's your hesitation? Allah will enter Mujahideen in the highest heaven unconditionally, without any trial!?'

'Yes.'

'Then, tell me, how can a mujahid be tried for petty sins by an average human?'

Zuber's eyes popped. He slapped Khalil and asked furiously, 'Couldn't you have told me this earlier?'

The twin murders brought Pathri Aali to a new low. As though, the twin peaks, Tatt-Kutti, were obliterated. If the community had once been polarized, the sentiment was now one of unconditional subjugation. The villagers' terror dwarfed their sorrow. When their men wrote letters from Saudi Arabia and enquired about their village, the mothers, sisters and wives of Pathri Ali dicated, as Ashwar wrote, 'Everything is fine.'

Twenty

Thousands of miles away, oblivious to the happenings in his village, Hanif also lived a life of subjugation. But his oppression was being perpetrated by one person only—his employer, Sheikh Saleh. Hanif despised being his servant; all his former ideas of his employer's generosity and goodness had hit the dust. Six months ago, Hanif had approached the Sheikh and asked him to terminate his contract.

'Why? What happened?' The Sheikh had been offended. 'I cannot terminate your contract before the term ends.' He had pocketed Hanif's passport and brushed him away, indicating that he didn't want any further discussion on the subject.

In the last two years, the Sheikh had issued seven visas on Hanif's recommendation, five of which had gone to his relatives. Hanif was back at his old job—looking after the Sheikh's deer. After he had refused to keep up the surveillance task, having surpassed all limits of moral endurance, the Sheikh had given his assistants the pink slip.

One day, the Sheikh's eldest wife asked Hanif, 'Why don't you come to the villa anymore?'

'Ask your husband,' he replied. 'He believes I am ignorant and he is steadfast.'

'And which part do you doubt more?' she joked.

Hanif couldn't appreciate the joke. He had lately realized that all the malicious tales he had heard about the Sheikh had been true. Earlier, Hanif had invariably disbelieved in the dirty gossip brought to him by the Sheikh's driver. But when a new driver, whom the

Sheikh had employed after the previous one left, recounted similar tales, Hanif was forced to re-evaluate his stand. The new driver, a man from Kerala, had come to him with the tapes one day. His face was distraught.

'Why do you look upset?' Hanif had enquired.

'I can't see what my sister is going through,' he broke down.

Two years after the man had been employed, he had requested the Sheikh to allow him to bring in his sister. The Sheikh had generously offered her a visa. Her work profile was to include babysitting the Sheikh's infant daughter and, occasionally, assisting the wives with their shopping. At night, she was supposed to sleep in the room adjacent to the Sheikh's youngest wife. It seemed an innocent enough job, but the naïve girl soon realized what it entailed. Whenever the baby cried, she had to jump in to calm it. If she made even a moment's delay, the wife would 'sensitize' her with slaps. Her hair would be pulled until her scalp turned red. The Sheikh also joined in the disciplining. He would call her to his room and keep her quiet while she endured punishment for her errors. The girl complained about the Sheikh's behaviour to his wife, but it was futile. For one, she spoke only Malayalam, and the wife understood only Arabic.

Unable to tolerate his sister's sorrows, the driver asked the Sheikh to terminate her visa and deport her. That was the day Hanif requested the termination of his own contract as well.

'She is crazy, insane!' said the Sheikh. 'Anyhow, what has she to do with you?'

'Did you rape her?'

'Rape? Are you crazy? She was my maid!'

'Does that mean she was your toy?'

'Don't be presumptuous! Go back to the farm.'

'No, give me my passport. I want to go home.'

The Sheikh spoke to him calmly; it took a lot to ruffle his feathers. 'Look, you are getting unnecessarily emotional. These things don't matter at all.'

'They matter to me. As a human, as a Muslim.'

'You think you are a more devout Muslim than I am?'

'What can I say? You raped a poor, helpless woman.'

'Enough!' he yelled, 'She was my maid, and I paid her enough.'

'Enough? What's the price of one's honour? How many women do you wish to sleep with anyway?'

'Hanif, don't test my patience. Just count the favours I have bestowed upon you and your relatives.'

Hanif continued as if he hadn't heard. He had long had it coming. 'Tell me, why do you spy on your wives? Don't you trust them? Do you fear they sleep with other men?'

It took a slap to silence Hanif—the first time his employer had ever raised a hand on him.

'I didn't want to do that, but you compelled me.'

That was six months ago. The day finally came when Hanif was allowed to leave, as his contract was over. He had packed his luggage and was ready to leave for the airport when he got a call from Sheikh Saleh.

'Come to my house with your luggage.'

He got a marvellous farewell—one he could never have expected, especially after the bitter argument he had had with his employer. His luggage had been just one suitcase, but he now found a multitude of gifts laid out for him—blankets, tea sets, dinner sets, cassette players, and some gift-wrapped boxes that shone alluringly. In addition, each of Sheikh Saleh's wives gave him a fistful of Saudi Riyals.

Hanif was overwhelmed. 'The airline will charge me heavily for this extra luggage,' he said quietly.

'Don't worry, I will pay for it.'

Sheikh Saleh went to drop him to the airport. It was a quiet journey; neither of them spoke. If the Sheikh had been able to speak, he would have assured Hanif that his son would always have a respectable job in Dammam.

Hanif sat in the aeroplane, thinking about the ups and downs he had experienced in his life. Several challenges were waiting for him back home, and he was diffident about resolving them satisfactorily.

A few months ago, a suitor had called for his daughter, Shamma. Ashwar had seemed keen to get his approval for the marriage. His wife's behaviour had surprised him. When they had first got married, Ashwar had been determined to secure a good education for both Manzoor and Shamma. She had even encouraged Shamma to study hard so she could set an example for the villagers. But then, all of a sudden, Ashwar stopped talking about Shamma's education. The only thing on her mind was getting her married. She kept demanding money too, never mentioning why she needed it. Was Ashwar avenging her own misfortune? Had she stopped loving her children? They were after all her step-children.

Hanif's mind was in a whirl.

Twenty-one

'But that's where my family is! That's my home,' Hanif said to the owner of the mule. He had hired a mule to transport his luggage back to Pathri Aali.

'Do what you feel like, sir. But I will again warn you—if possible, don't go there. It's a dangerous place.'

Hanif thought the mule owner was rather eccentric. How could his tiny, peaceful village suddenly turn so dangerous? But one thing did surprise him though—he was walking home alone. There had always been well-wishers who would walk proudly with a Haji, a Saudi-returned. And there were wayfarers who would take a detour to help transport Saudi merchandise. Occasionally, he thought he saw heads popping out from smoke holes, but he warded this off as imagination.

He was pleased when a little boy hugged his knees and demanded, 'What have you brought for me?'

'How are you, little Humza?' he asked his son, marvelling at how much he had grown.

The boy nodded and stared at Hanif's bags.

Lal Jaan came to visit him as soon as she heard of his return. 'Hanif, take your family with you and leave. Don't argue with them. They are not human.'

'What are you saying? Who isn't human?'

'This village is unlivable. It is full of snakes!' Ashwar cried. Her usually stolid exterior broke at the sight of her husband. 'I have braved poverty, misery and calamities over the years, but this constant fear and intimidation is beyond me. Our children are not safe here.'

Hanif didn't know what to say. He prepared to unload the mule, but Lal Jaan stopped him, 'Don't! Your journey is not complete. Take your family along and leave now.'

'No, *Daadi*,' Ashwar interrupted, 'I won't go anywhere. But Hanif, please take your daughter and son with you.'

Hanif was exasperated. This wasn't the sort of welcome he had expected at home.

Were they speaking the truth? Or was Ashwar trying to send him off so she could elope with another man? 'You want to get rid of me, don't you?' he asked his wife, his face blank.

'Are you insane? The militants are after Shamma!' Lal Jaan exclaimed. 'Do you know that she doesn't stay here anymore? She stays in Buffliaz, at her aunt's house. She came along today only to meet you.'

'Why?'

'Because if she stays here, they will abduct her and do unthinkable things. You don't know what they are capable of.'

'Over my dead body!' shouted Hanif. 'No one touches my daughter without killing me first.'

'That won't stop them,' Ashwar said quietly. 'That's what they did to Haji Mir Baksh and Avdal.'

'What?!'

'Yes, they were butchered like sheep. Do you know why they were killed? Only because they vowed to protect the modesty of a daughter of Pathri Aali.'

Hanif felt faint. Saghir Khan's voice rang in his ears. *I can see you'll do nothing when the Indian Army pulls down the salwars of your women, just like they did in 1947.*

'What about the Army? Why don't they do anything?'

'They left us. We are at Allah's mercy.'

Hanif couldn't believe that Saghir Khan's prophecy was turning true. It wasn't the Army assaulting his women, but what did that matter? Would he really be unable to do anything? If he had accepted Saghir Khan's offer, would his reality be different?

'We cannot do anything. Please take our children and go.'

'Leave it to me,' scowled Hanif. 'You have already made your choice, haven't you? You are free to pursue it.'

'What choice?'

'I don't want to discuss it,' Hanif said flatly, leaving Ashwar confused.

'You are wasting your time, son,' said Lal Jaan. 'Your daughter is not safe here. Every moment she spends here is a threat to her life.'

'What do you want, *Daadi*? Should I abandon my wife and run away like a coward? Have you asked her why she wants to stay back?'

'Do you know what happened after they killed Haji Mir and Avdal?' Ashwar spoke up in a steel-like voice. 'The villagers had no choice but to let those snakes fulfil their whims and fancies. The daughters, sisters and mothers of Pathri Aali became their prey. It would be sinful to name who was raped and who was spared. We, the woman of Pathri Aali, have decided that we will never narrate our personal shames, not even before our husbands, fathers and brothers. Why should we share our sorrows with men who have left us at the mercies of those scavengers? So, you will have to hear this: we are not chaste anymore. We have suffered a collective rape. And I cannot leave this village to let the remaining women suffer the shame alone.'

Hanif remained silent. 'It was Ashwar who brought all the women to this understanding,' added Lal Jaan.

'Okay, so you are a heroine. But what's your plan? What heroism will you achieve after you send me away?' mocked Hanif.

'You may mock all you please, but that won't change a thing. Do you know what I have gone through here, alone, afraid? I was really hopeful for Shamma. She was doing so well at school, and then, one day, the militants set her school on fire. The area commander, Zuber, directed his lustful gaze at her. I have protected my daughter all these days. No, I don't have a plan. How can we, people who hide in trenches from their cruel predators, have the time to think of a plan?'

'In trenches? Like what?'

'Yes,' Ashwar pointed to a heap near the end of the village. 'That is where we, the women of Pathri Aali, and our children, spend our nights.'

'It looks like a long grave to me.'

'And so it is; it is a communal grave. We call it *Saanjhi Qabar*. Every evening at sunset, we go there and lie low all night. It is big enough to accommodate forty women and their children.'

'It was Ashwar who designed and sponsored the construction of that structure,' Lal Jaan explained.

'I am sorry I spent the money without your permission,' said Ashwar, 'but we had no time to lose.'

'Are you safe there?'

'No. We are in mortal danger inside the *Saanjhi Qabar*.'

'Then what is the point? Why did you design a structure that jeopardizes the lives of women and children?'

'After they killed Haji Mir and Avdal, it became evident that nightly raids would become a regular affair. Every night, they would barge into one house or the other. During the mourning of forty nights, all of us women stayed together. They knocked at our doors, but each time, *Daadi* would announce that all the women were together and would not open the door under any circumstances. We spent most of our nights squatting on the floor; there was never enough space to sleep. One night, they did manage to break down the door of an unfortunate household. The women who had been hiding there were mercilessly tortured. It was then that I decided to construct that structure. If nothing else, we could at least be together and feel safer than we would in our separate homes.'

'But can't they break down the door of the structure you have built? What will you do then?'

'The door is hinged on a wooden pillar supporting the roof. Of course, they can break it down if they try hard. But if they do, the structure will collapse.'

'Haven't they tried yet?'

'No, but they have beaten our men in retaliation. Sometimes, they have threatened the men at gunpoint, warning them that they would shoot if we didn't open the door. But so far, we have resisted. I know our resistance is no match to their devilish desires, but, well, it has at least delayed our predicament. They satisfy themselves with easy prey from neighbouring villages.'

'Your wife has transformed this village into one family,' said Lal Jaan. 'We don't just have a common dwelling, but she has helped the villagers understand that all of us work for each other. Being together is our strength. Now, we share our daily chores too. If someone grazes the cattle, the others milk the cows. The remaining men bring groceries for everyone. Any decisions that need to be taken are made at our night dwelling.'

Hanif realized how foolish he had been to doubt his wife. 'So, this village is now managed by women,' he smiled weakly. 'I don't know how to respond to the two of you. I don't know if I would have been able to face what you have been through. But I do know this—I won't leave. I can also take a beating, just like other men.'

'No!' cried Ashwar. 'You must leave. They know that I am behind this idea of resistance. They will be sure to avenge it.'

'You are a changed woman,' Hanif shook his head. 'You aren't the one I married.'

'Perhaps, every husband returning to Pathri Aali might feel the same way about his wife.'

Calamity seldom arrives with a warning. Hanif didn't leave Pathri Aali despite repeated warnings from Ashwar and Lal Jaan. By the time he realized his folly, it was already too late.

'To the shed! Everyone, to the shed!' Mothers clutched their children; fathers raised war cries. Dinners were abandoned; hearths were left to die out on their own. Inside the communal grave, there was utter commotion. Lal Jaan stood with her hands on the latch of the gate. Even if everyone hadn't reached the site on time, she had to latch the gate. Ashwar refused to enter the dwelling; she was frantic with agony.

'Where is my child?' she wailed. 'Where is my Humza?'

'You go in; I will find him.' Hanif tried to reassure her, but she shook her head. She wouldn't go in without her son. 'Tell Lal Jaan to latch the gate. I must get my son.'

Shamma wanted to stay back as well; she cried her heart out for her little brother. Lal Jaan forced her inside. She, too, was beside herself with fear. She feared the worst for Ashwar, the daughter she had never had.

The predators arrived sooner than anyone had expected. Ashwar and Hanif were locked out, in direct sight of those plunderers.

'Do you think they are safe inside?' Zuber pulled Ashwar's hair and threw her to the ground. 'Do you think it's some fortress we can't enter?'

Someone held a rifle to Hanif's chest. 'Are you the one who came this afternoon with a mule-load of merchandise?'

'Yes, sir,' he managed to say, his lips trembling.

'Are you her husband?'

'Yes.'

'Listen to me carefully, or you will be responsible for the massacre of this entire village.'

'Ji, *Janab*.'

Inside the shed, the women and children were crying. Shamma's shrill cries could be heard over everyone else's. Lal Jaan slapped her to make her shut up. 'Where is my Humza?' she kept asking everyone. One of the women whispered, 'My son told me that he saw Humza going to the Pathri Pir stream to fill his new water bottle.'

Outside the structure, Zuber demanded that the door be opened. 'We have learnt that the Indian Army is distributing radio sets to help you send them information. Ask your wife to get the gate opened. We want to see if the stories are true.'

'The doors will not be opened!' Ashwar screamed. She screamed again when one of the militants slapped her sharply on the cheek.

'Where is Wazir?' Zuber looked around.

'I am here, *Janab*,' Wazir appeared before him, submissive, apologetic.

'Wazir, do you want your usual beating today?'

'No.'

'Then tell this man to command his disgusting and hot-headed wife. She assumes we won't dare to break open the door. She fools herself that I care what happens to those inside!'

Before Hanif or Wazir could reason with Ashwar, a child came running and clung to her. It was Humza. Ashwar hugged him to her chest, anticipating that it could be the last time she had the chance to embrace him.

Zuber smirked. He snatched the new water bottle that Humza was clutching to his chest and crushed it beyond recognition. Humza started wailing.

'Shut up!' ordered Zuber, his voice venomous. 'Tell your mother to get the door opened.'

'*Janab*, what if you find no radios inside?' asked Hanif.

'Do you think you can negotiate with me?' Zuber poked the butt of his rifle into Hanif's jaw.

'Tell them to open it,' Hanif said to Ashwar, giving up. He couldn't look her in the eye.

'Yes, I will,' said Ashwar.

But Lal Jaan had other plans. 'This gate will open tomorrow morning,' she said each time Ashwar requested her to open it.

'But they have gone away. Open it now,' Ashwar lied.

Lal Jaan stood firmly behind the latch, refusing to let anyone else come near the door. Shamma tried to convince her that her mother was speaking the truth. But Lal Jaan slapped her yet again. 'Hold on to your senses,' she commanded.

Ashwar turned to Zuber, 'What can we do now?'

'Plenty! We shatter the door.'

'Please don't,' Hanif and Wazir pleaded with the men. 'Please wait until the morning. We assure we will fully cooperate with you, without any resistance.'

Zuber looked at his fellow men; they exchanged a glance that Hanif could not read.

'Okay,' he announced. 'We will wait until the morning. Let's wait in your house.'

Surprised as he was, Hanif had to guide them to his house. Perhaps, some dates from the holy land could infuse mercy in their hearts. Ashwar started preparing dinner for the guests. Humza was still terrified.

Zuber sucked on a date, so did the other Mujahideen. His mood had suddenly become jovial. 'We are not bad people, you know. We are the Mujahideen. We are fighting in the name of Allah and for *your* cause. We also want to live a normal family life, just like everyone else.'

'Ji, *Janab*,' muttered Hanif.

'You must accept us as your family members.'

'Ji.'

'So,' said Zuber 'in the name of Allah and in line with the *Sunnat* of our prophet, I seek your daughter's hand in marriage. Accept me as your family member, your son-in-law.'

A few heads looked up, smiling sheepishly at the proposal of their area commander. Hanif stared at the floor, stupefied. He had never expected the direction the evening would take. He couldn't even imagine what Ashwar must be feeling; she didn't utter a word. Shamma, his daughter, was only a child who still played with her dolls. He had disliked it when Ashwar had mentioned the suitor in her letter.

'So? What do you think?' Zuber poked Hanif's back with a finger.

'In our culture, a marriage can only be decided by the relatives and the elders. I will discuss the matter with them and tell you what the decision is. There can be no compulsion in Deen-e-Islam, you know.'

Zuber was furious. The last time someone had tried to lecture him about Islam, the man had lost his life. He was now armed with the knowledge that would silence Hanif—the Mujahideen had special privileges. But he decided to save that for later.

'Very well,' he reflected. 'But let me make it clear, we will come back tomorrow to listen to the decision. Whatever is decided, you as the father have the power to veto it. There is no compulsion in Islam, but then, there can be no comparison between *Shariat* and your profane traditions. The desire of a mujahid will always hold precedence over the whims of ignorant villagers. But let's see what you decide.'

Long after the militants had left their house, Hanif and Ashwar sat frozen on the floor, as if already dead. Humza sat in his mother's lap, clutching his crushed water bottle and staring at the fire in the hearth.

Ashwar broke the silence. Her hair was dishevelled, her face distraught. 'I will go with you,' she announced. 'But we have to leave right now.'

'But how can we leave without Shamma? Will *Daadi* open the gate?'

'Don't worry, she will.'

An hour later, armed with a bag of essentials, Hanif, Ashwar and Humza reached the communal graveyard once again.

'Open the gate,' whispered Ashwar.

'This gate opens tomorrow morning,' replied Lal Jaan.

'But it's morning already.'

The gate opened then, and Lal Jaan hugged Ashwar. 'I feared the worst. I was waiting eagerly to hear you say the password.' Ashwar hugged her back, her eyes full of tears. Lal Jaan had been everything to her, but it was now time to leave. Taking Shamma along with them, the little family departed from Pathri Aali.

Dawn was still far away, and Ashwar and Shamma often missed their footing. Hanif had to switch on his pen torch even though he didn't want to; he had planned on using it only after they entered the jungle. There had been a time when Hanif had walked along roads far darker than this. But tonight, it was different. It was the walk of his family for their honour. When they crossed Pathri Pir, it felt like a small triumph. All of them prayed to the Pir to guide them along the way, to show them the path of divine light, far from this life of misery and fear.

But the Pir must not have heard. Suddenly, a search light from the Pir's shrine froze them in a frame of blinding light. A bullet flew past Ashwar's right ear like the hiss of death; it went past Shamma's eyes but kissed Humza on the left knee. The child screamed, and so did the whole family. Another bullet pierced Hanif's chest even as he yelled, 'Run!' It was the last word he ever uttered. The last bullet Ashwar heard that night went right through her belly, almost as if the Mujahideen had impregnated her. Shamma, terrified, expected a bullet to come her way too. All expectations were murdered that night.

Trick or Treat:
The Compromise

Twenty-two

After his promotion to the rank of a colonel, Dharam Pal Singh practically lived out of suitcases. In three years, he had been shifted six times from one station to another in Jammu and Kashmir. How he longed to be posted at the powerful corridors of South Block, New Delhi! The least acceptable was a posting in the Regiment Center in Bareilly, Uttar Pradesh—a place not too far from his family in Dehradun. Being Colonel Quarter Master in yet another insignificant town, Udhampur, infuriated him no end.

Kavita Singh didn't like her husband's reputation as a briefcase officer, perpetually being shifted from one station to another. Finally, when Dharam Pal got posted in Udhampur, she sternly told him that no matter what, she would stay with him. He should avoid another transfer like the plague.

Dharam Pal winced when Kavita came to stay with him in Udhampur. He had tired of her constant demands, complaints, and cunning manoeuvres that he never grasped until it was too late. Soon after they had moved to their new residence, and the trunks and cartons of household articles had been unpacked, they entered into a fierce argument. 'Who was this girl who was murdered in Budhpora? What did you have to do with it?' Kavita enquired, her eyes scanning some papers in Dharam Pal's files.

'Don't look through my things without permission! Those are confidential papers.' Dharam Pal snatched the papers from her hands, but only ended up flaring her apprehensions further.

'What are you hiding from me? I know there is something; don't attempt to lie.'

'I have had enough! Haven't I always been a *bloody* good husband, a jolly brother-in-law, and a *fucking* excellent son-in-law?' Obsolete, condemned merchandise, once consigned to nostalgia was retrieved to bear witness to his goodness and her meanness.

'Don't recount things you bought with petty money! I can also bring up a million things that I faced only for you. Do you want me to narrate in depth the meanness of your mother and relatives? The way they tortured me for dowry? The menial chores your family made me do?'

Kavita was furious, and Dharam Pal soon lost steam. Words, anyway, had never been his strength. He could only fire what he was good at—abuses. Provisions of Armed Force Special Power Act were vaguely demonstrated to her along with a slew of ready expletives. Unarmed, bare hands have their limitations. Weeks later, he would talk to himself, in his drunken state, about his acts as, 'Introducing her to the Bare Act of AFSPA!'

Kavita returned to Dehradun with a swollen face and her sons. And Dharam Pal took to '*bloody badminton*'.

Sepoy Arif Ansari was the pride of his small village in the Terai of northern Bihar. He was the first Muslim boy from his village to graduate, and he eventually made it to the Indian Army. He grew to become the favourite handyman of Colonel Bhupesh Singh. Arif was excellent at shorthand and never made an error in typing. Colonel Bhupesh Singh was so confident of his handyman's abilities that he signed all his letters without bothering to read them. Naturally, Arif's colleagues soon grew jealous. While they had to endure all sorts of petty tasks, Arif Ansari enjoyed a white-collar job.

One day, one of these jealous colleagues sent in a hushed word to Colonel Dharam Pal Singh. It wasn't fair, was it, to treat someone with such favouritism while the others slaved away?

Suddenly, Arif found himself under the dictatorship of Colonel Dharam Pal Singh. Arif had to make his shoes shine and ensure that his linens were spotless. Meanwhile, his duties as a typist and stenographer continued. It was an unfortunate time for Arif Ansari who had become a shuttlecock between the two colonels. He even hesitated to ask for leave when his parents arranged his engagement with a girl from the neighbouring village. But fortunately for him, Colonel Bhupesh Singh approved his leave immediately. 'Don't worry,' he said to his favourite handyman, 'By the time you return, things will get better.'

Arif's fiancée was eagerly awaiting his homecoming. She had never seen him before and stayed up at night wondering if he would look like the actor Akshay Khanna from the Bollywood film, *Border*. She wondered whether he would carry his luggage in a holdall and wear an olive green uniform just like in the pictures of armymen she had seen.

A disappointment awaited her—not because Arif didn't look like her favourite movie actor, but because the wedding couldn't be scheduled for at least six months. Her family had hoped for a definite date for the wedding, preferably not later than three months after the engagement. But Arif was certain that he wouldn't be able to take leave for the next six months. Arif wanted to put the ring on his fiancée's finger. It was denied by the girl's father and sneered at as un-Islamic, filmy and unbecoming of respectful people.

A day later, the girl got a cousin to arrange a clandestine meeting with Arif. And that afternoon, when the two finally got a chance to talk without a hundred onlookers scrutinizing their every move, they found the words flowed freely. Arif told her all about the rigours of training, the terrain of Jammu and Kashmir, the beautiful snowfall, and how the senior officers valued him.

'Do you have a picture of yours in Army uniform?' she asked, unable to stop herself.

'No, I don't, but I will surely send you one.'

'Okay,' she nodded and handed him a letter.

Later, when he reached home and opened her letter, he saw that she had enclosed her photo in it. Why, oh why, hadn't he asked for a photo of her? She must have expected him to! 'Keep this in your wallet,' she had written. 'It will guard you against all evil.' She had also apologised for her father's behaviour.

'I will get myself photographed in my uniform at the first opportunity,' resolved Arif Ansari. He felt morose as he boarded the convoy bus to Udhampur from the Jammu railway station. The photo of his fiancée was in his wallet. 'Thank you, Naazneen,' he said out loud. What a pretty name it was! He found himself wanting to repeat it, to gently say her name out loud again and again as the bus took him farther away from her. A jawan sitting next to him gave him several curious glances, but Arif didn't care. Not anymore.

At the gate of the Army base, a message awaited Arif Ansari. 'See Colonel Dharam Pal Singh immediately upon arrival.' Arif felt nervous; why did the Colonel want him so urgently? What could he have done wrong? As it turned out, Arif had returned to a bit of a nightmare. Colonel Bhupesh Singh had proceeded on an international training, and Sepoy Arif Ansari was at the mercy of his new master.

Arif's days began to be frenetic. He had to run until he was exhausted and then report to clean the Sahib's backyard. But Sahib was never pleased. There would always be *"bloody pebbles"* on the lawn and *"bugger dust"* on the leaves. Arif would spring-clean Sahib's bathroom, polish his shoes, dust his curtains, and kill the pests in the storeroom. Somehow, the pests never stopped proliferating. Arif would gaze fondly at Naazneen's picture every night at bed-time and say her name out loud until he got drowsy.

It was Friday morning. Arif Ansari had planned to get himself photographed in his uniform after offering the Friday prayer in the Jama Mosque. When he worked under Colonel Bhupesh Singh, he would be permitted to go for the Friday prayers without a gate pass. But this was a different time. He had been requesting a Subedar to get him permission from Colonel Dharam Pal Singh, but nothing had come in yet. He decided he would have to ask for the consent in person.

Arif opened the door of Sahib's car, and the man got in, the picture of importance. Arif Ansari sat on the front seat with Sahib's briefcase in his lap. In the trunk of the car lay Arif's neatly ironed uniform, a beret cap, shined shoes, and a lapel that spelt his name. He would wear it that day for the photograph.

At 11.00 a.m., when he was sure that Sahib must have had his morning tea, Arif Ansari peeped in. He had thoroughly revised what he wanted to say, having carefully selected every word.

'Sir, may I please have your permission to offer prayers at the Jama Masjid today?'

Sahib didn't respond. It was then that Arif realized he was in the middle of a phone conversation, and the conversation was not a happy one.

Kavita was making life difficult for Dharam Pal. 'The boys have their summer vacations,' she was saying, 'I can't keep them from fighting and breaking things. They are just like you!'

'Bring them here,' said Dharam Pal.

'Why? So they can learn even worse behaviour?'

'What do you want me to do?'

'Come here and take one of them with you. They can't stay together.'

'Is it them who can't adjust or is it you? What kind of a mother are you?'

Kavita could afford to say whatever she had to. Words like miser, savage, diabolic, drunkard and corrupted were used against him. A bad husband, a bad father and a bad officer were pitched in innuendoes. Dharam Pal Singh smashed the telephone set. Arif Ansari was summoned immediately. Dharam Pal needed someone to shout at.

'What the fuck are you doing here?' he yelled in response to a stiff salute .

'Sir, I was here to ask your permission to go for Friday prayer.'

'Motherfucker! You think you are in some bloody Madrasa? And who told you to wear this uniform? Will you wear this uniform to offer namaaz? Bastard, haven't you got some respect for it?'

Arif's body stiffened. Containing his anger, he stammered to say, 'N...N...N...No, not in uniform, sir. Just for permission... permission for gate pass.'

'Permision my foot. What do you think of this organization?'

'Colonel Bupesh Singh Sir always permitted...'

Arif had said the trigger word. Dharam Pal Singh jumped out of his chair.

'Motherfucker traitor! *Ghaddaar*! Will you tell me what I should do? You think you are in Pakistan Army?'

'I am not a traitor! Don't call me that,' Arif's immediate response came out in the manner of an Army man saying 'Yes Sir' to his senior's order. 'Bastard! How dare you talk back to me? You need to learn discipline, and I will make sure you learn it right here. You can go back to your bloody Madrasa after I have plucked you from the Army for terrible discipline!' Dharam Pal Singh clutched Arif's lapel and pulled it off. He tossed Arif's nameplate on the floor and yelled, 'Now run to your room and come back in your civvies in two minutes. I need to show you what it takes to be in the Indian Army before I formally remove you. Get out, you traitor!'

Arif Ansari ran like never before. Faster than ever before, furious than ever before. He ran for one last time at the command of Colonel Dharam Pal Singh.

Meanwhile, Dharam Pal Singh called for another telephone set to apprise his seniors of the indiscipline of a sepoy and his intention to initiate disciplinary proceedings against him.

Shortly thereafter, Arif Ansari pointed an assault rifle at Dharam Pal Singh. 'I am not a traitor!' he vowed. 'I am no *ghaddaar*. Who are you to call me that?'

Sitting stunned on his chair, Dharam Pal Singh breathed heavily through dilated nostrils. He shook his head up and down.

'So you want to shoot me?' he asked.

'I am no *ghaddaar*.'

'You will never get away with this.'

'And do *you* think you will get away with this? You think I am going to put my gun and belt on your table and surrender like a militant? No!' Arif shouted.

'If you kill me you will prove yourself a traitor, and—,' Sepoy Arif Ansari fired an entire magazine into Dharam Pal Singh's chest from a very close range. Apart from the bullet burst, the only sound that echoed in Dharam Pal Singh's chamber was an Army man's vow, 'I am NOT a traitor!'

Kavita Singh sat with two Army jawans in the jailer's office. Her face was sullen. A week ago, she had been the paragon of sophistication in observing her husband's last rites. She had shed tears without crying and developed dark circles under her eyes.

'Will you have some tea, madam?' offered the jailer.

'No. Thank you. I just want to have some words with him, if you permit me.'

'Ji, madam. Why not?'

Arif Ansari was produced before Kavita Singh. Immediately,

she jumped out of her chair and slapped him repeatedly.

'Murderer! You ruined my world!'

'Madamji, please!' pleaded the jailer.

It didn't take much to contain her sudden outburst. She wiped her tears and did her hair. The jailer dragged Arif Ansari to a chair across the table.

'Why did you do it?' she enquired. 'Just tell me your motive.'

Arif sat still, his lips sealed. That day, after he shot the Colonel, he had surrendered to the police. Since then, everyone asked him the same question, 'Why did you do it?' But he never offered an answer.

'Madamji, he will not speak so easily,' said one of the jawans. 'If you allow me to interrogate—'

'No!' said Kavita. 'Let me talk to him. Could both of you please wait outside?'

She emerged from the jail an hour later, still without an answer. A couple of day later, Kavita returned for her questioning.

The jailer didn't like her frequent interactions with a convict. 'Madamji, I think you are wasting your time. He won't speak. If you wish, I can share with you the statement he voluntarily made on the day he surrendered.'

'No, Sahib. Please understand my position. I need to hear it from him.' She asked her companion to present a jute bag to the jailer; inside were bottles of subsidised Army liquor.

'Madamji, there is absolutely no need for this,' said the jailer, tucking away the bag in the cabinet quickly.

That day, Arif Ansari had been taken outside for some fresh air and sunlight. Kavita addressed him gently, 'Please understand my plight. You are like my son. Do you know I have two sons who are only a few years younger than you? When I met you the other day, I thought I would scratch your face with my nails. But when they told me you had made a voluntary statement, I realized you weren't a criminal but a victim.'

Arif stared at her, taken aback.

Kavita continued, 'I have heard that you got engaged a month ago. I can understand the pain your fiancée must be going through. What's her name?'

'Naazneen.' Arif's eyes welled up as he voiced the name of the woman he loved and pined for.

'Arif, I think it was our bad luck that got us into this situation. I am going to tell you something. It may appear strange to you, but it's true.'

Arif wiped his tears and looked up.

'My husband was a harsh, crude man. For most of the years that we were married, we didn't live together. What you did to him was long coming. Anyone could have done it, but you just got unlucky. I know that despite the fact that you surrendered, they will leave no stone unturned to ensure that you are hanged.'

'I am not afraid.'

'Please don't think that I am scaring you. I am here for a different reason.' Kavita met his tired, tear-stained eyes, and said, 'I need to redeem myself.'

'Redeem yourself? For what?'

'I am also guilty of murder. I murdered my husband too. Never did I try to counsel him through my love and care. We always quarrelled.'

Arif stared at her as she wept, unsure of how to console her. 'Why are you telling me this?'

Kavita fished out a bottle from her handbag and gulped some water. 'Arif, if the charges against you are proved, I will fail again. I'll commit an even more heinous crime.'

'Madam, I don't know what you mean.'

'Do you know that my sons are exactly like their father? They are quarrelsome, egocentric and prejudiced. I tried to keep them away from my husband, so they didn't learn his ways, but I failed as a mother. Now that they have learnt that their father was killed by a Muslim sepoy, they are furious. They have vowed to avenge their father's death. One of them even said that he would join the Indian Army and kill you and your family. "All Muslims are like that", he says."All of them deserve to be killed".'

'They are not alone in thinking this, madam. What can I do?'

She drew closer to Arif and whispered, 'Listen to me carefully. There is no evidence against you. They only have your confession. No one saw you kill my husband.'

'So?'

'I will convince my sons that their father was killed by militants. It is my only chance to stop them from meeting the same fate, a similar disaster.'

'I cannot change my statement.'

'Think of Naazneen,' pleaded Kavita. 'Don't punish her. Think of my sons. Think of your mother!'

Three days later, Kavita returned to the jail. 'Jailer Saab, I will disturb you for one last time today.'

'Not at all, madamji,' he replied, glancing at the jute bag she carried. 'Please go ahead.'

Arif Ansari hadn't changed his mind since the last time they had talked. But today, she was here to make one final attempt. This was her last chance to broker a deal of a lifetime. Stakes were much higher than Arif Ansari could have imagined, and she wanted to make sure he realized it.

'What do you need to change your statement?' she demanded, abandoning her tone of sympathy and assuming a shrewd, business-like demeanour. 'I can manage everything else if only you retrieve your confession.'

'Madam, I know that you are resourceful. You can make big things happen. Instead of forcing me to change my statement, why don't you ask your sons to shed their prejudices and hatred? Why don't you tell them the real reason their father died? Why don't you help them understand that they shouldn't join the Army for such murderous reasons?'

'Don't preach to me. I haven't come here to be enlightened about how I should behave. Listen, I will give you two lakh rupees. Your job and dignity will both be restored. You can happily marry Naazneen and forget that any of this ever happened.'

For the first time, Arif appeared hesitant. Kavita jumped at the opportunity.

'Don't over think it, young man. You have a life to live. I am giving you an offer no man in his senses would refuse. Consider yourself lucky!'

'Madam, I am confused because I cannot understand you. Which is your true face? Is the mournful widow real? What about the visionary mother? Or are you just a cunning woman who is here to make a business offer against her husband's ashes?'

'You don't need to understand me. The reality is simple: I have been widowed by you and am alone with two fatherless sons. Do I have a choice? No! But I do understand business! I can get compensation from the government only if it can be proved that my husband was killed by militants. And that I can arrange.'

'Ah yes,' nodded Arif, 'what's the going rate these days? I think some forty-fifty lakh rupees and a plot in Delhi. It seems a fair bargain for one's conscience.'

'Look, I am willing to up my offer to four lakh. That's my final offer. But you will have to change your statement today, in my presence.'

'Okay,' said Arif, agreeing suddenly. 'I will make my statement today.'

Kavita sighed in relief. 'Very well,' she said and walked out of the cell. She needed to go to the Magistrate's office for he would oversee the change in the statement.

But it wasn't as straightforward as Kavita had hoped. References and personal requests couldn't win her any favours with the Magistrate. He would not appear for any changes in statements until the chargesheet had been filed. Frustrated, Kavita flew back to Dehradun to wait it out. She ensured to tip off the investigating officer about a hefty compensation if he filed the chargesheet as soon as he could.

Twenty-three

Shamma's feet were scratched by the gravel; some of her wounds had started bleeding. She somehow dragged her feet along, unsure of the direction in which she was headed. In happier times, she would play on these slopes with Manzoor; they would use planks from the deodars as sledges. But her present fate left no time to ponder over happy memories.

Down below, in the village of Pathri Aali, people attended their chores as usual. Smoke holes issued silvery smoke as always, the chickens scampered without a care, an elderly woman spread her washing on the clothes line, and a stray dog snooped from one heap to another. Yet the village appeared very strange to her. Sometimes the normal is difficult to accept.

The world, anyway, didn't run as per her expectations. People had their lives to live; lives which couldn't care much for the abduction of a helpless girl; lives that were compelled to ignore the devastation of a family in the neighbourhood; and lives that continued the routine, pending their own devastation.

Shamma had debated taking her life several times since that night. But something stopped her, something that warmed her heart in the form of hope. What if someone had managed to survive that night? What if her little Humza was alive somewhere, waiting for her? She could have gone down to the village and made enquiries, but she didn't have the courage. Shamma didn't want to obliterate the ray of hope that was keeping her alive.

She followed the stream to the shrine of Pathri Pir, stopping every few minutes to ensure no one was following her. She hid among the bushes to observe without being observed. How many new graves had been dug since that fateful night? Were they big or small? Was one of them of Humza's size?

She couldn't tell fresh from old, big from small. And she couldn't go any further, for she considered herself a defiled body, not worthy of entering the shrine, nor the graveyard. And she broke down then, wailing, 'Why did you leave me, mother?' 'Why do I have to bear this? Why doesn't death come for me? Oh, call me, wherever you are!'

Unknown to Shamma, the entire village wept with her. Sorrow can spread even faster than tidings of joy, and house after house sobbed for Shamma and her destroyed family. Suddenly, a gentle voice called to her from the bushes, 'Let's go home.'

It was Humza, her little brother! He was alive! Shamma embraced her brother and kissed him frantically, before pushing him away. 'Don't touch me. I am dirty.'

'No, you are not,' came Lal Jaan's voice from near the graveyard.

Lal Jaan, Wazir and Humza were there to bring Shamma home; three generations representing wisdom, strength and innocence. 'Your father died a martyr's death,' said Lal Jaan, 'One should not cry over a martyr's grave.'

'I am responsible for his death,' Shamma wailed.

'No, you are not. Don't belittle his sacrifice and his martyrdom. Get up and get moving. And see how your mother, Ashwar, is determined to face our enemies.'

'Is she...'

'Yes, she survived.'

Propping herself behind an equally bent cane, Lal Jaan took upon herself the responsibility of addressing the villagers.

'Snakes!' she managed to say, panting. 'Progeny of snakes! Sons of Shaitan have occupied our lands.' The communal sobbing gave way to a momentary hush which soon became utter silence as all eyes and ears were turned to the old lady.

'We had heard from our ancestors that Shaitan had entered Eden guising himself as a serpent,' Lal Jaan continued. 'The cunning serpent then misguided Adam and Hawwa to eat the forbidden grain. And the Shaitan was successful in getting them banished from *Jannat*. Our *mulk*, our nation, our meadows, they say, is a paradise on earth. And yes, indeed it is. We never felt we were not free before *they*,' she pointed her cane towards the hills, 'occupied our Eden, our meadows. Now we must strive, we need a jihad for our freedom. Yes, freedom from those snakes who are ruling over us, freedom from those sons of Shaitan who are ruling this Eden.'

Alas! There was no applause. The old woman had ignored the fact that she was addressing a crowd of mostly timid women who had accepted submission as their only defence. 'Sons of Pathri Aali, why are you silent?' Lal Jaan demanded of the half dozen middle-aged men present. 'Be brave! Face them! Pick up axes, snatch their rifles and shoot them. You are capable of lynching them with your sticks!'

The men hung their heads. 'How would an issueless woman know how it feels to lose one's son?' Hamida retorted.

'Oh yes!' Lal Jaan yelled in despair. 'An issueless, old woman. But who was there to pull out your babies from your wombs to this world? Why did you trust an issueless woman to help you during birthing? I will tell you why. Because you were helpless then. And now, when this village is helpless, like a woman in labour, you are unable to feel it, and instead you question me?'

'Who would feel it better than me?' Hamida yelled.'My husband sacrificed his life for this village. My son was banished from this village, that you call our Eden, as if he had committed an unpardonable crime—all for the honour of this village. You call it Eden? Ask me. It's hell! Yes it was Eden once. But what you are proposing is a fairy tale. Fighting demons with bare hands is like snatching the golden comb from the *Bann Budhi*. Only the illustrious Great-grandfather could do it.'

The crowd muttered in agreement. Lal Jaan scowled and returned to her hut. Her creaky door shut with a thud. She would vent her anger on her pots and ladles; her husband had died the previous winter.

Ashwar was bedridden. She had been unable to recover from the injury to her belly. The villagers had discovered the bodies of Hanif and Ashwar only a few yards from each other. Humza lay in the fronds nearby, wailing intermittently. If it hadn't been for his cries, Ashwar might never have been discovered. She might have bled to death. The villagers brought Ashwar's unconscious body to Swarnpur hospital. There was no doctor on duty, only a nursing orderly. 'It's a police case. Go to police first,' the orderly had said.

When the villagers presented a few currency notes, he suggested an alternative, 'Go to the doctor's residence.'

There, at the lady doctor's residence, all efforts were made, by men and by their meager pockets, to convince the gynaecologist for an unusual delivery. She counted her miseries of police harassment, court attendance, and above all, deprivation of a peaceful life. She was humble enough to quickly translate those complications into an equivalent monetary value. Half an hour later, a bullet was delivered through a C-section. However, Ashwar was referred to the Jammu Hospital as the lady doctor was not equipped to stop her internal bleeding. A day later when she opened her eyes, Ashwar was informed by a nurse that her womb had been removed to stop the bleeding. 'No worries, sister,' Ashwar reflected, 'in the part of the world where I come from, no mother would like to bear any more children.'

Ashwar couldn't move for several days. She slept sporadically, lapsing into long periods of unconsciousness. Lal Jaan had told her that the militants had destroyed the *Saanjhi Qabar*. Whenever Ashwar regained consciousness, she had only two things to say, 'Has Shamma returned? Have the villagers started building the shelter again?'

When her daughter finally returned, mustering some strength, she caressed Shamma's hair and said, 'You are back to me now. All this will be over. We have lived our horrors.'

Shamma kept quiet. For many days after her return, she couldn't stomach any food. Lal Jaan tried to counsel her. 'Be brave like your father,' she would say. 'And look at your stepmother. She is so ill, but she hasn't given up.'

But nothing worked. When Shamma had shown no signs of recovery even after a fortnight, Ashwar's brother and sister-in-law took her to Swarnpur Hospital.

'Is she your daughter?' asked the lady doctor. Her manner was haughty, and she sounded exhausted after seeing the dozens of patients who had turned up that morning.

'No, she is our niece. Why? What's the matter with her?' Ashwar's brother enquired.

'Don't pretend to be innocent. Don't you know what she has been doing? These days girls are so clever that as soon as they are caught, they pretend to be innocent.'

'I don't understand, Doctor Sahiba.'

'Don't you know that she is pregnant?' the doctor said coldly.

'What? But she is not married!'

'What does that matter? Look, this is a difficult case. I don't want to be embroiled in the ugliness of police investigation. Arrange ten thousand rupees for abortion as soon as you can.'

'She is an orphan, Doctor Sahiba. Please show us some mercy. We are very poor; how can we arrange ten thousand rupees?'

'Well, then take her away. This isn't a charitable trust.'

Somehow, Ashwar's brother managed to negotiate a deal with the gynaecologist. She agreed to perform the abortion in return for a second-hand wristwatch and a goat for slaughter 'to please Allah'. Shamma had to bear the horrible pain of a vacuum-suction abortion. But then, beggars cannot be choosers.

Twenty-four

It was hours past midnight but Himanshu was unable to sleep. He had a lot on his mind. The next day, he was going to Pir Panjal to spend a few months there. He had to visit his uncle's house—never a pleasant proposition—to ask him for a favour. Finally, he would meet the young, beautiful, jet-setting photojournalist who had convinced him to be a part of a documentary. It was called 'Impact of Militancy on the Fauna and Flora of Pir Panjal'.

After he had refused to prescribe multivitamins and health tonics, his clinic started doing poor business. His second Short Commission with the Army was over, and the clinic owner said to him politely, 'I can't afford you, doctor. You may be bound by your ethics, but then, there is nothing ethical about starving my children either.'

The jet-setting photojournalist, Lucy Kaul, lived in Bonn and Srinagar, and worked for a German wildlife magazine as a freelancer.

Lucy Kaul had befriended Dharam Pal Singh during his posting in Kashmir. She was keenly interested in exploring the habitat of Markhors. Dharam Pal Singh, not remotely interested in wildlife himself, had recommended Himanshu to her.

Himanshu didn't *want* to think about her. He had grown really fond of her during their telephonic interactions but presuming that she had the slightest romantic interest in him would be presumptuous. 'So?' he thought, 'You *have* to tell her what you feel. Haven't you always dreamt of marrying an independent and modern girl?' Himanshu tossed and turned in bed, willing sleep to come, but his eyes remained wide open. He didn't want others to sense his feelings for Lucy. That Pinky Sharma, for instance, would be sure to ask some very pointed questions.

Pinky Sharma was a teenager with no one to call her own in the world. One afternoon, Himanshu had seen her in his clinic. She was asking for cough syrup for her grandmother. Something about her manner didn't seem quite right to Himanshu.

'Who are you buying this for?' he enquired. The girl was wearing a school uniform. She clutched the brown bag with the medicine tightly.

'For my grandmother. She has a cough.'

'Wait! Keep it back!'

'Why?

'No, we cannot sell it to you unless you show me the prescription.'

The clinic owner looked on but said nothing. The girl ran away, with the cough syrup, withot making any payment.

'Why did you do that?' The clinic owner was enraged. 'Do you know I haven't made any sale today?'

'It is dangerous to sell drugs to children when they don't have a prescription. Why do you think she ran away?'

The clinic owner grunted. He found Himanshu too meddlesome.

A few days later, a woman from the neighbourhood came to Himanshu's residence. With her was the same girl. Today, she held a sick infant in her arms.

'Who is she?' Himanshu asked her, pointing to the girl.

'She is my niece. Why, Doctor Sahib?'

'Well, I think I have seen her somewhere. Maybe with her grandmother, who perhaps suffered from cough,' he joked.

'You must have confused her with someone else, Doctor Sahib. Her grandmother died decades ago. She is an orphan and lives with me.'

'I am her maid, not her niece,' declared the girl as the duo walked out. 'Haven't you any manners?!' retorted the woman, giving her a slap on the back.

Three days later, when he was jogging in the park, Himanshu noticed the same girl sitting on a bench. She was staring at him, almost unblinkingly. 'What are you doing here?' he asked.

'I don't talk to strangers.'

'Oho! But you do stare at strangers. That's interesting.'

The girl said nothing. She sat on the bench, tearing pages from a notebook. 'What's wrong with you?' he asked, his voice gentle. 'Are you angry with someone?'

'No! I am not just angry; I feel like killing someone!'

Himanshu was surprised at the vehemence in her voice. 'This is just a phase,' he tried to calm her. 'It will be over soon. And I presume that I am not that "someone"?' Himanshu smiled at her genially, and got a rather watery smile in return.

Pinky Sharma was seventeen years old. Her parents and younger brother had been killed—or roasted, as she asserted—by militants. She had somehow escaped by hiding in a cornfield.

'After my family died, relatives lined up to take me home. I was pleased to see how many people loved me until I realized that it was the money they loved. All they wanted to do was appropriate the government's compensation in lieu of my family's death. My so-called aunt treats me like her maid. She doesn't even give me proper food. And as for her brother, I am sure he is a rapist.'

'Does she at least send you to school?'

'Yes.'

'And you sit here and tear your notebooks?'

'Where else can I go? I cannot live with her. I detest the sight of her!'

'You can go to school, can't you?'

'What good will it do? I don't want her to succeed in her evil plans!'

Himanshu didn't know what to say. He tried to reassure her that things would settle down, that she could always talk over her problems with him. 'Remember, Corex isn't the solution. It is never a solution to take drugs.'

'I don't take Corex.'

'Why were you buying it then?'

Pinky confidently lit a cigarette and said, 'Well, I figured some weeks ago that I need to be intoxicated if I have to live this life. I started smoking. But it gave me a bad cough. Now that you know the truth, can I have that cough syrup?'

'No, Corex isn't for this kind of a cough. You should not smoke, Pinky.'

'Why? Because it kills? My parents and fourteen-year-old brother were roasted. Were they smoking cigarettes?' Himanshu didn't know how to reply to that.

Two weeks later, early in the morning, the landlord rapped on Himanshu's door. 'Your cousin is here to see you,' he announced.

Himanshu was half asleep when Pinky Sharma, exhausted and famished, walked into his room. What could have happened to her?

After the landlord left, Pinky spoke, sitting on the bed, 'I am sorry I lied about being your cousin.'

'Sit on the chair, not on the bed. Why are you here, Pinky?'

'I am going.'

'Going where?'

'I don't know. But I am not going to stay with that witch. Last night, I couldn't take it anymore. I took my bag and ran away.'

'You ran away in the night? Where did you go?'

'I didn't want to disturb you at night. So, I waited in the park.'

'Are you mad? You spent this cold night in a park?'

'Doctor, could I please sleep for a few hours before I leave? And give me something to eat.'

Himanshu wavered. Here was a young, immature girl seeking

asylum. He felt certain his landlord had sniffed a rat. How would Pinky's aunt react to the whole thing? After he had served her tea and buttered toasts, he watched her sleeping in his bed, and sat still for several hours, wondering what to do.

By afternoon, Himanshu had made his decision. He convinced Pinky to live in a girl's hostel, whose monthly fee he would pay. Pinky was apprehensive. 'Why don't you send me to an orphanage?'

'You are my cousin, aren't you? You are not an orphan.'

About a month after Pinky had started living in a girl's hostel, Himanshu went to pay her a visit. He had received several complaints from her warden; she kept complaining about Pinky's behaviour. Apparently, she smoked, did not attend school, and bullied the other girls.

Himanshu spoke to her sternly, 'Why do you behave like this? Don't you want a better life than this?'

'I am sorry,' said Pinky. 'I will behave better.'

'I know you will. You are a good girl.'

'Am I? Really?'

'Yes.'

'How good?'

'What do you mean "how good"?'

'I mean, am I good enough to fall in love with?'

'Why? Do you love someone?'

'Yes.'

'Who is it?'

Pinky didn't respond. Instead, she grasped Himanshu's hand and asked him: 'Will you marry me?'

Himanshu was stunned. A proposal of marriage from his 'cousin' was the last thing he had expected that morning.

'This is unacceptable, Pinky. You are a child; I treat you like my cousin. I am more than twice your age. Does my hairline look like that of someone you would like to marry?'

'Well, if hairline would have been important, I would have married Khadim Hussain.'

'Who?'

'The hostel gatekeeper. He has so much hair you can hardly see his forehead.'

He shrugged. 'Pinky, do you remember you had an urge to kill someone? Just like that, this is just a phase. It will soon be over.'

Pinky looked thoughtful. Himanshu got up and declared, 'I am going now. I have some important work to do, so I may not visit you for the next few months.'

'What is it that you have to do?'

'I am going to Pir Panjal. I want to save an endangered species of deer in the mountains.'

'I am endangered too,' said Pinky. 'I am the last surviving member of my family. Save me first.'

☙

Lucy Kaul was a lovely comapanion to have. She always smiled, and her dimples only made her more charming. The morning she met Himanshu, he noticed that she had placed her overcoat in the seat next to her in the car. 'Has she reserved that seat for me?' wondered Himanshu. But he soon met five more people who were accompanying her—driver, cameraman, vet, ex-forest ranger, and a freelance environmentalist. Himanshu felt himself fall deeper in love with her as she sat looking out of the window, smoking and smelling like a million bucks. 'And there's nothing wrong with a girl smoking,' he thought, 'a mature, independent girl smoking,' he corrected himself. He had managed to pay another visit to Pinky before leaving for Pir Panjal. 'Here is some money,' he had said to her, 'don't spend it on cigarettes! My uncle will be here every month with the hostel fees.'

'Are you going alone?' asked Pinky, pocketing the money.

'No, I am going with Lucy Kaul. I think I am in love with her.'

'You think?'

'Of course. I might just ask her to marry me.'

'Oh?' was all she said as he bid adieu.

They halted for tea at the foothills of Pir Panjal. The environmentalist was a chatterbox; he kept regaling Lucy with trivia about the vegetation in the area. Standing on a cliff that overlooked the valley, he shared a cigarette with Lucy and chattered about the pristine nature that 'wasn't polluted like our big cities'. For possibly the first time in his life, Himanshu felt jealous of a man. He walked up to them.

'Cigarette?' she asked him.

'No, I quit smoking years ago,' he replied. 'And I love the smell of the pine trees in this region.'

'You're right! They do smell wonderful,' she stubbed her cigarette and took deep breaths, savouring the delightful pinewood smell.

As they climbed the steep hill to the Army battalion, Himanshu shared novel ideas with her. He had quite a few, but the one Lucy found the most fascinating was that the militancy in the area might have actually benefitted the flora and fauna. 'The local hunters and timber thieves are so scared that they don't hunt down the animals.' The environmentalist scowled. 'Wishful thinking!' he said, even as Lucy winked and smiled at Himanshu. His heart was pounding all the time.

About a month after the trip, Himanshu and Lucy decided to camp out in Shimla. Lucy wanted to do some filming there which wasn't a part of the script. 'It's behind the scenes material,' she explained. Himanshu nodded, pretending to understand whatever she meant. She had chosen Shimla because camping out in Pir Panjal would be too dangerous.

It was bitterly cold in Shimla. The biting winds of December brushed their cheeks whenever they stepped out of their sleeping bags. One frigid night, Himanshu asked Lucy, 'Don't you think it is a little crazy to camp out in Shimla in the winter?'

'I like crazy,' Lucy replied.

Himanshu could smell the cigarette from Lucy's tent; it was right next to his. Even though he had quit smoking, the fragrance still got to him sometimes. He sat near the entrance of his little tent, gazing at the twilit landscape.

'Close your eyes!' Lucy shouted suddenly.

'Why?'

'Just shut them.'

Himanshu did as he was asked, abruptly realizing that she needed to relieve herself.

'All right, you can open them now.'

'Okay,' laughed Himanshu.

'Why are you laughing?' Lucy inquired. 'What is so surprising about a woman peeing?'

'Nothing. I just remembered something.'

'What?'

'When I was a child in Karanprayag, my father had a driver who claimed that he could smell the piss of tigers and leopards from a distance. He told me he could detect from the smell what the animals had eaten for dinner. And I had a knack for smelling piss too.'

Lucy giggled. 'Oh!' she said, 'What did you smell?'

'Nothing.' Himanshu was embarrassed.

'Come on, tell me. Am I in heat?'

'What?' His heart pounded like never before. He wondered if she could hear it.

'You call yourself an expert, and you couldn't detect even that?'

The sleeping bags had a rough time that night; they were hastily unstitched and transformed into a mattress and a quilt. 'Behind the scene material!' Himanshu laughed, several moments later, stroking Lucy's hair. She snuggled onto his chest, unclothed under the quilt even in the bitterly cold night. 'So? Where's the funny part?' she whispered.

'It's here,' he guided her hand, laughing at his own joke.

Later that night, when Lucy was gently snoring, Himanshu wondered how we would tell Pinky about his love.

Twenty-five

'You have to learn your numbers,' Shamma instructed Humza. 'I won't let you go and play until you trace out all the numbers I have etched on the wooden tablet.'

Humza looked bored. 'I promise I will make a paper windmill for you as soon as you are done.' Shamma was an expert at bribing her little brother into studying. He was young, and incentives mattered a great deal.

'He has to finish reciting his tables too,' Ashwar added, walking up to her two children with breakfast. Humza ran up to Lal Jaan, hoping that *Daadi* would play with him and end the tyranny of scary-looking numbers.

Lal Jaan had moved into Ashwar's house. She found it difficult to sleep ever since her husband had died; she could only manage to nap in fits and starts. 'Don't go out too early in the day. It's still too cold,' Lal Jaan warned Humza as Ashwar handed her a bowl of salted tea, in which floated crumbs of corn roti.

After his breakfast, and after doing a rather rushed job of tracing the numbers, Humza ran out to play with his ball. Ashwar turned to Shamma; there was something she needed to ask her, something that had been troubling her for a while.

'Shamma,' said Ashwar, 'Did you get your periods after that doctor performed the abortion?'

'No.' Shamma's voice was strained. It was possible that she didn't understand the significance of the situation, but the pain in her mother's voice was palpable.

Ashwar held her head in her hands. 'Allah! It can't be!'

'Let me take a look at you,' said Lal Jaan, weakly getting up from the cot. As she examined Shamma, her eyebrows went up. A deep pallor fell over her face.

'Allah's wrath! She is one finger above the belly button!' cried Lal Jaan.

'What does that mean?' Ashwar appeared confused. The look on Lal Jaan's face frightened her.

'She is pregnant, Ashwar! Five and a half months pregnant!'

'No! That can't be! They had aborted her pregnancy.'

'Who can abort Allah's doing?'

'Don't worry, my child,' Ashwar hugged Shamma to her chest as the girl started crying. 'We will go to the doctor again.'

'It would be pointless. Those doctors are nothing but greedy quacks. All they care about is money, not the lives of people like us.'

Ashwar felt helpless. She had emptied the money containers in her house and had managed to ferret out only a handful of currency notes. It would not be enough.

'But we have no choice, we have to go to them again,' she said.

'I will bear the child.'

Both Lal Jaan and Ashwar stared at Shamma. 'What are you saying?' Ashwar cried. 'Do you even know—?'

'I know. I will bear the baby.'

'But why? What will people say?' She turned to Lal Jaan. 'What do you think, *Daadi*? We will never be able to live down this ignominy.'

'Why should we care about people? We owe them nothing. You should think about what your daughter wants.'

'What *do* you want?' Ashwar was frantic as she addressed Shamma. 'Why do you want to bear this baby?'

'It's Allah's will. I am convinced it's Allah's will.'

Ashwar shook her head. Her immature daughter had got all sorts of wrong ideas. 'Why would Allah wish for you to suffer?'

'I don't know. All I know is that this baby has already survived three deaths. When they shot you, I remember something hitting my head. I fell unconscious. When I woke, I saw Satan lying by my side. They tied me with a robe to the cot, like I was a mental patient. I can't even tell you what Zuber and Khalil did to me. But I bore the torture; I believed that I was responsible for your deaths and this was my punishment.'

'Oh, my dear child,' wailed Ashwar. 'It wasn't your fault at all.'

Shamma went on speaking, her voice steadier than it had been in months. 'One day, Zuber took me to a maze of trenches in Hill Kaka. There were big guns, machines and militants everywhere I looked. When the militants objected to my presence, Zuber hushed them. He would kill me in a few days, he assured them. By then, I was relieved to hear the news of my impending death. I only wished it would come sooner. When Khalil took me to the forest to shoot me, I was praying for a quick death. He untied my hands, placed his gun on my forehead, and was about to pull the trigger when a wild goat appeared from nowhere. Khalil forgot me for a moment and ran after the goat, rejoicing in how he had finally found it. I ran away, and heard a gunshot fired. The poor goat lost its life to save me. That was the second death that my baby managed to survive. Finally, during that horrifying abortion, when I felt as if my innards were being pulled out, I lay on the bed praying that it would soon be over. But look, here it is. My baby lives on because it's Allah's will.'

Ashwar was not convinced; she couldn't see her daughter suffer anymore. But Lal Jaan was moved.

'I think she is right,' nodded Lal Jaan. 'Allah chose Maryam to bear Isa even though she was a virgin. At times, we fail to spot the signs that Allah so clearly lays out for us.'

'*Daadi*! Not you too!' Ashwar complained. 'What possible message does Allah want to send us by unleashing these horrors in our lives?'

'He wants to tell us that we must strive to reclaim our lives. We have been pushed back in time by many, many centuries; it is the time when the serpent entered Eden, when the Pharaoh oppressed the righteous, when Allah brought Isa to the world from Maryam's womb. By compelling us to suffer, Allah wants to remind us of our duties. To restore goodness, we have to make sacrifices.'

'What sacrifice, *Daadi*? And how many more sacrifices? They are already slaughtering us like sheep! Doesn't Allah see that? Why doesn't Allah punish them now?'

'Allah will punish them only after we follow what he has ordained for us.'

Ashwar grimaced; Lal Jaan could sometimes get incredibly trying. 'And what has he ordained for us?'

'Didn't I just tell you? Sacrifice! Have you forgotten how Ibrahim was ready to sacrifice his son? But here, mothers are discouraging their children to return to the village, to even step forward and protest. Allah doesn't pick up the sword himself to slay wrongdoers. No, he gives strength to the men so they can triumph over evil. If our men are unable to invoke Allah's blessing, how can you blame Him?'

'So, you are saying that Allah is intentionally bringing on this affliction because we are refusing to sacrifice as blatantly as he would like us to?'

Lal Jaan frowned. 'Ashwar, you have to understand this without losing your head. Do you know what Allah did in Noah's time? And then He destroyed with brimstone all those who transgressed during the life of the Prophet Lot.[3] We can ask Allah only for two things: the strength to defeat our enemies on our own or the willingness to let Allah unleash his annihilation. If we ask for the

---

[3]Lot, or Lut, as he is known in the Old Testament, is a prophet of God in the Quran.

strength, we will have to make sure we use it. But if we ask for the latter, no one will survive to see the aftermath.'

Lal Jaan's ideas may have held water, but they appeared to be practically impossible. Wazir and a handful of other villagers had agreed to follow her command. They had readied themselves for the Abrahamic sacrifice in lieu of strength to deal with the wrongdoers. But their desire was denied. Ironically, it was some more of Allah's disciples who denied them this strength, sitting smugly in their places in the district administration office.

Wazir and his men had gone to the Army base, seeking their help in exchange of crucial information. A rather bored senior officer of the Rashtriya Rifles' Romeo Force met them. He listened to their revelations about the trenches and heavy guns in Hill Kaka. At least a hundred militants hid there, revealed Wazir.

The officer hemmed and hawed. He propped his elbows on the glass table, right next to a crest of two crossed beyonated rifles over the motto '*Dridhta aur Virta*' (Firmness and Bravery). A dozen golden-edged trophies stood on the shelf behind his desk. For a moment, Wazir felt anguish for his dead father. He too had once stood behind another cross. He too had lived a life of firmness and bravery, but no one had presented him with any trophies. Indeed, he hadn't even been awarded a quiet, peaceful death. Wazir was asked to leave the office with the half-hearted assurance that they would 'look into it'.

Not to be discouraged, Wazir then approached the superintendent of police. 'Why don't you approach the Army again?' the officer asked him. 'Sir, we have been to the Army already,' replied Wazir. 'Go there again,' said the superintendent with a lopsided smile.

Adhering to philosophies and mottos is easier said than done. And yet, there are people—exceptional people—who manage to do it. Haji Mir Baksh was one of them, and he didn't give up on his *asool* even once in his lifetime. Another was Vishnu Shah. He was the one who had relegated the once illustrious Adalat Shah to the status of 'the other Shah'. Over time, Vishnu Shah had developed a reputation in the world of retail. He had also cemented his perception as a man who could make things happen.

Wazir and his men went up to meet Vishnu Shah in his retail shop. The authorities had failed them so far, and they had decided to turn to this last straw of hope.

The villagers of Pathri Aali were walking on a double-edged sword. The militants would send them off to buy prohibited merchandise like dry fruits and batteries. They would brave terrible weather and tight security to secure these items. If they failed, the militants would be sure to behead them. But if they were caught by the police, they would spend months in dark interrogation cells. But Vishnu Shah was different. He had good connections. On Eid and Diwali every year, he would carry baskets of select merchandise to the powers that be, sometimes pleading for the myriad issues faced by the minority Hindu Khatri community in Swarnpur. His people stood behind him, for he stood up for them.

He came up with an ingenious plan for Wazir. 'Hide the dry fruit inside cattle feed. Put the batteries in your milk containers. Tell Mujahideen that I can arrange for snow boots and mackintoshes too.'

In those terrible times, Vishnu Shah turned out to be one of the few people who lived up to his motto. For him, the motto was 'Customer is God.' And God mustn't be sent home empty-handed.

It was an overcast morning in January. Humza wore a balaclava as he rode his wooden horse—Lal Jaan's cane—to the hollow of the big oak tree near his house. There, inside the hollow, he would sit and stare at the snowcapped Tatta-Kutti peaks. The Great-grandfather had crossed those mountains, his mother had said, and he imagined he could still see him there, trudging along against the wind. It was getting progressively colder, and Humza decided to return home. He would ask his mother to make him some popcorn. It felt delightfully warm and crunchy.

On his way home, someone suddenly emerged from a bush. His face looked as wild as that of a beast, and he held a gun in his hands.

'Come with me,' the man ordered the frightened child.

'No, I am going to mummy.'

The lone militant brandished his gun in front of Humza. 'Do you know what this is?'

'Yes, it's a gun,' said Humza, trembling.

'Good. Now get this clear in your little head—I will not shoot you if you do as I say.'

'Ok,' tears rolled down Humza's eyes.

'Here,' said the militant, opening his zipper and holding his penis, 'suck it like you sucked your mummy's tits.'

The Tatta-Kutti peaks would have witnessed the shame of their youngest admirer, had nature not covered them with clouds. Humza ran home as fast as his legs could carry him, fluid dripping from his mouth.

Ashwar was petrified when she saw her son squealing. 'What happened, my child? Did someone hit you? What is this in your mouth?'

The neighbourhood gathered to inquire about the commotion. 'Did a militant catch hold of him?' 'Perhaps they made him eat something forcibly.'

Ashwar was hysterical. 'Did someone do something wrong to you? Please tell me, Humza.'

Humza vomited and wiped his tears. 'He did it in my mouth, mummy.'

'What?!' Ashwar was appalled. Children whispered in confusion; men dropped their gaze in embarrassment; women walked away. Ashwar wailed, unable to believe that her little child had suffered a trauma he would probably never forget.

'Allah,' she cried, 'is this a new message for me? Why do you always direct your wrath toward me? Don't I, at least occasionally, deserve your blessing?' She then turned to the hills—that abode of the shameless where they dwelled in trenches and descended on the village like predators. 'There will be a reckoning of your crimes,' she vowed, 'in this world or the next. The cries of the helpless won't be in vain. One day, your fangs will be removed, and your ugly heads will be crushed. I will wait to see you perish, oh serpents of our meadows!'

Ashwar was inconsolable. So was Humza. 'If you continue crying like that, your son will keep crying too,' people advised the mother. 'If you continue crying like that, your mother will keep crying too,' they advised Humza.

Shamma tried to placate Humza. 'Do you want popcorn?' she asked him. 'I will make popcorn for you. Tomorrow, it will snow, and then we will build a snowman. We will shovel the snow. You like doing that, don't you?'

Ashwar stared at her daughter. 'Is this the world you want to bring your baby into?' For once, Shamma had nothing to say.

That evening, Wazir came to Ashwar's house with seven men from the neighbouring village. The incident of that morning had revolted the men so much that they were now ready for the ultimate sacrifice.

'We have decided that we will take them on,' said Wazir. His voice sounded uncannily like his father's. 'We have knocked at all possible doors, but no one is ready to help us. We have to figure things out on our own.'

'What are you going to do?' Ashwar asked.

'We have decided that we will cross the border and go to Pakistan. We will present ourselves as recruits for the Mujahideen. And then, we will return with guns and roast those serpents alive.'

'Oh, no! No!' Lal Jaan emerged from behind a pillar. 'That would be suicidal.'

'What are you saying, *Daadi*? Wasn't it you who asked us to fight those demons even if it meant sacrificing our lives?'

'Yes, but your plan is sure to be a mass murder! If you go to Pakistan, don't you think they will consult the militants already in their team before they recruit you? They will soon realize that you are impostors.'

'Yes, we have thought about that. We are going to go to these serpents first. We will make sure they recommend us.'

Lal Jaan shook her head. 'The Army will shoot you at the border.'

'We are ready, *Daadi*. We can't sit back and watch our children get bitten by those snakes.'

'Brother Wazir,' said Ashwar, 'you have done a lot for this village. Now, let me do something. Promise me you will support me in this.'

'What is it, Ashwar?'

'I have given this a lot of thought; it isn't a reckless decision. But I'll share it with you only after you promise me your support.'

'Ashwar, you have always shown great courage to inspire us. I have no doubt that your decision will be for the good of this village. I give you my *lafz*; I am with you.' The remaining men nodded, all of them promising Ashwar their support.

Ashwar had stopped reading letters from Saudi Arabia. Earlier, the villagers would often come to her house, asking her to read out letters from sons, husbands and brothers who were earning great riches and glories in Saudi Arabia. But now she sent them away, refusing to either read or send out replies. That night she sat under the lamp and wrote letters. She prepared twenty-two identical letters and sat gazing at them till midnight.

'What are these?' Lal Jaan inquired.

'These are your words, written in my style.'

'What? Whom are you going to send them to?'

'The sons of Pathri Aali. The men who can't hear your words. Why did you stop Wazir from going to Pakistan?'

'I had my reasons. Wazir had misunderstood my message. I wanted the men of Pathri Aali to fight like Haji Mir Baksh, to salvage the village like he protected Mehar Bi's honour. Can you imagine one lean boy challenging twenty skilled fighters? The logs on the door weren't a magical barrier; they were a mental barrier. He could have kept the door shut, but he chose to keep it ajar. Do you know why? It was so they may see the steeliness of his resolve. Even a little mynah bird can fight off a ferocious snake when she wants to save her chicks!'

'I understand, *Daadi*. That is why I thought of an alternate plan. I know that we need to prove to the militants that we aren't afraid. We are ready to die for our children, for our women, and they can fight us until death, but we won't give up.'

'Have you described your plan in these letters?'

Ashwar folded all the letters but one. Twenty-one of them would be posted to various addressees in Saudi Arabia. The twenty-second letter was to be posted to a long erased address. While the address was vague in her memory, of one thing she was certain— the addressee would definitely live up to the reputation of the Great-grandfather. He was the son of a man who could snatch *Bann Budhi's* golden comb. He was Aslam, the estranged son of Haji Mir Baksh.

'I will read it out to you, shall I?'

How do you define misery?
How do you define sorrow?
What about horror?
Intimidation?
Subjugation?
How about unimaginable humiliation?
And systematic annihilation?
We are facing them all at once, and then some. Words almost fail me when I attempt to explain what we are going through.

I can't believe that you're unaware of our misery, oblivious to our suffering. And if you indeed don't know anything, well, you don't deserve to. But let me give you the benefit of the doubt.

I won't shock you with all the naked facts; I don't want you to relive your worst nightmares. For now, let me just tell you that Pathri Aali, our beloved village, is possessed. Our home, our Eden, isn't ours anymore—it belongs to monstrous snakes that lurk about in the meadows. These creatures have enslaved us; we are little more than their flock, petrified servants who have no choice but to do their masters' bidding. I don't have the courage to tell you what our masters make us do. They are bestial and ruthless, not thinking twice before trampling all our desires to satisfy their macabre whims. These new masters of the meadows are certainly not human or humane; they aren't even animals. They are vile ogres.

I am not asking for your help. My world has already been ruined, and you cannot salvage it. Chances are that by the time you read this, I would have been murdered. Sometimes I let myself dream that I will survive until the summer and eventually be buried in Pathri Pir. And then it strikes me—Pathri Pir isn't a shrine anymore, it is a graveyard.

You probably think that you are better off where you are, earning your bread in a distant land. But let me correct you—all that you are earning is ignominy. You may be saving your skin, but here at home, someone is paying for your cowardice.

I don't know if you'll be fortunate enough to survive this madness. But even if you do, what stories would you tell your children? Would you tell them tales of your spinelessness? Sing them ballads about how you abandoned your people because you were a selfish deserter?

I can't foresee any respite from our suffering. Not now, not in a decade. For us at Pathri Aali, there are only two choices—live like slaves, like instruments of their pleasure and abuse, or die with dignity. I have made my choice. And no, it's not the one you might assume I would make. Indeed it's the first one—a life of subjugation. It isn't a choice that can save my skin. Indeed, I want it devoured, if that can help some innocent.

Come back! Be the brave soul you were born to be. Death is inevitable; don't fear it. Bring to the children of our village something they have utterly forgotten—hope. If you can save Pathri Aali from annihilation, I assure you will find redemption. You will earn dignity to bequeath to your children, not tales of cowering behind walls. Don't just live to narrate the stories of your cowardice. Someone will tell a better story of how you died, rather than you telling your children how you lived.

—*An unfortunate daughter of Pathri Aali*

The Resistance to the Resistance

Twenty-six

Aslam was incensed and almost hysterical with rage. 'How was he killed?' he grabbed Wazir by his collar.

'The militants killed him.'

'I know they killed him. How? Tell me the details. Where were you then?'

'Control yourself,' said Hamida, 'you will hurt your brother.'

'Brother, do you remember the one word he always told you about, the one thing he wanted you never to give up?' Wazir smoothed down his collar.

'*Asool*,' muttered Aslam.

Haji Mir Baksh was no more, but his *asool* lived on. Aslam didn't need any further explanation. He knew he was guilty of failing his father. And his family had erased him from their memory. The realization broke him inwardly. 'I know I was a bad son,' he turned to his mother. 'But does that mean I didn't even deserve to be informed of my father's death? If it hadn't been for Ashwar's letter, I would have lived on in ignorance. You didn't even let me attend my father's burial!'

Hamida put a loving arm around her son's shoulders. She was seeing him after a long time, and it still felt unreal. 'You need to leave for a safe place, son. You are not safe here. They killed Hanif the very day he arrived from *Soodia*.'

Aslam had his family worried as they accompanied him to the Pathri Pir shrine where his father was buried.

The graveyard at Pathri Pir was flooded with fresh graves, many of which he identified as friends and relatives. He looked around at the world he had once left behind—devastation was evident everywhere. There was the spot he had sat with Ashwar once upon a time, making plans for the future. How many times had he dreamt of revisiting that very spot! Ashwar would be beside him, and he would ensure that the thorns of the Datura never pricked her. But gone were those days when people could dream; only the shards of broken hopes remained. He held Ashwar's letter in his hand and proclaimed, even as curious onlookers stared:

'Heaven or hell, only time will tell. Eden or Satan, I don't give a damn. Pride and dignity? I don't care about any of this. I only want my revenge. By the shrine of Pathri Pir, I swear I will avenge not only the murder of my father but everything my village has lost!'

'You are coming with us, brother,' Wazir told Aslam as they started walking away from the shrine.

Aslam was unwilling. He wanted to be at home with his mother, to spend time with her and compensate just a little for all the lost years.

'I beg you,' Hamida implored. 'Please listen to your brother. I know you don't listen to anyone, but please listen to him just this once.'

'Come—to safety and to meet someone,' Wazir waited for his mother to move away before continuing, 'we have pledged too, just like you, to fight them. But we must have a plan. Come.'

Aslam waited as the old man smoked his hookah, coughing intermittently. The old man, or Haaku, as the villagers called him, was Parveen's grandfather. It was rumoured that Haaku had once fought *Bann Budhi*, along with his dogs. Haaku lived at the edge of the jungle, away from everyone else. 'They came here once,' said Haaku, his face golden in the light of a kerosene lamp. 'The militants. My dogs almost broke their chains barking at them. They warned me to control my dogs or else they would shoot them. I begged them to spare us, but I knew my prayers didn't mean anything. So, I lied.'

'What did you tell them?' Aslam decided that gossip would be better than sitting still in that secluded safe house Wazir had dropped him at.

'I told them that my dogs bark even louder when the Army comes. I said, "The moment the Army moves from Buffliaz, my dogs smell it and start barking in strange ways."'

'Did they believe you?'

'Not immediately. They threatened me: "If you are playing smart, then be ready to play dead too". But they did leave my house, instructing me to inform them should the Army arrive. And guess what, they never returned.'

'You must be relieved.'

'I am. They say that Allah doesn't send his angels of mercy to a house where a dog barks. But I believe it is my dogs that keep Satan away.' His voice suddenly changed. 'Someone is here.'

'Militants?' Aslam stood up, ready to attack if need be.

'Don't worry; it's your brother with a few others.'

Aslam had never imagined meeting Ashwar in such a situation. She took the lamp from Haaku and walked closer to where he stood transfixed. She looked different, a glowing face flanked by her red shawl. She was more beautiful than he remembered her. There was no guilt in staring at the only woman he ever loved. There was no guilt in finding a few moments of affection in a horrible, hateful world. There was no guilt in soliciting a speck of bliss amid oceans of sorrow. For the moment the darkness could wait. And she was not shy of gazing at him either, contrary to what he had imagined.

Ashwar was transfixed, gazing at him as if lost to her surroundings. The spell was only broken when Wazir tinkered with some utensils. 'You must have your supper before we discuss anything,' Ashwar said. It was only then that Aslam realized there were several men in the room he hadn't noticed. A white bearded man greeted him with a salaam from near the door. Another man, of almost the same appearance, nodded at him, holding his hand 'Recognized me?' he asked, as Aslam nodded to everyone in greeting.

'Before we discuss our matter, let me warn you that you are not safe here,' Ashwar said, extending a plate of rice and daal to him. Aslam nodded again in acknowledgement. Ashwar stood up, took out some papers from a bag and walked to the lamp.

'You must pledge that whatever Ashwar proposes,' Wazir addressed Aslam, 'you will adhere to it. Just as all of us present here have already sworn.'

Aslam realized that Ashwar was that *someone* he was destined to meet. She was not just there to serve him daal and rice. 'I am listening.'

Ashwar held some papers in her hand as she addressed the men. 'We have been denied any help by both the Army and the police. We must now launch a resistance against our oppressors on our own. I propose Aslam's name to lead this resistance.'

Aslam was confused; this was entirely unexpected. 'Why are you choosing me?'

'You are free to say no,' said Ashwar. 'No one will blame you if you refuse both the idea of resistance and the willingness to take any responsibility for it.'

Responsibility was Aslam's nemesis. He had never liked that word; it had eluded him all his life. He distinctly remembered the evening when Badar Kaanchwala had come to drop him at the railway station. He had felt compelled to apologize: 'Please forgive me, Badar Bhai.

The two men I had identified as conspirators in your factory could have been blameless. They weren't good men, but I don't know if they ever conspired against you.' Badar Kaanchwala hadn't rebuked him, but he could sense his disappointment. On the way back to Pathri Aali, he had tormented himself with the belief that his father had been right. He was untrustworthy and irresponsible.

Ashwar continued without any emotion in her voice. 'Twenty more men are coming from Saudi Arabia this week. But they can't come like you did. They are not safe here.'

'How should they enter this village then?'

'With guns! The leader of our resistance will lead them to the superintendent of police, the Army brigade, and the district administration. I have written applications to all of them, requesting them to give us guns to form a Village Defence Committee. They might consent to that much. Perhaps they will realize that since they have failed to do their duties, we must do it for them.'

'But what if they refuse yet again?'

'Then, you will have to lead your team to the next higher authority—the deputy inspector general of police, the Army GOC, and the divisional commissioner. If required, we will go to the chief minister, the governor, the Army chief, the defence minister, the prime minister, and even to the president of India.'

'I need time to think,' Aslam managed to say. He had returned to the village certain that he was going to fight, but he hadn't thought of involving others. Now that the lives of twenty young men, including two of his nephews, were at stake, how could he make a decision? Anything he did could potentially endanger the lives of his men.

'We don't have much time,' said one of the men. 'Make up your mind as soon as possible.'

Aslam's head was bursting with pain. Haaku's non-stop chatter only made his headache worse.

Suddenly, Haaku sat up straight. 'This is strange.'

'What is strange?' said Aslam. His head hurt so much that all he wanted to just then was sleep.

'The dogs are barking rather oddly. But then, I overreact. Maybe they are just excitable. No stranger can ever enter this house until I let him. As long as my dogs are alive, we are safe in here.'

'Ok.'

'Don't worry about it. Dogs do need to bark sometimes, you know,' Haaku continued.

'Just like we sometimes talk, even when it's not needed?' Aslam

'Right,' he agreed. 'Now I will tell you what happned to this village.'

'Now, if you don't mind, I need to sleep. Let's talk tomorrow.'

'It *is* strange; take my word for it. They never bark like this.'

Haaku's refrain continued the next night, after he had narrated detailed tales of the village to a tired Aslam.

Late one night, when Haaku was narrating yet another story, one of the dogs howled ferociously. 'It must be a bear!' Haaku yelled. 'You stay here; I will go and see what's happening.'

Aslam did as he was told. He heard Haaku's voice a few moments later. 'What are you up to?' he was asking someone. 'Why are you sneaking about like thieves do?'

'I am here to meet him,' a woman said.

'No, you are not. Leave immediately, or I will unleash my dogs on you!'

'I must meet him. Please!' she implored.

Aslam peeped from a crevice in the wooden door and saw Zaitoon. 'Let her in,' he said.

'No, she has been trying to sneak into my house for the last two nights. She cannot be up to any good.'

'Let me talk to her, Haaku. Don't worry.'

Hesitantly, Haaku left Zaitoon and Aslam alone for a few moments. 'Remember, I give you only a few minutes. My dogs and I are both waiting right outside for you!'

'I am sorry to trouble you,' Zaitoon told Aslam. 'But I really needed to talk to you. I fed those dogs biscuits, did everything I could to befriend them, but they are such horrible creatures!'

'But why did you risk your life to meet me?'

'It must be something very important then, worth risking my life for.'

'Whatever it is, just say it. I am listening.'

'You are still the same. I thought you would have changed, but... I mean you are still so arrogant. Didn't you think even once when you left us, when you rejected me?'

'I am sorry for what I did. Trust me, I have thought about it a million times. Yes, it's only about you and my sister-in-law, Parveen, that I felt contrite. If I had known what was going to happen, I wouldn't have done that. But then, you never get a second chance.'

'That's enough for me. Your father died to protect my honour. His legend will live on in Pathri Aali forever. By now you probably know what happened to my father. Zuber took him to the hills to transport some ration, but he never came back. I kept pleading with the militants, but when has that ever done us any good? Sometime back, my worst fears were confirmed: a militant told me they had killed my father. But this man isn't like them; he is against the Mujahideen.'

'Against? Like what?'

'Like that young militant, Humza. He wants to kill them. He is ready to give us guns. He told me he would meet you whenever you can find the time.'

'What is this amazing friend of yours called?'

'Bilal.'

'And where is he now?'

'I don't know. He must be in the hills.'

'Really? Or maybe at your house? Waiting for you to return with some good news?'

'No! Do you think I am lying to you? I came here to help you. I know we need guns to fight them, and that you are unable to decide if you can assume the role of the leader of the resistance. I know all about Ashwar's proposal. I know how smitten you are with her, but tell me, where was Ashwar when your father was killed? What happened to her plan then? Why didn't she write a letter to inform you? Why didn't she call over the men from Saudi Arabia when her husband was killed? When her step-daughter was in captivity for over a month? Why did she become a saviour only when her son was in danger? She wants to secure her son's future, but she doesn't care for the lives of the dozens of children she is misguiding to fight with the militants.'

Aslam was unmoved by Zaitoon's harangue. 'Here,' she took out a gun from beneath her shawl, 'here's a proof of my truthfulness. He gave me this for you.'

'Thank you,' he held the gun and cocked it, 'thank Bilal for this gift and…'

'So, when are you meeting him?' Zaitoon couldn't contain her excitement.

'Soon,' he said as he took out the magazine and inserted it back again. 'But,' he said pushing the gun in his belt at the back, 'you must warn Bilal about the outcome of this rendezvous. The best I can guarantee him is a clean death,' he smiled.

'You have rejected me all over again!' she cried.

'Haaku!' Aslam called out, 'Please escort her away.'

'Why? Please answer why? What should I tell him?'

'He should have taken his revenge by now, if he wanted it

and if he has guts. Tell him this. And yes, tell him that I will give him a clean death, not to worry.'

'You are still arrogant!'

'Go! And remember, my father lost his life protecting the honour you still have to prove you possess. Don't befriend dogs!'

※

Early the next morning, someone knocked at Ashwar's door. 'Who is there?' she asked.

'The leader of the resistance.'

Ashwar instantly knew who it was. She opened the door and smiled warmly at Aslam. Lal Jaan welcomed him with open arms. 'I live here now,' she said. 'My husband passed away last year.'

'I am sorry. How did he die?'

'He died of asthma.'

'Asthma?'

'Yes. I can understand your surprise. Natural deaths appear unnatural in our village.'

'May Allah forgive all his sins.' Turning to Ashwar, he said, 'The last time we met, just before I left this village, I offered you a gift. You refused to accept it.'

'Let's not talk about the past,' Ashwar interrupted him.

'There can be no present and no future unless we learn from the past. I want you to remember that.' Aslam looked forlorn. 'Anyhow, I am willing to assume the responsibility you have entrusted me with, Ashwar.'

'We are all grateful for that.'

Aslam looked around the house, searching for Humza. He was eager to see the little boy. Did he look like Ashwar?

'Can I see Humza?'

'Yes, of course,' she pointed to the cot in which Humza lay asleep. 'He is sleeping.'

'Don't wake him. I only wanted to see him. And here's a gift for you.' He brought out the handgun, much to Ashwar's amazement. 'You have earned it,' he told her, 'let me show you how to use it.'

As Ashwar and Lal Jaan watched, puzzled and rather taken aback, Aslam left the house. 'It may take a couple of weeks or maybe a month,' he called out. 'But I will come back soon, with guns and with my team.'

Twenty-seven

Pagers had a thing for beeping at inopportune times. Lucy Kaul and Himanshu were inside their fishing boat, enjoying themselves in Wular Lake, when Himanshu's pager beeped. 'Call back immediately—*Mamaaji*.' That was the short but curious message that somehow spoiled the afternoon for the couple.

'What is the matter?' Himanshu called his uncle from a telephone booth. He could sense it was an emergency of some kind.

'A man called Aslam is here. He is from Swarnpur and says he wants to talk to you.'

'Put him on the phone.' It had been years since he had communicated with Aslam, and Himanshu wondered why he was calling him so urgently. 'Where have you been?' he said to Aslam 'Is everything all right?'

'Nothing is all right, sir. Our world has been turned upside down. The snakes are killing all the markhors!'

Himanshu cancelled fishing with Lucy. Aslam had made a distress call, and he had to respond. 'Please understand,' Himanshu pleaded with his girlfriend. But all he could see, now, was a boat dashing away and Lucy's middle finger raised high above.

*

Aslam's team had arrived. He had the responsibility of leading twenty men, mostly teenagers, to take on an enemy with which the mighty security forces were yet to lock their horns. But the problem was the team didn't recognize him as their leader. Except for four of them, including two of his nephews, Riaz and Kabir, the rest outrightly rejected anything he proposed. The hotel room in Jammu, where Aslam had organized their initial meeting, turned into a turf of recalcitrance. The men who were against Aslam wanted to adhere to Akram Khalifa's methods. The polarization was lopsided—five versus sixteen.

'That is the problem with our people,' ranted Aslam, 'you resolve to do something, but everyone only wants to engage in petty squabbles. No one remembers the larger cause.'

'Really?' replied Khalifa, 'that is quite a revelation coming from someone who ran away from the kachehri, his family, and all his responsibilities.'

'Don't get personal, Akram.'

'Why not? Your father and my father both died horrible deaths. But this village reckons that your father died a hero's death, while my father died a villain. Where were these villagers when my family was humiliated and outcasted? Why should I bother to risk my life for this village now? It *is* personal!'

'If it is personal to you, why don't you walk away? Why are you brainwashing these young men into believing in a concept tainted with your personal biases?'

'Oh, Aslam! Perhaps you have failed to understand that they are not as much with me as they are against you. What if you get them ready to face the militants, and then, the next morning, you board the first train to Bombay?'

Aslam took a deep breath. He had returned to the village to seek revenge, not get into heated arguments. 'You know that I have pledged before Pathri Pir,' he said, 'that I will take my revenge on those snakes. I will have my revenge anyway, with or without you. If anyone of you has the same enemy as I do, and wants to defeat him, you are welcome to come and stand with me. I don't care what your motive is—revenge, freedom from their tyranny, salvaging your pride, performing an act of valour, or merely redeeming your conscience. If our enemy is the same, we must fight him together!'

'Fair enough,' observed Akram Khalifa, 'now let me put forth my proposal. All I want to say is that we mustn't be fooled by the idea of fighting an enemy who doesn't discriminate between children and adults, women and men. Those snakes that Aslam talks about have been trained to kill people, to butcher them. We had left this village, this hellhole they are claiming was Eden, because we couldn't earn our bread there. We had no roads, no electricity, no infrastructure, no education, no health services, no employment—is that what Eden is like? This village has been crippled by militants only because they were looking for such a place! The government doesn't care for us. No one does!'

'So, what's your plan?' Aslam demanded.

'I want us to accept that we don't have to fight anyone but our foolishness. Let's not deny the fact that our village is—and has always been—a backward shithole of a place. Let's not call it Eden. All of us have earned enough money. This purported Eden had no role to play in our fortunes except that it compelled us to leave. And now that we have made enough money, let's buy some land or a small house in Swarnpur and move there with our families. Once we are safe and sound there, we can sing as many praises of our meadows as we like; we could organize a poetry recitation about our oh-so-beautiful homeland.'

'I think Akram *Bhai* is right,' said one of the men. The entire team but for four agreed. 'Yes!' they shouted. 'This is a much more sensible proposal.'

'All the best then,' Aslam said, 'buy your new houses and live in them. But don't be misled into believing that you won't have to fight for your rights to live. You don't value our meadows, our Eden, because you inherited it for free. But even your entire month's salary won't buy you the beauty of your homeland in your tiny, one-room houses!'

'All the best to you too,' smiled Akram, 'we will be waiting to see if you survive—from the safety of our new homes!'

※

Hanif's son, Manzoor, was among the youngsters who had joined Aslam. He clasped his hands as he stared at the floor, sitting outside the office of the superintendent of police. Himanshu was also with him. He had travelled with Aslam and four others, including Manzoor, to the commanding general officer and then, the DIG of police.

Aslam was nervous, almost like the four teenagers who had agreed to follow him. The meeting between Himanshu and the SP had been going on for much longer than expected. Now and then, he brought out the application that Ashwar had given him. It had five signatures. Five! That was, surely, too paltry a number to convince the superintendent of police about the Village Defence Committee.

What would he do even if the SP agreed? How would Aslam train those teenagers to operate a rifle? He remembered the days of his brief arms training when he had been a security guard. It had been nerve-wracking.

On their way to the SP office, he had administered an oath to his four companions. 'The four of you will be the guardians of Pathri Aali. No matter what, you won't leave the spot that I assign to each of you. When the militants come to our village, you shoot to kill them. But don't venture out of our village at any cost. I may not always be there to command you, so ensure you adhere to this oath.'

Himanshu finally emerged from the SP's office, dejected.

'Don't worry,' he said to the small group. 'I will go to the GOC again.'

'What did he say?' asked Aslam.

'He says that if you are willing, he can recruit all of you in the STF, but he can't give you weapons.'

'What is the STF?'

'Special Task Force. They have started a group to deal with the militancy. They pay fifteen hundred rupees per month to a team member.'

'But if we join the STF, will they allow us to guard our village?'

'No. That was precisely what I requested. But he declined.'

Aslam was angry. What would be the point of joining the defence group if they couldn't defend their own village? He stormed into the SP's office even as Himanshu tried to stop him.

'Sir, I am from Pathri Aali. Why aren't you giving us guns to defend ourselves?'

The SP didn't respond. He pressed a bell kept on his table, and a security guard immediately came in. 'How did this man enter my office?' the SP shouted.

'Wait!' Aslam shouted back, even as the guard tried to pull him out. 'Who will help us if you turn a blind eye? If you refuse, I will go to the DIG, your boss! I will go to the governor, the chief minister, and, if need be, even the prime minister!'

Himanshu shook him after managing to drag him out. 'The SP could have you arrested!'

'A militant is offering me guns.' Aslam replied. 'Did you know that? I am going to get them.'

'You have lost your mind, Aslam. But if you are going to behave like this and insult the very authorities that can help us, don't expect any support from me.'

'I am sorry, sir,' said Aslam. 'But I am desperate. This boy here,' he touched Manzoor, 'he is unable to visit his father's grave and say his prayers because the authorities aren't giving him protection. And the SP asks me how I entered his office!'

'We have to stay calm, Aslam,' Himanshu patted him on the back. 'We cannot give up hope.'

The Village Defence Committee didn't seem to be taking shape. A week after the SP had rejected their demand, Aslam and Himanshu ran from pillar to post, begging the authorities to help them out. But no one cooperated. It seemed to Aslam that he had only one option left—to accept the proposal of the militant.

'Sir,' said Aslam to Himanshu, 'I am left with no option but to seek that militant's help. But it could be a trap.'

'Why don't you guys join the STF, at least for the time being?'

'No, sir, the moment we join the STF, the militants will kill our families. It is certain.'

'Okay, let me try something. I know a young journalist in the *Jammu Times* newspaper. I will write a detailed article about the plight of Pathri Aali and give it to him. Once our plight comes out in the media, surely some alarm bells will ring.'

Himanshu wrote a well-thought out article for the newspaper.

> Prevention is better than cure; pre-emption is better than war. Take my word as an ex-Army man. The entire nation criticized how the lack of intelligence and General Musharaf's backstabbing led to the Kargil War. But no one cares about the ISI's latest victim. They have burrowed deep inside our hinterland. Hill Kaka is a small, insignificant village; it is usually abandoned during the winters. No one expects you to know where Hill Kaka is. But then, no one expected you to know where Kargil was until it announced itself. Hill Kaka, too, is preparing to make its

presence felt, and I can assure you that it won't be pleasant.

Let me try to explain Hill Kaka to you, and you'll see why it is of great strategic importance. A depression on a high hill in Poonch district, almost like a naturally built fortress, it has been offered on a platter to intruders. They have developed a maze of trenches and hideouts inside this fortress. It is located 40 kilometres inside the border and is higher in altitude than the closest location occupied by the Indian Army.

The locals from the nearby villages claim that more than a hundred militants dwell in Hill Kaka. They have installed heavy weaponry and stored enough ration to feed hundreds of men for an entire year. Their handlers, their Aaqas in Pakistan, watch every movement of the Indian security forces around this fortress. For now, they aren't worried. After all, we are still busy discussing and decrying 'Kaargil'.

The figurative snakes that haunt the hills are also killing markhors. The Markhor, Pakistan's national animal, is depicted on the emblem of the ISI; in the emblem, it holds a snake in its mouth. It is ironical, but the ISI is probably too thick-skinned to care. Their emblem, if anything, probably inspires them. Just like the snake trying to sneak out of the markhor's mouth, the Mujahideen are burrowing their way out. In the process, they are clawing deep into our land, defiling everything that was once serene.

A man from a village near Hill Kaka claims that he has approached all the senior authorities to alert them of this development. But the security forces have been indifferent. They have also been unable to protect his village from the onslaught of the militants who, not surprisingly, have inflicted unimaginable atrocities on the residents of the village. The locals also claim that despite volunteering to fight against the militants through a Village Defence Committee, the security forces turned down their demand. They were not issued weapons, and how can they protect themselves with their bare hands?

Hill Kaka may appear to be insignificant, but it isn't. We have been unable to realize it, but the ISI has. Let's not waste another moment in taking cognizance of our follies. They have already won the first round of the combat; they have successfully pre-empted into our world and destroyed it. But we can still knock them out and restore peace. Let's trust the locals and empower them. Animated debates and discussions about Kargil can wait a while.

Every day Himanshu keenly flipped through the pages of the *Jammu Times*. He had penned down the piece with great care. He had toyed with the idea of making the article a little more shocking by hinting at the prospect of an imminent war. But then he had checked himself; the idea was to inform and not to scintillate. Yet Himanshu could never find his article.

He called up his journalist friend to find out. 'It is not going to be printed,' his friend informed him. 'My editor said it wasn't up to the standards of the *Jammu Times*.'

'Well, I know I can't match your editorial standards, but couldn't you extract the news from it and print it?'

'The editor says there was hardly any news in it.'

Twenty-eight

Lucy Kaul reacted to Himanshu's apology with the manner of a stranger. 'It's fine,' she said, blandly. Himanshu wanted her to be angry with him, to complain about his absence for more than two weeks. He tried to tell her how occupied he had been, how traumatized by the attitude of the security forces, the callousness of the administration, the apathy of the press. 'It's fine,' she said and made no further comment.

Himanshu decided to change the subject. 'So, what did you do after I left that day? Did you catch any trout?'

'No,' she replied, 'I didn't try, actually, and I don't feel like sharing any more of my life with you.'

'What?' Himanshu stared, not comprehending.

'Stop boring me with grisly details of your life. Stop imagining something could ever happen between us in the future. We were rather silly, that's all, and I would be pleased if you forgot all about it.'

'So, you are asking me to leave?'

'Well, if you are willing to work with me on purely professional terms, you are welcome. Otherwise, you are free to move on.'

Himanshu suddenly saw through her; he had never been more than a passing fling for her. 'All right,' he said, 'I am willing to work with you as a professional. Tell me, can you help me run a news story? I know you have good connections—'

'No personal favours please,' she interrupted him. 'That would be unprofessional.'

How fickle she was, thought Himanshu! How easily she had

plucked him from his life and now, was unwilling even to help him out professionally. How misguided he had been!

Back in his hotel room that night, he found himself thinking about Pinky Sharma. He called her hostel and requested to talk to her.

'Is it urgent?' The warden sounded irritated. It was almost midnight.

'Yes', he replied.

Pinky greeted him warmly. 'How are you? Where are you?'

'I am back in Srinagar.'

'When did you return?'

'Listen, I need you to tell me something.'

'What? Why do you sound so disturbed?'

Himanshu couldn't ask her anything. He remained silent, beating around the bush. Pinky sobbed over the phone. 'I have missed seeing you,' she cried.

'Please don't cry,' he consoled her. 'You are not alone. I will always be there for you.'

The next morning, Himanshu had a surprise visitor—Lucy Kaul. 'I am sorry for my behaviour,' she smiled at him. Himanshu stared at her, thoroughly confused and unable to convince himself that this smiling, apologetic Lucy was real.

The young Army Major had a commando haircut. 'Hi, I am Navniet Sekera,' he introduced himself. 'You can call me Seki.' He was a handsome man, well-built and well-groomed. Lucy Kaul couldn't take her eyes off him; Himanshu noticed her instant attraction. She hung on to his every word, telling him all sorts of things, being more giggly and flirtatious than he had ever seen her. The Army Major was quite responsive to her attention. 'Do you know why this place is called Buffliaz?' he asked her.

She shook her head.

'Well, today, you are visting history. This place was the easternmost extent of Alexander's invasion. His horse, Bucephalus, died here; it was here that he was buried. Alexander was deeply aggrieved by his horse's death. He decided to move back to Babylon. The town came to be known after Bucephalus. But like the Greeks corrupted our Sindhu into Indus, we took revenge, right here, on his horse's dead body and Bucephalus became Buffliaz.' The Major and Lucy Kaul shared several moments of laughter, even though, thought Himanshu, it wasn't really that hilarious a tale.

Lucy stuck to the Major like a leech all day.

'Do you gel your hair?' asked Lucy, inching so close to the Major that her face almost touched his hair.

'No, not at all,' he replied modestly, 'They are naturally spiky. In the military academy, they used to call me "copper wires."'

Himanshu felt disgusted. If he spent more time watching Lucy, he felt he might lose sight of himself. But he couldn't abandon her abruptly. After all, it was his suggestion that had brought Lucy there. Himanshu had promised to get her valuable footage of markhors in their natural habitat. But this was only a half-truth. What Himanshu really wanted was some footage of gunmen roaming freely where markhors should have been. It would be a win-win situation for both Lucy and Aslam. He wondered if he should tell Lucy about his real intentions. But one glance at her ogling the Major's hair, made him decide otherwise.

'Let's call it a night,' he declared loudly, getting up from his chair.

'Good night,' said Lucy shortly. 'Seki and I will sit here for some time.'

Himanshu met Aslam the next afternoon. 'We will record videos of the militants and their hideouts,' he proposed. 'We can do it together.' He was done with expecting Lucy's help.

'How, sir?'

'We don't have to go very close. Our cameras are powerful enough to capture clear images from miles away.'

Aslam appeared doubtful. 'But sir, they don't believe us at all. Would a video change anything?'

'It might. Words are just words; people believe what they *see*. News channels will vie with each other to broadcast these videos. But we will let them do so only on one condition—that they also include an interview with you. Make sure you are well prepared with what you want to say.'

'They want news, don't they? I will give them news.' Aslam sounded decided. His apprehensions seemed to have dimmed. Himanshu glanced at him nervously; you could never be sure what the man was up to.

Earlier that morning, Himanshu had gone for a walk by the Swarn river. With him was a jawan who wanted to accompany him because he felt it wasn't safe to wander about the banks alone. In front of him lay the Swarn river—the river that always made him nostalgic. He remembered the first day he had stood there; he had been eager to offer water to the Sun God. The ice-cold water had slowly dripped from his hands, forming memories that would last him a lifetime. He found himself thinking of Pinky. He realized that he had been so aware of falling in love with a girl half his age and its social fallout, that he had avoided confronting his feelings. But he couldn't anymore. Pinky, Himanshu felt certain, would help him reconstruct his world.

The jawans and officers at Buffliaz were taking excellent care of Lucy Kaul. While she was enjoying her breakfast with Major Sekera, Himanshu decided to call Pinky Sharma. He didn't want to waste another moment of his life without her by his side.

'Oh Mister Himanshu,' came the rather anxious voice of the warden, 'we tried to contact you yesterday. But you weren't available.'

'What happened? Where is Pinky?'
'She ran away.'

Himanshu was stunned. 'Ran away? How could she run away from the hostel? I will sue all of you!' He banged down the receiver and fell on a chair, his head in his hands.

Twenty-nine

It was dark when Aslam knocked at Ashwar's door. 'Can I borrow your gun?' he whispered, coming inside. He didn't want Shamma and Humza to know what he had gifted Ashwar two weeks ago.

'What will you do with it?' Lal Jaan asked.

'Nothing, *Daadi*. Just in case I have to use it.'

'They aren't giving you guns, are they?' enquired Ashwar. 'And families are ready to move out of here?'

'We are trying our best. I am going to make some news that will change everything.'

Leaving the two women confused, Aslam tiptoed out of the house. He walked out of the village towards Hill Kaka. Aslam had been doing a lot of thinking for the past few days, consumed by vengeance. He had considered abducting Zuber, cutting him into pieces and hanging his corpse from a tree. But it all seemed rather impractical. He had finally decided to sneak into the militant's hideout and then see what he could do. After all, Zuber wasn't the only one who needed to be killed.

In the darkness of the night, years after the tradition had been discontinued, Aslam mounted a dhaal on the maple tree near Pathri Pir. He wanted to mark the commencement of his journey—a journey that could well be his last. But he didn't care for the price he might have to pay; it was the only option he had, to infuse some hope in Pathri Aali.

Walking uphill in the dead of night was a treacherous task. There were patches of snow that frequently made him lose his footing. But he knew he must walk briskly or he wouldn't be there before dawn. He crawled over slippery cliffs and trudged through waist-deep snowfields, all the while fuelled by the hope that he would be able to sneak into the enemy's bunkers. He would map it with his eyes and memorize all the details. He would then return with a dozen AK-47s, six on either shoulder, and present his loot to the security forces.

'Here,' he would tell them, 'look at the rifles we have been begging you for. You couldn't spare your outdated guns for us, but we managed to get much better without any help from you. I hope you finally realize that it wasn't just the guns we were asking you for. We were requesting the authority to use them.'

※

It had been over ten hours since he had started his uphill journey from Pathri Aali. He had been set back by several hours because he had lost his way; the darkness and the snowfields had fooled and almost frozen him. Finally, he knew he was almost there. Aslam remembered there was a cave directly overhead. He found the cave and curled inside it, like a wild animal who had found shelter after days.

He woke up to the sound of what appeared like a cricket commentary on the radio. His knees felt stiff; he was unable to straighten them. Down there, below the cave, were two militants, both of them in black salwar-kameez and brown jackets, just like him. They had their backs to him. They appeared to be busy cleaning and tuning the dozens of radio sets they had arranged on some of the boulders.

Aslam figured it was an excellent chance to kill at least two militants. He took out the gun and pointed it but stopped himself just in time. No, it wouldn't do to lose patience and be impulsive. His plan was to sneak into the bunkers and memorize the location of the hideouts. He knew he had to wait till darkness fell again.

※

Night fell sooner than Aslam had expected. It was now time to attempt what no one in his village had attempted before—to sneak right into the jinns' dens. He climbed down the cliff using a pine tree and walked cautiously, keeping low,, hiding behind boulders until he could hear them chatter and smell food cooking in their kitchen. He hid behind a rock and waited while they finished their supper. He didn't move until all the torches had been switched off and the men had retired to their makeshift beds.

Bent at the waist, Aslam walked into the bunker that he had identified as the biggest. Moving about in the darkness, unnoticed, Aslam followed two men right inside. The trench was even bigger than he had imagined; about twenty men were sleeping on the floor. In the far corner of the hall, sitting under a lantern, some men chattered in low voices. He could make out guns—dozens of them. Behind every sleeping man was a gun, quietly leaning against the wall.

Aslam felt brave. He crept inside an empty sleeping bag and strained his ears to listen to what the men were planning. But except the repeated mention of helicopters, he couldn't gather much.

Suddenly, 'Who took my sleeping bag?' shouted someone.

'Let it be,' someone suggested, 'you can sleep with us.'

If only my gun had a silencer, Aslam wished. *These snakes would never have woken up. I could have gone from trench to trench, decimating all of them.*

After he was convinced that everyone was indeed asleep, Aslam gathered guns and stacked them near the exit ladder. Just as he was about to exit the trench, his eyes fell on something that the men had hidden behind a boulder right next to the ladder. 'It is worth a dozen guns,' thought Aslam, 'or perhaps a hundred!' Moments later, with the precision of a seasoned burglar, Aslam walked out of the enemy's trench with a rocket launcher dangling on one shoulder and five live cartridges wrapped in a sleeping bag on the other.

§

Early the next morning, Aslam went to meet Ashwar. 'Here is your gun,' he handed his gift back to her. 'I didn't have to use it.'

Ashwar's eyes widened in surprise when she saw what dangled on Aslam's shoulder. 'I will need a sack,' said Aslam, trying to suppress a grin at her evident shock.

'Where did you get it?'

Ashwar and Lal Jaan listened in disbelief as Aslam revealed how he had been to Hill Kaka and returned with what would be their last effort in trying to stir some sense in the authorities.

'I have to leave for Buffliaz now before it's too late,' Aslam got up after drinking the tea that Lal Jaan had brought him.

'Aren't you going to meet your mother first?' asked Lal Jaan. 'I will come with you.'

'Why?'

Lal Jaan patted Aslam on the shoulder, her eyes welling up. 'I have to tell her that the legend of the Great-grandfather is not just a story. He stands right here in front of us. He has been inside the jinns' dens and snatched the golden comb from the *Bann Budhi*.'

§

'It's a Carl Gustaf!' Major Sekera exclaimed in disbelief, 'Carl Gustaf M3!'

Himanshu smiled at Seki's disbelief.

'What is it?' asked Lucy.

'It's a rocket launcher,' explained Major Sekera. 'A bazooka, you can say. Where did you find it?' he turned to Aslam.

'I went inside the militants' bunkers in Hill Kaka and stole it from there, sir,'

'Just like that?' Major Sekera shook his head, disbelief written large on his face. 'You walked into their bunker, hung the launcher on your shoulder, and walked back? And what's there in that sleeping bag? Have you got some more stuff?'

'Yes, sir,' he brought out all the shells as more officers and jawans gathered to see the exhibits.

Major Sekera shouted, 'Be careful! They can go off if they hit something hard. I still can't believe you got all this stuff just like that.'

'Not just like that, sir,' Aslam said quietly. 'I walked from Pathri Aali to Hill Kaka in twilight, guided by patches of snow. I climbed cliffs like a lizard, slept in a cave like a bear and sneaked into the cobra's pit like a snake myself. Not "just like that", sir!'

'Can I take pictures?' asked Lucy, readying her camera.

'No, you can't!' Himanshu yelled, 'It's a matter of national security. You should know better than that.'

Lucy frowned. She realized that this was a different Himanshu, not the one she had known. She turned to the Major. 'With this bazooka on your shoulder, you will look like Arnold Schwardzenegger from the *Terminator*.'

'No,' said Major Sekera unsmilingly, 'I cannot allow you to take photos.'

Lucy was offended. She lost all interest in markhors—if she ever had had any. She packed up and left for Srinagar, taking her cameraman along. That was the last both Himanshu and Seki saw of her.

After Lucy left, Major Sekera called his seniors. 'Sir, we have got a situation here,' he transmitted over the hotline, 'Our source has recovered a MANPAD, a Carl Gustaf M3, with five live Large Calibre Ammunitions. He also has some vital and highly sensitive information. I would request you to make a personal visit ASAP, sir.'

Major Sekera turned to Aslam, his face serious. 'The GOC

will fly to Swarnpur in twenty-five minutes,' he said. 'Let's ride to Swarnpur and get you ready for the meeting. Perhaps you should change into a uniform—'

'It is guns that I need, sir, not a uniform.'

'Have patience,' Major Sekera interrupted. 'Today, after I brief the GOC and you narrate your account to him, I will request him to send a message to the Police Chief. I will then send a truck full of my men to the SP's office. They will ensure that the SP doesn't leave his office without issuing rifles to you.'

'Thank you, sir.'

'So, are you now ready to wear a combat uniform—one that befits the commando in you?'

Aslam smiled, looking in turn at both Major Sekera and Himanshu.

Himanshu, however, was lost in his own thoughts. The night before, he had made one of the hardest decisions of his life. He had decided to find Pinky and bring her back. He couldn't always live for others; it was now time to live his own story.

When Aslam was ready to leave, proudly wearing his combat uniform, Himanshu was prepared to leave too. But he was embarking on a search for his destiny.

'Aren't you coming with us?' Aslam asked as he got inside the jeep.

'No, I can't,' Himanshu replied, 'go and destroy your demons and free all the lives they have held hostage. I have to go in search of my own life.'

Sarp Vinaash: Destruction of the Snakes

Thirty

'It's him! It's him again!' A woman from the neighbourhood came running to Ashwar.

'Who is it? What happened?' Ashwar was preparing supper and coaxing Humza to wash his hands.

'That shameless militant! The one who took Humza to—'

Ashwar lost no time. She immediately sent Lal Jaan, Shamma and Humza to her brother's house. The very thought of that militant enraged her still. Humza would often wake up at night, spitting and screaming, haunted by nightmares he couldn't even describe.

Four militants were robbing the livestock of the villagers. He was one of them. They were butchering goats and shooting chickens, competing with each other shamelessly. 'Five hundred rupees if you shoot it midair,' declared one. 'One thousand rupees if you shoot that one in its left leg,' promised the other. After they had had their fill and packed their loot in bags, the militants walked past Ashwar's house. She stood at the door, staring at them without blinking.

'Salaam,' she said.

'Friends,' said the militant who had tortured Humza, 'I will join you later.' He smiled at them mischievously, fixing his lewd eyes on Ashwar.

Ashwar welcomed him inside, much to the shock of her neighbours. 'She should not do such a thing,' they muttered, 'If she doesn't do it, he might torture her son again.'

'But she is crossing all limits! She jeopardized our lives in that *Saanjhi Qabar*, and now she doesn't care for her own honour!'

The men, who had been lamenting the loss of their livestock, now sat talking in hushed whispers. 'All that preaching,' they shook their heads, 'it was all humbug! Look how she has succumbed to them!'

'What can she do,' said another, 'the Saudi-returned never came back with guns. Some of them are looking for property in towns. I think she has lost all hope.'

'Well,' interrupted the first man. 'I have certainly lost all the respect I had for her.'

Inside Ashwar's house, the militant eyed her lustfully. 'I always fantasized about you,' he said. 'I wanted to feel how it is to sleep with a skinny, lonely woman of the mountains.'

Ashwar locked the door. 'We women of the mountains have our fantasies too. Why don't you relax and lie down on the bed? I will fulfil all your fantasies today.'

'I can't wait. Come quickly,' the militant lay down immediately. He couldn't believe his luck.

'I'll give you the ultimate pleasure,' she pressed his eyes with her palms, 'Open your mouth.'

'Why?' The militant was beside himself with delight.

'It is my fantasy; you have to taste it to experience it.'

Excited, he shut his eyes and did as he was told. The thunderous noise of a bullet pierced the hubbub of the afternoon.

'*Ya* Allah *Khair,*' the neighbourhood echoed, 'She is no more.'

The militants, halfway to their hideouts, complained, 'What a loser! He is still trying to shoot chickens midair.'

Later that evening, Aslam marched into the village with sixteen more men, all of them with rifles dangling from their shoulders. By then the entire neighbourhood had heard what Aslam had done. Here was a man of true valour, they said. Under his leadership, winning their freedom would not be impossible. Only Akram Khalifa and three of his followers appeared unmoved.

Major Sekera had kept his word. His men hadn't left until the GOC confirmed that the Inspector General of Police had agreed and Aslam and his men would be issued rifles immediately. Aslam could also recruit more men from Pathri Aali as Special Police Officers to launch a massive defence programme for the village.

As the days panned out, however, the Special Police Officers or SPOs were in for some nasty shocks. The title was rather a joke, and comprised misfit shirts, drop-crotch trousers, ragged boots, and outdated guns. This was the condition of the first line of attack against the militants. The first line of command was to shield those who had discarded these uniforms long ago and were equipped with state of the art rifles. Many in the police made fun of the 'grand SPOs', laughing at their clothes. About half of Aslam's troop embraced the SPO tag. The inspector general of police had ordered that they be deployed in Pathri Aali. Eventually, Akram Khalifa and his three followers also joined the Task Force, but they preferred to stay in Swarnpur.

Thirty-one

Saghir Khan was angry. His family's special status had been snatched away. General Musharraf had supported the war against terror launched by America; if he hadn't, the Central Intelligence Agency (CIA) would have unleashed the war right inside his office. Soon after, the ISI disowned Saghir Khan's family, retracting all their luxuries and even seizing his passport. His spacious bungalow in Muree was now occupied by a relative of the General; the family was compelled to move to Lahore. After the General had initiated a movement to identify all religious institutions that received unreported foreign aid, Saghir Khan's Madrasas had also been shut down. Everything that General Zia Ul Haq had bestowed upon Saghir Khan was taken back by General Musharraf, including his illustrious name. In retaliation of his deprivation, Saghir Khan had, allegedly, joined hands with a banned organization that directly received funds from Al Qaida. No one knew if these stories bore any truth.

His children had, however, become well-established. His sons no longer ran the slaughterhouse but exported leather goods. The youngest daughter studied journalism in Lahore University, while the elder one married a lawyer and quit her job.

Two hours after Sagir Khan and his family had commenced their road trip to Peshawar, a traffic officer stopped their car. 'Where are you going?' he demanded. 'Can I see your identity cards?'

'Why is this checking being conducted, officer?' Saghir Khan enquired.

'Mind your business. There has been an accident ahead, and

there's a massive traffic jam,' replied the officer, returning the identity cards. 'Take the Lilla exit and go via Mianwali.'

Half an hour later, the car reached the Salt Range.

That day, the road looked abandoned. Saghir Khan and his wife napped in the back of the car. His son didn't notice that surprisingly, theirs was the only car that had been diverted on to this road. No one saw it coming until ear-splitting noise burst upon them, strewing bones and flesh of everyone in the car onto the Salt Range. Saghir Khan's name was struck off the list of the ISI and, in turn, that of the CIA. 'His car was hit by a drone,' it said in the reports prepared for the weekly briefing of the war against terror.

In February 2002, Adalat Shah was released on parole. A month before his release, he had divorced his wife. She had accepted the divorce and the offered alimony without any protest. The alimony included his house and a cement store. The day he was released, Altaf Dastarkhan didn't come to welcome him, much to his surprise. His girlfriend, however, was present, holding a garland of currency notes. Adalat Shah looked around. It felt good to be a free man again. But there was one thing he needed to check—the makeup box. All the way from the prison gate to his girlfriend's house, he had enquired about it endlessly.

'Here it is,' she handed it to him, rather annoyed. 'This seems to be more important to you than me.'

Adalat Shah breathed a sigh of relief as he weighed the makeup box with his hands. His fingers deftly worked the combination lock.

'Here you go,' he tossed the lipsticks and nail polishes to his girlfriend.

She stared in surprise as he cut open the bottom of the makeup box to reveal another cavity. There was nothing inside.

'What the hell!' he shouted at his girlfriend, slapping her.

'Why are you hitting me?' she ducked when he raised his hand a second time.

'You plotted with him, didn't you? You lousy woman, I should never have trusted you!'

'I have no idea what you mean. Why are you so angry with me?'

'I had hidden gold bars under this box! But do you see anything now? All my savings, my hopes are now gone!'

'But it's not possible,' she cried. 'I hid the box very carefully in a place no one could ever find.'

'If it's not you, then it can only be him.'

Adalat Shah cornered Altaf Dastarkhan the next day, grabbing him by the collar. 'What are you saying, *Janab e Aala*? I don't know anything about any gold.'

'Don't play games with me. If I don't get my gold back by tomorrow, you can't imagine what I will do,' Adalat Shah threatened.

'How can you doubt my honesty? I helped you when no one else did, and yet you accuse me of theft. This world is so unfair!'

Adalat Shah wasn't swayed. 'You better return my gold unless you want to spend the rest of your life in prison. I will plead guilty of perjury and name you my accomplice. I will kill you and every member of your family. You haven't seen the real me yet!'

Altaf was unresponsive; he had lapsed into silence. Adalat Shah now spoke gently, 'Brother, you are younger than me, but I still treat you like my elder brother. Please don't do this to me. I have spent years in prison; I have divorced my wife, and I have nothing left except those gold bullions. I will be dead without them! If you want, I can make you a deal. Fifty-fifty? Aren't we old partners?'

'This is an unreasonable accusation, *Janab e Aala*,' said Altaf Dastarkhan, 'I don't know what to tell you.'

Adalat Shah gave up, at least for then. 'I will teach you a bitter lesson, Altaf,' he promised as he walked out, 'I know Saghir Khan and you hatched a dirty plan to nail me down. I knew he was untrustworthy, but I trusted you. How foolish I was! From now on, the only one mission in my life is to destroy you.'

'Yes, you were foolish in behaving as you did,' said Altaf Dastarkhan, finally speaking up. 'You thought you would fool all of us. You never paid salaries to the young boys who lived the miserable lives of militants, who died believing whatever rubbish you promised them. You lied to me about what was really there in that makeup box. You probably took me for a fool too, didn't you?'

'Bravo, Altaf Dastarkhan!' Adalat Shah clapped, 'You sound like a politician now. You can impress voters for sure. But don't try your newly acquired skills on me! You keep the gold, but don't forget that I will soon bring you what you truly deserve.'

Altaf Dastarkhan was a busy man. He canvassed for election candidates, including the one who had substituted Adalat Shah in the State Assembly elections. Altaf was quite good at this job. He spent money, made alliances, and made sure to ask for votes after feigning shock at the present living conditions of the people. He delivered speeches on Eid and sat in the middle of the first row, right behind the Mufti. A month ago, when Aslam was struggling to get rifles issued, Altaf was granted a Personal Security Officer. 'You see the situation now, *Janab e Aala*. We endorsers of peace are under constant threat,' he had pleaded. 'Give me a security officer, please, not an SPO. I want a regular constable.'

'Dear friends and elders,' said Altaf Dastarkhan, stealing Adalat Shah's words, as he addressed the Eid congregation, 'before I read out the next message, I must share with you an outrageous incident that happened yesterday.' He held a folded paper in his hand; it had been passed to him by the Mufti to read out during the congregation.

The crowd murmured in anticipation.

'Yesterday, some people from my neighbourhood came to me with a complaint about a man who has recently moved here. When I confronted him about his bad behaviour, he almost fired at me! If it hadn't been for the timely intervention of my personal security guard, I might not have been standing here today.'

Agitated and anxious murmurs came from the crowd. 'Who was he?' shouted someone.

'He is an SPO from Pathri Aali. This isn't the first time I have received complaints against SPOs. These men used to graze buffaloes before our government decided to give them rifles. I appeal to the government to take back their rifles; they have become dangerous and out of control. I strongly believe that they have no civic sense and no experience of living among civilized people. We don't want to fall prey to them, do we?'

The crowd shouted in agreement.

Altaf was referring to Akram Khalifa. Ever since he had become an SPO, Akram had unleashed his own brand of terror in Swarnpur. He had settled in the town with a few other men and their families. The town dwellers couldn't tolerate the newly ousted villagers, protected by gun-wielding SPOs. The problems of the local residents were myriad: they had to acknowledge tribal people as their neighbours, people who didn't care for their urbane clothes; they had to endure the bland folk songs played loudly to drown their heart-wrenching songs of love and infidelity; they had to tolerate newly-inducted SPOs flashing their rifles, and attracting the attention of their schoolgirls; and they had to accept unbearable villagers as their tenants.

It was partially this constant detestation that irked Akram Khalifa. He started retaliating against the humiliation in his own way, giving men multiple fractures and haemorrhages and recreating fighting scenes from Bollywood films in the backyards of the townsfolk. The police hesitated to take any action, for Akram Khalifa enjoyed the protection of the deputy superintendent of police.

'Now, I'll move to the next message,' said Altaf Dastarkhan, glancing at the note. It had no name but only a signature. The signature was familiar; in fact, he knew it very well. 'Who gave it to you?' he asked the Mufti. 'I don't remember,' the Mufti replied.

While the Mufti recited the Eid *Khutbah*, Altaf Dastarkhan cautiously pulled out the message that he had lied about to the crowd. 'It is yet another complaint about the bad behaviour of the SPOs,' he had told them. But the real message had unnerved him.

> *Swindler of hopes, burglar of words, the snake in my sleeve, fifteen years ago, you entered my life, greeting me Eid Mubarak. Slowly, you swallowed me, and now you have taken my form. But you won't be able to digest me. I will slit your innards! Perhaps, you don't know what happened to your accomplice, that smuggler of gold and salt. You will be lucky if you meet such an end, but I think that would be asking for too much. Your end will not be easy, not sudden. You will feel it coming and fear its advent every moment that you breathe. Take cover if you like; get your security guards to brace themselves. But nothing will stop your annihilation. Every member of your family will meet a bitter, well-deserved end.*

Altaf found himself sweating profusely. Adalat Shah could be lurking anywhere. He had jumped his parole sometime back, and people believed that he had crossed the border to Pakistan.

Thirty-two

Aslam's team wanted to announce itself to the enemy. What good was it to unleash a menace unless it was well and truly announced first?

'This is not a marriage procession,' Aslam refused, annoyed. 'This is a death squad. Let me remind you what you learnt during the training—the enemy can't kill us, but our indiscipline will.'

The teenaged boys looked sulky. Aslam had lately sensed that they disliked his constant cautionary advice. 'Listen, if you want to announce yourselves, I will arrange for it. But remember your discipline. You will never leave the places that I have assigned to you. Your rifle is a part of your body. Eat with it, sleep with it, cry with it, and go, when you have to, but never leave your rifles alone.'

Aslam had supervised a week's training for his team. Major Sekera had been assigned the task of handling Aslam. The men were trained to use weapons and radio transistors. On the last day of the training, Major Sekera had assured them, 'I will be here for any help and reinforcement you may need. Remember, you don't have to go to their doorsteps like this man here,' he pointed to Aslam. 'Individual bravado cannot win this battle, but your team can as long as you fight as one unit. You only have to guard your doors, not pursue them. Leave that to us.'

'Yes, sir,' nodded the men. They were keen to assume their positions as guards for their village, their people.

'There is one final thing I think you need to hear,' said Major Sekera. 'It is a message from Doctor Himanshu. Aslam, could you step forward? He wanted you to stand in front of your team when I read this message.'

> *Dear young men of Pathri Aali, If this message is being read to you, I am sure that you have received training to fight your enemy. You are now ready to take on your demons. I am not sure if Akram Khalifa is among you. If he isn't, I'd like one of you to tell him the real story of his father's killing. It might disappoint you, as your fathers and elder brothers may have been among those who killed him. But here's the truth—it was not an act of valour. Twenty men against one, and he still fought like a brave warrior. Whether or not his crimes deserved such a death, I will not discuss today. But I think it is important that you remember this story because you cannot defeat your enemy like those men killed Akram's father. Trust me; you won't.*
>
> *So, how should you fight? Let me tell you another story—that of a skinny boy who lived with a beast. The beast, surprisingly, had a kind heart. The boy wanted to encourage it to take on an enemy. But the creature was timid and fearful of failure. The boy pushed it, threatening to kill it if it didn't fight. But the beast still hesitated, unsure of its strength. The boy became so agitated that he fumed like a beast himself. I was a witness to this. I could read what the boy was thinking, 'Oh Allah, give me strength so I can take on the enemy myself.'*
>
> *Do you know who the boy was? He stands in front of you. It is none other than Aslam. And the fight I described was the last bullfight in Pathri Aali. When the beast fought, he stood in the arena, never leaving its side. And guess what, they won!*
>
> *So, young men, I want you to fight like Aslam, your*

leader. Never show your backs to your enemy, and never doubt your capabilities.

※

Zaitoon was surprised at her visitor. 'I can't believe that you came to my house,' she said to Aslam. 'You are always welcome here.'

'Have you spoken to Bilal?'

'I lied to him,' she said, 'I told him you were unwell and hospitalized. But he was happy that you had accepted his gift.'

Aslam sipped the tea Zaitoon's mother brought him. 'I am here to ask for a favour,' he said, trying to gauge her reaction. 'It isn't for me, but for our people.'

Zaitoon stared at Aslam. 'You have hurt me, not once but several times. But after I came home that night, I realized I had been foolish. I was going to attempt something I was clueless about. All I wanted to do was to help you. It was a mistake.'

'All of us make mistakes. I have made many mistakes far graver than you can imagine.'

Zaitoon looked away. 'Anyway,' she said, 'I assure you that I will do anything for my people. You told me I don't have the honour that your father died protecting, but I do. In my whole life, no one has ever asked me what I want. They think I am a woman who doesn't have honour. I am treated as if I have no self-esteem. But I am not like that.' Zaitoon's voice broke. 'Tell me!' she wiped her tears and said to Aslam, 'What can I do for you?'

'I have brought you a radio set. I will show you how to operate it. You only have to inform me of their movements as and when you get any information. It is risky, but I am sure you can do it.'

'I will do it.'

A day later, Aslam and his team braced for their first combat. Zaitoon was not completely sure of the information she had given, but Aslam thought it was worth exploring anyhow. The battleground was familiar; it was the Changa riverbed where Khalifa had been confronted, where the Army had lost several of its officers. And now, it was here that the resistance in Pathri Aali was set to begin.

The whole team was present at the site except two men who had been commanded to guard the village. Daylight was close, and the men found various hiding places. Manzoor and Riaz crouched behind a fallen deodar trunk. Manzoor appeared still troubled by his father's death. But Riaz felt it was something more and he couldn't understand it.

It had been more than four hours since they had crouched for an ambush. Aslam waved to them now and then from behind a tree below, asking them to be patient. Some of them had started to look tired; they emerged from their hiding places to rest comfortably. Aslam frowned; it was the first real test of their stamina, but it was turning out to be what he had anticipated.

Manzoor spoke softly to Riaz from his hiding place behind the trunk. Riaz was not far off, sitting quietly by himself. 'Do you recognize Zuber and Khalil?'

'How can I forget their faces?' Riaz replied, 'Kabir and I can recognize them even if they wear a hundred masks.' Once Zuber had pointed his gun at Kabir and said, "I don't like a furious face. Not on a dog, and certainly not on a man." Khalil had laughed at our terrified faces and said, "Yes, that's right. We like terrified faces much better."' We didn't see them for a long time after that; our father sent us to Saudi Arabia. When we learnt that they killed our grandfather, we swore to kill them at the first opportunity. I know they killed your father too.'

'Yes, they did.'

'We will take our revenge. That is certain. I know you are still upset about his death, and understandably so. No one can fill the vacuum of a parent's loss.'

'It's not that,' said Manzoor quietly.

'Then what is it?' Riaz had feared as much.

'You will know it. The whole village will know it,' tears welled up in Manzoor's eyes, 'you will all see the truth in one month.'

'We cannot cry now,' Riaz tried to console him. 'Please tell me what is troubling you.'

'Don't you know it already? My sister, Shamma, is eight months pregnant!'

After four and a half hours of waiting, Aslam finally ordered his men to get ready for action. The militants were approaching. The boys, much to their surprise, found that their hearts were thumping and their hands were wet with sweat. One of them fainted from mere exhaustion, or perhaps, from fear of what was to come. Aslam raised his hand to command Riaz and Manzoor to fire. They would, in turn, transmit the signal to the others.

At the count of one, the firing began. But it was among the ugliest firing that the mountains had seen. Aslam's men lacked coordination; the short training had done little to teach them the nuances of war. Three guns were jammed; the ones that worked missed their targets. Despite all this clumsiness, Aslam and his men managed to hit six militants. The rest of them took combat positions immediately. Aslam wasn't worried that the militants had rushed off to hide. In fact, he had been hoping they would. He felt certain that they had assumed the very positions he had hoped they would. Down went carefully aimed hand grenades, not making the slightest sound until they had caught their targets unaware. Unlike the firing, the grenades were almost on target. Aslam was right in assessing the effectiveness of the hand grenades on the gravel—'twice as effective,' he had guessed.

'We have arrived!' Aslam's voice echoed in the hills. His men joined him, their fears and apprehensions washed away by this first victory.

8

The news spread like wildfire. It was all over the news channels; newspapers splashed it in their headlines every morning. 'Security forces down sixteen militants in the foothills of Pir Panjal; huge cache of arms recovered', reported *Jammu Times*. There were press conferences about 'one of the biggest operations in the history of counterinsurgency'. Aslam and his team were not mentioned at all; they were referred to in passing as 'members of some Special Groups'.

In any case, they didn't have time to sit back and enjoy these brief moments of fame; they had to plan their next strike. 'Let's not get complacent over our first success,' Aslam cautioned his team. 'Our battle has just begun.'

Nonetheless, Pathri Aali was rejoicing. Children simulated the incident through encounter games. Lal Jaan visited almost all the houses in the neighbourhood, her back straighter than before. If her voice hadn't been strained with age, she might have broken into song. But the other women weren't so excited. 'We want guns too,' they demanded of Aslam. 'Valour isn't exclusive to men, is it?' Most of the women had been incredibly impressed when Ashwar had dragged the corpse of the fallen militant from her house. It had left behind a red trail, as if a humongous snake had emerged, dead, from a pool of blood. 'We can do what Ashwar did if only we have a gun,' declared the women, not to be overshadowed in this show of valour. 'But how did she know how to use a gun? It's not just about having a gun; you must have the courage to pull the trigger at your enemy.' 'Oh, we can do it. When you have a gun in your hand, the rest of it comes to you naturally.'

While the women of Pathri Aali made plans, there was one

woman who wept in silence. No one asked her why; no one cared for her tears. As always, she was excluded from the celebration. She could confide only in Aslam. 'Bilal was among those killed,' wept Zaitoon. 'You gave him a clean death, exactly as you had promised.'

Not everyone was pleased with the Changa encounter. Major Sekera was somewhat unhappy. 'Why didn't you inform me about your plan?' he frowned at Aslam. 'I told you never to plan anything without informing me.'

'I didn't imagine it would become such a success,' said Aslam. In the next two weeks, Aslam and his team helped the Army kill thirteen more militants in several skirmishes.

As the resistance in Pathri Aali became stronger and more widespread, a rather disturbing situation made itself evident. Amidst all this, realized the security forces, something had gone entirely amiss.

Top echelons of intelligence agencies were having frequent confrontations with the security forces. The militants had claimed Hill Kaka and the surrounding villages as Liberated Territory. Many people issued statements regarding the developments around Hill Kaka, but many of these statements contradicted each other. What on earth was going on?

The district police backdated its records, entering the names of Aslam and his team members into Special Group III and Special Group II. 'Yes, there has been a misunderstanding,' they admitted. But the 'error' was never pronounced beyond its admission.

Hill Kaka suddenly came into prominence—something it would never have expected to achieve. Plans in both the Northern Command and the Defence Ministry were made around Hill Kaka. Aslam had the honour of briefing high-ranked generals. He would point out errors and suggest corrections in the simulation model of

Hill Kaka that they had prepared from satellite images. The cave over the cliff, where Aslam had spent a day in reconnaissance, was named Aslam Point. To their utter confusion, the herdsmen were ordered not to migrate to their summer abodes—the reason was kept under wraps.

One morning, Major Sekera called Aslam and gave him a command that took him by surprise. 'Today, you will ride a helicopter to Hill Kaka.'

'Why, sir? What would be the point?'

'We need one final aerial reconnaissance before they make the announcement.'

'Announcement?'

'I can't tell you now; you'll know soon. So, are you ready to go?'

'Sir, I don't think it's a good idea.'

'Why?'

'It's dangerous. Plus, wouldn't we be alerting them?'

'Don't worry about the danger. You will ride with a man who is skilled at manoeuvring a helicopter. I haven't seen it, but people say he can even fly it belly up. Just have a strong heart and an even stronger stomach.'

The helicopter ride turned out to be a joyride for Aslam. 'Do you see that cliff over there? The one that looks like a bird's beak? That's Aslam Point,' he pointed proudly to the two cameramen sitting next to him. 'And those dark broken lines are bunkers.' The helicopter did a few quick rounds between the hills before the pilot commenced the return journey.

Upon return, Aslam was taken to the GOC and the Northern Command. He sat in the office, sipping tea and munching on the snacks that the jawans offered him. The GOC had asked him to wait until further instruction. 'You may have to fly with me to New Delhi,' he had said.

The big announcement that Major Sekera had hinted at came

with a bang. 'The Defence Ministry has declared war on the militants hiding in Hill Kaka. The operation will be called Sarp Vinaash.' Major Sekera announced with a smile, patting Aslam on the back. 'You did it, Aslam.'

Aslam was elated. 'It's because of you and Himanshu Sir that we will finally launch our attack on them.'

'The credit goes to the GOC and you and your team,' replied the Major. 'I only did what I needed to.'

'Thank you once again, sir.'

'Aslam, I want you to listen to me carefully. While the Army launches a helicopter attack, you and your team will guard your village. I will lead my men to close in from the right flank, the ridge southwest of Hill Kaka.'

'And what about the left flank?'

Major Sekera shook his head in disappointment. 'I have failed to convince them; they say it's too risky to position the Army there. You know, the Army will have to cross the Changa river, and without road connectivity, it will be impossible for us to attack. However, we will ensure that we do maximum damage during the first aerial foray.'

'This sounds pointless, sir.' Aslam looked thoroughly upset. 'Nothing will happen. Nothing! Don't you think we have already alerted them by our helicopter ride? They must be well prepared for aerial attacks. The escape route from Hill Kaka is towards the northeast, along the left flank. It goes straight to the Kashmir Valley, which you are leaving unmanned. It's as good as offering a clear, safe passage to them.'

The Major looked doubtful. 'You may be right, Aslam. But you had convinced us that Hill Kaka is occupied by the enemy and needs to be recaptured. We can't suddenly predict that the enemy will not defend its position and run away at the sound of the first bullet.'

'Sir, you know the situation. We will help the Army in reaching the spot, but you *have* to intercept them on the left flank. That is the only option to ensure this mission isn't a total failure!'

'You don't understand my position. You and I are no different when it comes to influencing the plans of the government. In fact, you are more powerful than I am as far as any say in this operation is concerned.'

'Sir, I have one solution, if you will permit me to execute it. I will position *my* team on the left flank.'

'No!' cried the Major. 'Are you out of your mind? Do you think this is like the Changa attack where you could kill them only because you caught them unawares? No, Aslam, they will go all out on you. Seventeen of you with rudimentary rifles would be no match for them with their modern artillery.'

'Sir, if recapturing Hill Kaka is the mission, then you can announce right away: "Aslam Point captured". I am going to position myself there.'

'Don't do it; trust me. Recapturing Hill Kaka is not our mission; our mission is the total destruction of the enemy. But give me a day or two. I will inform them of your request, and let's hope they concede. But even if they don't, I advise you not to be disheartened. The left flank would still be under tremendous aerial and ground shelling.'

Thirty-three

The trial, finally, began. Kavita Singh sat in the front row in the courtroom, right next to the witness box. Kavita had been sitting there since morning and had listened carefully to the proceedings of the first four cases, irrelevant as they were to her. It was all part of her homework. In the last few days, she had been busy writing scripts and getting them rehearsed. The roles and actors were precast; the dialogues had been written accordingly. She did it diligently, fully utilizing the apprenticeship of the early years of her marriage: the letter of unwritten words, and the telegrams.

The lead actor in the trial had refused to rehearse the dialogues in front of her. She hadn't been pleased, but she couldn't afford to annoy him. 'If you don't want to say anything,' she had said to Arif Ansari, 'it will be fine. You can tell the court you don't remember anything.' Arif Ansari had declined the offer. 'No, I will speak. Don't worry, madam.'

When Arif Ansari was summoned to court, Kavita tried desperately to meet his eyes. She wanted to signal several things to him. But he didn't look in her direction.

The prosecuting officer read the charges without much interest. The defence lawyer, arranged by Kavita Singh, vowed emphatically to demonstrate that every allegation against his client was untrue. 'Your Honour,' he began, 'the only evidence against my client is his own statement taken through coercion and intimidation.'

'You may make your statement now,' the judge addressed Arif Ansari. Arif finally looked at Kavita Singh for one brief moment. He then brought out a piece of paper from his pocket. It looked like the paper on which Kavita had written down his dialogues, hoping to make Arif memorize them.

'Oh God, is he going to read it?' Kavita trembled in her seat. 'What if the judge asks me to explain the script?'

Arif Ansari's voice resounded clearly in the silent courtroom. 'Your Honour, I have written this statement in my full senses, in my own handwriting. If you permit me, I can sign this document. You can consider this my statement before you.'

'Yes, you are permitted to submit the statement,' said the Judge. 'However, adhering to the spirit of court procedure, you have to read out what you have written. The court scribes will record it.'

'Thank you, sir,' Arif replied and started reading. 'Pride is what defines me. I am the pride of my village, and my pride lies in being a soldier of the Indian Army. I underwent rigorous training to earn my pride. I believe I have been a disciplined and devoted soldier.

'We, the soldiers of the Indian Army, live and die for our country. Our country and our pride mean the same thing to us. The bullet from an enemy doesn't discriminate between a Muslim and a Hindu soldier.

'During my tenure in the Army, there was something that troubled me. I was made to feel that being disciplined and devoted was not enough, that I was born with an inherent defect. I always got the feeling that being born a Hindu makes you a patriot by default, but a Muslim has to prove his fidelity every day. I was under a trial of sorts, merely for being who I am. But I chose to live with it. I believed that every profession and organization has some inherent failings. I still feel proud that I never allowed the filth of some of my bosses to taint my mind toward all of them. Dharam Pal Singh breached all my beliefs. The person that he was, killed the officer in him; I killed the person. I have no regret about doing what I did. He attacked my pride and delivered the judgement of my unnecessary, unfair trial, labelling me a traitor while I had been anything but a traitor. I had to defend my pride.'

'Traitor!' Kavita Singh jumped out of her seat. 'Oh no! You traitor!

'Traitor!' Kavita Singh kept repeating long after the courtroom had emptied, to the utter annoyance of the lady constable who finally dragged her out.

Thirty-four

The youngsters of Pathri Aali were angry and resentful. The batteries of their radio sets had drained, just like their hopes. All eyes and ears had been directed at Aslam's radio set; Major Sekera could send in a message anytime, confirming that yes, they were to defend the left flank of Hill Kaka. But no message ever came. The mission that was to ensue had been named Sarp Vinaash, Annihilation of the Snakes. But in reality, it seemed that the snakes were only being poked and shooed away.

Ashwar's plight was even sadder. Shamma was about to deliver a baby in about three weeks. It was likely to be in mid-April, and the trio had assumed that it would be after the villagers had migrated to the upper meadows. It had been Shamma's idea to stay back; she didn't want any taunts for her and her newborn. But now that the villagers had been commanded not to migrate, women from the neighbourhood came in at all odd times of the day, invoking Allah's mercy and cornering Ashwar and Lal Jaan for having attempted to conceal the news. *The bastard, the rape child, should be buried!*

Burdened by the barbs of the villagers and unable to imagine a lifetime of stigma for her daughter, Ashwar turned to Aslam.

'Marry Shamma,' she said. 'Please accept her as your wife.'

'What?!' Aslam was stupefied. Was this his Ashwar who was making such a request? 'How can you be so cruel? You know that I have always loved you. But that isn't why I have to reject this sinful proposal. Shamma is like my daughter, Ashwar. I cannot see her as my wife.'

'You and I can never be together,' said Ashwar, between sobs. 'If you love me, can't you abate my sorrow by helping me?'

'Do you know why I ran away from my marriage with Zaitoon? I felt I was committed to you! The only way I could have freed myself of that obligation was if you had been happy, if you had achieved your dream. But you weren't happy, and your dreams were buried in the dust.'

'So, you will do nothing for me, is that right? You will only dig up the past and watch me suffer in the present.'

'Ashwar, I may not be as strong as my father. Indeed, I am unlike him in many ways. But I, too, am a man of my word. Here's my word to you—I will marry off Shamma to a suitable man, to a man who deserves a courageous girl like her. But allow me to return from my mission.'

'Your mission?'

'Yes,' said Aslam. 'I haven't told this to anyone, but I am telling it to you—I will take my revenge, with or without the Army's help. Or I will die trying. I will revisit Hill Kaka one last time. If I come back alive, and if today isn't our last meeting, I assure you I will keep my word.'

'Please let go of your revenge, Aslam,' requested Ashwar. 'This is not what your father would have wanted for you. You have already done a lot for this village; you *have* liberated us of our tormentors. I didn't kill that militant only to avenge my child's trauma. I wanted to tell the militants that we are now deadly hornets! Yes, I know that the murderers of my husband, the rapists of my daughter, and the butchers of the innocent are still alive. But they will meet their destinies. Leave it to Allah.'

'Ashwar, just tell me one thing. If I come back alive, will you marry me?'

'I can't, Aslam.'

'Why not?'

'I will never be able to give you the love you deserve. All the love I had in my heart died with my husband. I believe I am responsible for his death. You need a woman who can love you, who can bear you children. I can't even do that.'

'You should decide *your* reasons, not mine. Stop blaming yourself for sins you never committed.'

'You should decide *your* reasons, not mine,' retorted Ashwar.

Aslam smiled. 'All right, Ashwar. I will take your leave. The last time I met you, I would have done anything to change my present. I had been afraid I would never see you again. But I did, and it was upon your invite. Nothing will ever again compel me to return now. There would be no point.'

'Aslam, listen to me,' Ashwar kept pleading for a long time even after he had walked away.

Stepping into the shoes of his father was even harder than fighting his enemies. Aslam realized it when he called his family for an urgent discussion.

'I don't deserve to ask you this, but I am helpless,' he said to his mother, sister-in-law, brother, and nephews. 'But let me assure you, while I may be undeserving to ask anything of you, the person I ask for isn't.'

'Don't talk in riddles, son,' said Hamida. 'What do you want to ask us?'

'I have a marriage proposal for Riaz. I want him to marry Shamma.'

Parveen's eyes widened in shock. *How dare Aslam propose such a thing!* Wazir shut his eyes and breathed deeply, possibly trying to comprehend the full weight of Aslam's proposal. Riaz did not react. He sat staring into infinity.

'No!' cried out Parveen. 'I reject this shameful proposal.'

'She is right,' agreed Hamida. 'From grandfather to grandchildren, why should our family be burdened by unimaginable sacrifices? Why doesn't anyone else ever come forward?'

'It wouldn't be a sacrifice,' said Aslam. 'Shamma is a good girl; she would be a suitable match for Riaz. What happened to her wasn't her fault. Does anyone have a say in his or her misfortune? Can we, the villagers of Pathri Aali, be blamed for what happened to us? If anyone can be blamed, it's the men who failed to guard the honour of their mothers and daughters. But the women have still chosen to accept them as their partners. Tell me, who is the one making the sacrifice?'

'It's easy to preach,' Parveen said, 'why don't *you* marry her? Why did you run away from your marriage and put all of us through horrible circumstances?'

'She is like my *daughter*,' argued Aslam. 'Yes, I ran away from my responsibilities, but I came back when you were nothing but helpless prey for those snakes! Not long ago, you had no choice but to obey every command of your predators. And now, suddenly, you are raising your voices and judging people! You are berating their shame! What will you do if I put my gun to your son's head and command him to marry Shamma? Isn't that what you have been used to? Isn't that what the militants have taught you?'

'Yes, hold a gun to my son's head. What better can I expect from you?' Parveen taunted, tears flowing. 'Shamma is more important to you than my son. Ashwar is more important to you than any of us. You are dancing to her tunes! I know that it's her proposal you have brought home. Why are you asking for our permission, anyway? Just intimidate my son and force him to accept Shamma as his wife.'

'You will never understand me,' said Aslam, 'I can do anything for Riaz and Kabir. I just wanted to change your opinion of Shamma; it pains me that you think ill of her because of the grave misfortune that befell her.' He turned to Riaz and said, 'Son, I will not force you to do anything. If the answer is no, just say the word. You don't have to run away, like I did. I was not given a choice, but you certainly have one.'

'I second Aslam's proposal,' Wazir said. He had been quiet all this while. 'I have been thinking about Shamma all these days, but somehow I hadn't the courage to bring this up. I think our father would have done exactly what Aslam is proposing.'

'Have you lost your senses too?' Hamida cried, 'All of us know what Ashwar and Lal Jaan are hiding. We know what lies in Shamma's belly, under her oversized *kurtas*. It's not just about accepting that girl as our daughter-in-law; it's accepting a rape child as our grandchild!'

'Oh yes! How can you accept an innocent child in your family?' Aslam said furiously. 'It is another thing to accept unchaste women, isn't it? Accepting cowardly men doesn't dishonour you. The child is innocent,' Aslam pleaded. 'Don't you realize how courageous Shamma is? She could easily have dumped the baby, but she didn't. It takes courage to stand up for innocents, even at the cost of your own peril. That's what my father did, and that's what Shamma is doing. I believe that Riaz, my son, my nephew, deserves a brave woman like her. But like I said before, I leave it to Riaz. Let him decide first.'

Riaz continued to stare into the distance, not responding.

Later that day, when Aslam was preparing to proceed to Hill Kaka, his radio buzzed. It was Major Sekera. 'Come to Buffliaz.'. 'Bring "Shikari" along with you.'

Who was 'Shikari'? Aslam was puzzled for a moment before he suddenly remembered that the Major had given this nickname to Kabir. He recalled that during practice Kabir had engraved a

'K' on the target board, all with his bullets. It was as neat as in children's alphabet books. Kabir, indeed, was quite the *Shikari*, the skilled hunter.

❦

'The conversation we are about to have will never be repeated. You will never mention it to anyone at all. It will be like it never happened.' Major Sekera addressed Aslam and Kabir, his tone grave and face grim.

'Yes, sir,' they said in unison.

'I tried very hard to convince my bosses about your offer,' he continued, 'and they have allowed it.'

Aslam let out a cry of delight.

'You can position your team on the left flank.'

'Ji, sir.'

'You must understand that a lot is at stake in this operation. This will be the first ever major counter-insurgency operation since the inception of the Rashtriya Rifles. So, in a way, the outcome of this operation will decide the fate of the RR. You and I are directly responsible.'

'Yes, sir.'

'The GOC has ordered me to impose two conditions. You have to adhere to them at all times.'

'What are they, sir?' enquired Aslam.

'First, you and your team will remain directly under my command and act as per my instructions. I understand that you have personal revenge to exact, but you will not pursue it. You must fight like disciplined soldiers. And second, if anything unfortunate happens to any of you, you will be the only one held responsible. No one from your family can blame anyone else. Do you agree?'

Aslam was quiet. All his vows to take revenge were now being dissolved. How could he disrespect the pledge he had solemnly made at Pathri Pir? It was the pledge that had kept him going all these days.

'I accept, sir,' said Aslam, 'but I must tell you about a pledge I had made at our holy shrine. I had vowed to seek revenge against two monsters—Zuber and Khalil. Not just me, but all of us feel that they do not deserve an easy death or a Muslim burial. But, anyway, I can guarantee that the left flank will fight like disciplined soldiers, under your command. But yes, we will ensure that Zuber and Khalil meet terrible deaths during the operation.'

'Only those two then?'

'There is another thing you must know, sir. I do not recognize either of them.'

Major Sekera smiled and signalled Aslam and Kabir to follow him to the armoury. 'We have an understanding then,' he said. 'You will have to position yourselves at the Aslam Point. When the operation ends, you will return your weapons and unused ammunition to me. The rest of your team will have to operate with bolt action rifles.'

'Ji, sir.'

The Major turned to Kabir. 'Shikari, do you know what rifle this is?'

'No, sir,' Kabir replied, glancing at his new possession from the armoury.

'It's a Heckler and Koch PSG1, a sniper rifle. It's a weapon that hunters like you must have during combat. You will also position yourself at the Aslam Point. I want you to update me with the score.'

'I will do it, sir.'

'Now,' Major Sekera ordered, getting into his jeep, 'hop in for the last part of your training.'

The Major took Aslam and Kabir to a hillock overlooking the Army camp at Buffliaz. 'Take a look down below,' he commanded, pointing his finger towards the camp. 'Assume that the Army camp represents the bunkers of militants in Hill Kaka, and we are standing at Aslam Point. Is the distance optimal or should we move closer?'

'As far as I remember, we have to descend some more. We should take another turn down below,' said Aslam.

'Now?' Major Sekera asked after a while. Aslam nodded. It looked all right to him.

'Okay, now tell me, what is the distance between that temple and the river?'

Aslam was embarrassed. He looked at Kabir for help, but Kabir only smiled sheepishly. 'Sir, I dropped out of school precisely because of such questions.'

Major Sekera laughed. 'Don't worry,' he assured him, 'I will make it easier for you. Can you tell me how many Army trucks can fit between the temple and the river?'

Aslam and Kabir started calculating. It took them a while, but they came up with a number they thought sounded correct. 'Twelve.'

'That's fine,' said Major Sekera, 'remember to be consistent about your conjectures. So, if I have to move to the river, and I am at the temple, I need to move twelve trucks forward. Is that correct?'

'Yes, sir.'

'Okay, assume that I have done so. My location is now the river, say, on that big rock protruding right below. Now, if I have to move from that big rock to the willow tree on the other side of the river, I have to move forward and then go right.'

'Yes, sir.'

'Now tell me, how many trucks forward and how many right?'

'Fifteen forward and six right.'

'Excellent. What about from that willow to the temple?'

'Twenty-seven backward and six left.'

This went on for some time till the Major exclaimned, 'Amazing! Your teacher may not have been good enough to teach you. You are now battle-ready.'

Thirty-five

Thirty-five days of fighting is the number the Army put on the duration of Operation Sarp Vinaash. But as far as Aslam and his team were concerned, the period was an eternity. On the tenth day, they were partially relieved of their duties. But it had been ten long days and ten cold, dark nights in thick forests, lying in anticipation of encountering the devils. The wait had seemed endless for the teenagers. They would take turns stretching their legs and resting their backs on lichens and pine leaves. They rationed potatoes and ate them half-baked from stone *chullahs*. At night, they hugged stones for warmth. For two nights and an entire day, they endured a vicious hailstorm while the fire pits stubbornly refused to kindle.

On the night of 21 April 2003, Aslam and Kabir marched towards Aslam Point. The rest of their team was divided into three smaller groups, each waiting in ambush along the passages leading out of Hill Kaka. Simultaneously, the Romeo Force of the Rashtriya Rifles closed in from the right flank. The next morning, as directed by Major Sekera, a group of five young men, led by Riaz, took position for the first action of Sarp Vinaash—the Shock and Awe tactic. As the Romeo Force fired a rocket to bust a post at the base of Hill Kaka, thirteen shocked militants were caught unawares. Rapid fire was coming in from the determined teenagers, one of whom yelled at the end of the spell, 'All out!' Their wrists ached; their muscles seemed to have become involuntary. It was surprising that the teenagers made their rudimentary rifles work as if they were automatic.

Down below, in lower Pathri Aali, villagers squatted on their roofs to witness the battle. They couldn't see much, but marvelled at the blasts and stared awestruck at the clouds of smoke. Some of the spectators showed off their knowledge of the ways of war. 'That's a 303 fire,' declared someone. 'That smoke is coming from the militants' hideouts.'

The encounter below alerted the militants in Hill Kaka. Their shock magnified when the aerial shelling began. After an hour of discomfort, Kabir got used to viewing everything through the telescope in his sniper. Aslam tuned in to the correct frequency on his radio set. He was occupied with cracking the codes that Major Sekera had predefined. *Get on elephant. Get on horse.*

The only response from the militants was radio communication; they were trying to alert each other of the Army's movements. It was only in the evening after the helicopters had stopped hovering, that Aslam and Kabir spotted two heads venturing out of the bunkers. That's when Aslam realized that the militants could escape during the night. The three subgroups would have to keep up a constant vigil.

That night, Aslam accompanied ten teenagers to deadly combat with two dozen militants. It was a blind firing frenzy; often, they seemed to be shooting at imaginary targets. The encounter lasted several hours. Eventually, it forced the militants to retreat to the safety of their bunkers. A handful of rookies had turned out to be a mighty legion that would need to be reckoned with.

On the fourth day of the operation, the hideouts were razed after Aslam guided the Major to their precise location. Major Sekera turned out to be a genious. The artillery was commanded by him to the precise angle and direction as Aslam gave the directions in terms of trucks: five trucks forward, ten trucks to the right etc. While Aslam helped the Army with calibration, Kabir counted the heads.

'Close to twenty,' Aslam updated Major Sekera. The Major seemed to be unhappy and had asked him to reconfirm the figure. 'Counting is a more difficult task than killing, sir. Kabir can't see much under the heap of dust.'

Later that day, the militants launched a counter-attack, complete with mortars and machine guns. The barrel of their launcher was the only thing visible from Aslam Point. The attack had been launched from their strongest hideout, shielded by a massive rock. It managed to stop the Army's forward march.

On the fifth day, the stalemate continued. Kabir's left eye remained continuously strained, staring through the sniper's telescope. He was getting weaker and disoriented, beginning to see the world in two dimensions. Aslam noticed that he couldn't even walk about in the cave without colliding with walls. It had been five days since they had eaten a proper meal. That night, Aslam sent him home. 'You have done your part, son,' he said, 'now go and help your teammates. Get them food, ammunition, batteries, clothes—whatever they need.'

The stalemate went on for another four days. The Army and the militants exchanged fire without any result. The protracted deadlock withered the spirit of the teenagers. Sometimes, just to keep them encouraged, Aslam would transmit over the radio, 'I have noticed some movement.' The youngsters would fire at phantom enemies, sometimes only to vent their frustration. Aslam was aware of their depleting energy levels. Lying on his tummy behind the sniper, he observed the hideout and worried about his team members. Sometimes, he felt that he shouldn't have involved them. But then again, they were the real heroes of the resistance. He was yet to kill an enemy during the operation.

During those four days, Aslam tried his best to distract himself and the boys from negative thoughts. He, too, was unbelievably fatigued; his mind seemed to function at a strained, unreal level.

Distraction was what he sought—from thoughts going over and over about what he had wanted but couldn't get; from repentance; from yearning; from the world that had suddenly become bipolar—life and death; love and revenge; Ashwar and Zuber.

The tenth day was when things took a decisive turn. Aslam hadn't rested for a single moment the previous night, worried about how much longer the stalemate would continue. He blamed himself for the situation. Surely, there was something he had been unable to figure out. Why had there been no movements from the militants' end? Why were they defending their position despite suffering huge losses and realizing that the Army was closing in? 'Was it a jackal and lioness riddle?' he asked himself. Perhaps Major Sekera would have been able to figure it out. Aslam held the Major in high esteem, especially after he had used Kabir so efficiently and had successfully bombed the hideouts of the militants without even seeing them.

Early the next morning, Kabir came to visit Aslam. 'Ashwar forced me to deliver this to you,' he said, handing him a metal lunchbox, 'here's some food for you. I have a feeling there could be a letter inside.' Kabir smiled at him affectionately—a flicker of hope after the darkness that had been the night.

Aslam decided to invest all his energies into figuring out the enemy's strategy. There had to be something he was missing. Around afternoon, after Aslam had eaten his lunch, he discovered some movement through a trench. Apparently, the trench connected the ruined parts of the hideouts with the bunker from where the militants fired the rockets. Immediately, he crawled behind the sniper and made a radio call to Major Sekera.

Aslam's hunch was bang on. For the next half an hour, he didn't even find the time to reply to Major Sekera's calls. 'Aslam Point? Come in, come in,' the radio blared, but Aslam was busy targeting the militants with the sniper. Behind the razed bunkers was a cave-like trench, the opening of which was not visible from his vantage point. But now militants were clearly frenzied; they were running helter-skelter from the cave's mouth. 'Position?' demanded Major Sekera. 'I am not sure, sir,' Aslam finally replied. 'May be all out.'

The dust at Hill Kaka was finally settling. The barrel of the launcher that had held the Army's forward march had disappeared. 'Perhaps, no other militant is now alive,' hoped Aslam. He looked all around himself, straining his eyes to detect the slightest movement. And then he saw it: the launcher was pointed right at him, towards Aslam Point. There was no time to think, no time to apprise Major Sekera about the imminent danger. 'I am under attack, fifty trucks back—' he babbled before the radio screeched and went off.

Major Sekera heard the deadly hiss of the rocket that was fired at Aslam Point.

'Are you there, Aslam?' Major Sekera shouted. 'Aslam, come in!'

'No, he is not,' replied a militant who was piggybacking the radio frequency. 'And you are up next.'

'That is surely a bluff,' declared Major Sekera as the jawans looked on, worried. The radio set was now silent. 'It's the time to display our *Dridhta aur Virta*. Now is the time when we must live up to our reputation. I need two volunteers, two brave men, to accompany me to Aslam Point. And we have to run up the hill, all the way!'

§

It was deathly quiet. When he regained consciousness, Aslam half thought he was dead and had been buried. He pushed the debris off his body. Gasping to catch his breath, he tried to sit up. His ears still buzzed; that rocket seemed to have exploded right in his ears. The boulder overhanging the cave had collapsed, and the debris had shut off the entrance completely. There was no trace of light, no way of even finding out the time of day. He crawled through the debris, digging at it; the air felt heavy. 'Perhaps, it's because of the dust,' he thought. 'Or,' he checked himself, 'maybe I am running short on oxygen!' He felt his pockets and discovered a matchbox. Ah, he could finally see something.

All the matchsticks were soon burnt. But they hadn't gone waste. Aslam had been able to locate his rucksack, radio set, the Kalashnikov rifle, and the lunchbox that Ashwar had sent. The sniper had been crushed under the sill. Except for the torch in the rucksack, everything was most likely useless. The LED indicators on the radio still glowed, but there was no sound coming from it. The radio was apparently damaged.

With every passing moment, the air became heavier. He panted and coughed; his head ached and made him feel nauseated. It seemed useless to struggle now, for death was sure to meet him within moments. He leaned back on the wall of the cave and closed his eyes. But his eyes fell open in an instant. No, he didn't want his dead body to be discovered like a resigned, broken man. He held his rifle tightly, pointed it at an imaginary enemy, and lay down in a combat position.

He lay for many long moments, thinking of Ashwar. He saw her throwing away the Datura blanket and holding her arms open to him. 'The angel of life has come to meet me on my deathbed!' he smiled to himself. He suddenly thought of the letter. Exactly as Kabir had hinted, there had indeed been a letter inside the tiffin box. He had read it almost at once, imagining how Ashwar must have looked when she was penning it down. 'I will die with that letter in my hands,' he decided.

> *Do you remember what day it is tomorrow? Well, if you don't, I will remind you later, but let me first give you some good news. Shamma delivered a healthy baby girl yesterday. We have named her Ayesha. Your mother, sister-in-law and*

brother were the first people who came to see her. And they told us that Riaz had asked them to do so. They told us that the first thing Riaz wants to do, after the war, is to marry Shamma and take her home along with the newborn. Shamma, however, is reluctant. She says she can't burden anyone; she can raise her daughter herself. But I am sure you and Riaz will be able to convince her. The women of the village have already started preparing for the wedding. I have never seen them so emotional. They have proved our apprehensions wrong.

And now, I want to confess something. That night, when I saw you at Haaku's house, I immediately read your eyes. And I have never felt as guilty as I did that night.

I am sorry that I imposed my guilt on you. I am sorry for that shameful marriage proposal I made to you for Shamma. I decided that the only way to wash off my guilt was to confess everything to you.

Aslam, you have won this war already. Everyone is talking about how the snakes have been brought to justice. Every day, we see the Army moving closer to Hill Kaka. Humza is waiting to hear the war stories—of Aslam Point, and of how Kabir killed twenty militants with a telescope rifle. I have promised him that you will tell him all about it.

Now let me remind you about tomorrow. It is the first of May, the day you had first expressed your love to me. Do you remember that you had asked me to marry you? You had said that I was sixteen years old and had asked me how long you would need to wait, I had replied, 'Sixteen more years.' Strange as it is, tomorrow, it will be sixteen years!

I will keep my promise, Aslam. Now you too must honour your lafz. I want to live for my family, but I also want to live for myself. I want to live for you and for our love. Come home and marry me, Aslam. I am waiting.

Aslam had been in tears when he had read the letter. He had read it twice before folding it and keeping it in his pocket. Now, certain that death was close, he found that the letter infused him with a fresh lease of life. Ashwar had, like a cherub, brought him the message of love and life. 'I must keep my promise,' he told himself and extricated a hand grenade from his rucksack.

He had seen dust falling from one of the corners of the cave. He could have tried to climb out, but it was too high up. In his state, any strenuous climb could lead to death. But wasn't death imminent, anyway? Aslam fixed his torch in the mud and slowly began to scale the cliff. He fell twice, once when he had almost reached midway. His plan was to fix the hand grenade between the crevasses, pull its pin, jump down to the rocky floor, and run to the other side of the cave for cover. It turned out to be an implosion, not an explosion. Things went terribly wrong.

Aslam broke his right foot when he landed on the floor, shoved right inside the cave by the impact. Once again, he was knocked unconscious. Once again, when he opened his eyes, he feared that he had been buried. But he had lived.

One good thing had come of the implosion—it had widened the crevasse, just enough for the radio to establish a connection with the outside world. And just enough to let in some fresh air.

'I am trapped,' he was finally able to transmit.

'Stay put!' Major Sekera's reassuring response immediately came in. 'I am on it. We just razed the very last hideout.'

The Major was preoccupied just then. Meanwhile Riaz informed him that they had just encountered five militants, one had been killed, but four had escaped. Zuber and Khalil were among the escapees. They had sheltered in the tent of a nomad, holding the nomad's family captive. Major Sekera was aware of the situation and had instructed Riaz to wait for him to arrive.

Aslam got another message from Major Sekera soon after the previous one. 'Can't you command your boys to be disciplined?' shouted the Major. 'It's a no-shoot order! Tell them not to shoot!'

It turned out that the militant who was piggybacking Major Sekera's frequency was someone named Buttshikan—the destroyer of idols. He was a big catch for the Army. On the fourth day of Operation Sarp Vinaash, he had been seriously injured. He had offered to surrender before Major Sekera along with three others, including Zuber and Khalil. But Riaz and Manzoor were finding it excruciating not to kill them at once; they refused to budge from their positions.

Aslam's foot ached unbearably, and he bled from various parts of his body. But somehow, crazy as it sounded, he felt sure he would survive. What he did next could only be put down as madness, but then, many acts of unconditional bravery often qualify as insanity.

Aslam grabbed a second grenade and, once again, climbed up. His broken foot made the climb even harder than it had been earlier. Another grande was exploded in one of the corners of the cave making a vent big enough for Aslam. But he had no chance of scaling the cliff. He felt that he was standing on the terrace of a skyscraper, considering making the final, fatal jump. 'Five trucks below and at least one truck away,' he estimated.

Like a flying squirrel stretched out on four limbs, he glided out of the cave's hole, in the direction of a large pine tree. Moments before he jumped, he told himself, 'Someone will tell a better story of how you died, rather than you telling your children how you lived.'

§

Aslam pleaded with Riaz over the radio. Riaz, however, was adamant.

He was refusing to obey all orders. 'At least, wait for me to come,' pleaded Aslam.

Aslam and Major Sekera reached the spot together. Four militants, all of whom looked savage but drained, squatted on their knees. Their heads were threadbare, and blood oozed from their wounds. Riaz and Manzoor held their guns to Zuber and Khalil's heads respectively.

'They have surrendered, boys,' said Major Sekera. 'Let me have them now.'

Both the boys shook their heads.

'If you care for my word at all,' Aslam addressed them, 'hand them over to Sekera Sir.'

Riaz and Manzoor stared at him. 'You told me to wait for your arrival,' complained Riaz. 'And I have. Don't expect any more.'

'Listen, son,' said Aslam eagerly, 'I detest them as much as you do. I had pledged to take my revenge on them. But it's not my hatred for them that brought me here.'

'Then what do you want?'

'I'm not the same person who entered that cave. I know now that the purpose of this war wasn't exacting revenge. They need retribution, and they will get it when they are hanged for their crimes.'

'This war is not over,' the Major said to the gathering. 'However, I do believe that this operation has been a grand success. We have displayed our *Dridhta aur Virta*. After every war, the Indian Army decorates its gallant men with awards befitting their valour. Some of them receive those awards posthumously. I am happy that in this war we lost no lives thus far. But here,' he tapped Aslam's shoulder, 'here is a revenant among us. He died during this war, only to come back to life. He has displayed valour that deserves nothing short of the highest gallantry award. In fact, all of you have displayed great valour worthy of being recognized. I know you have revenge to exact, and I would have gladly rewarded you these trophies,' he pointed his guns towards the militants, 'but I cannot do it. They have surrendered, and my seniors have directed me to take them in custody. I am going to recommend each of you for bravery awards and recommend permanent jobs for you. But if you display indiscipline, I'll be compelled to take you in custody.'

Major Sekera proceeded to arrest two of the militants, including Buttshikan. But Zuber and Khalil were still at gunpoint, held there by Riaz and Khalil.

'Well? Take off your guns!' ordered the Major.

'Sir,' vowed Riaz, 'today, you will definitely take four men in your custody with their guns.'

Apprehending what it implied, as Riaz and Manzoor nodded at one another, Aslam rushed to them yelling a loud 'No!' that blended with the two bullets fired into two savage heads which had never opened to anything better before.

Eternity

Early one morning in May, someone knocked on Ashwar's door. When the door opened, the visitor was stunned.

'Raise your hands!' shouted Lal Jaan. She held a rifle to the visitor's head. 'State your name and purpose of your visit.'

'I…I am a postman from the neighbouring village,' babbled the visitor. 'This is for Aslam from someone called Badar Kaanchwala from Bombay.'

'Oh!' said Lal Jaan, lowering the rifle, 'but why are you here so early in the morning, son?'

'Actually, I am late. I should have delivered this yesterday, but somehow I couldn't. I have to report at the head post office in Swarnpur by 9.00 a.m. Is Aslam home?'

'Yes. I will call him.'

Two weeks after the end of the operation, the high school in the village was repaired. Major Navniet Sekera had managed to arrange financial help for the cause. Aslam's savings that Badar Kaanchwala had sent through a special messenger also came in handy. Lal Jaan inaugurated the school building amid applause by the villagers.

'Thank you,' said Lal Jaan. 'Thank you for standing up for what is right. Finally, the children of Pathri Aali and the neighbouring villages will be where they should be—in school, Major Sahib,' she addressed Major Sekera. 'In our village, teachers refuse to come to the school. They excuse themselves citing security concerns. We don't blame them, but how can we do without them? I am sure that as long as we have your support, and our sons valiantly guard this village, our children will not be deprived of education. My daughters, Ashwar and Shamma, have already volunteered to teach the children, free. And we call such acts of charity, "*Sadqa-e-Jaria*", a charity that lasts forever, a charity that resounds until eternity.'

One fine morning of May, someone knocked on Himanshu's door.

'Buttered toast and tea,' demanded Pinky Sharma, stepping inside the house.

'Is this a restaurant?' Himanshu asked sternly. But he couldn't keep up the pretence; he was grinning from ear to ear.

'And yes,' she added. 'I am sleepy. Don't tell me to sit on that chair.'

'Marry me,' Himanshu said abruptly. He couldn't stop himself.

'What?'

'Marry me.'

'Well, I think it's just a phase. It will soon be over.'

'No, it won't be over. But if you want me to wait, I will. That's what I have been doing since you left.'

'Really? And how long can you wait for me?' Pinky rolled her eyes, a mischievous smile forming on her lips.

'Until eternity.'

Acknowledgements

I have borrowed ideas from various people and incidents that have intrigued me enough to adapt them here, in my own way. I thank Razaq—one who served our family for a decade and would probably never care for this gratitude—who, during my childhood, had narrated to me inspiring stories and the traditions of his village. Decades later, his village inspired me to write this book. Thank you Razaq and your village, Murrah.

I thank my parents for their belief in my capabilities. My father, Fazal Mushtaq, being an author himself, has inspired me in many ways to write this book.

To my wife, Falak, who was the first reader of the manuscript despite the fact that she is not a book lover—thanks for enduring me and my passion. Thanks to my daughters, Rania and Zinia, who have reinforced my belief in love and care, without which this work would have been lacking in these attributes.

Being the youngest in our family, my siblings have always loved me unconditionally and supported me in all my endeavours. Dear sister, Qamar-Un-Nisa and brothers, Ashfaq and Fareed, thanks for your support. Your love and affection is reflected in this book wherever sibling bonding is depicted.

I thank Sakshi Nanda without whose honest and extraordinary efforts this book wouldn't have been what it is.

I thank Kapish Mehra and Rupa Publications for giving me this opportunity to bring my work to the world.

Thanks are due to Elina Majumdar, Rudra Narayan Sharma and the team at Rupa.

Thanks to Mugdha Sadhwani and Muneer Ali Khan for the cover design and painting, respectively.

Thanks to Dharamveer Tiwatia, my friend and colleague, who painstakingly read my manuscript and who is as keen in getting this book out as I am.

I thank Brigadier (Retd.) Sukhvir Singh and Colonel Sanjiv Singh, who were troubled by me for information on many aspects of the Indian Army.

Thanks to Navniet Sekera, the celebrity cop who graces the last few pages of my book. It's an honour to have you here, sir.

I thank Devesh Tripathi, my friend, who has more confidence in my capabilities than I would ever possess.

And to my friends and well-wishers, I thank you all. I remain indebted for your support and encouragement.